Rebecca's Brother

Rebecca's Brother

a novel

White Bear Books
Sebastopol

Richard Welin

Chapter 1 Catherine

She lay drifting between thought and sleep, tired, more tired than she'd ever felt in her life. She ran her hand over her abdomen. It was flat almost, no longer a mound, mountain. Her baby was born, but not her little girl. She'd been sure it was a girl. "He's a fine boy, healthy and sound." She let that voice slip away. Dreaming now, she heard fat little Marcie Perkins: *I'm not ever getting married* – waving the card in her hand – *the old maid! I win! No screaming babies for me!* Marcie was nuts. The old maid, so ugly. That horrible long chin. Hairy wart on her big lumpy nose. Hideous red lips.

She opened her eyes... Alan. Beside her bed.

"How are you feeling?"

"Tired. Sore."

"Can I get you anything?"

"No."

"We had names for a girl but never fixed on one for a boy. What do you think?"

"Oh..." She took a deep breath, grimaced. A long sigh. "I can't think. I'm tired."

"How about your father's name?"

She closed her eyes. "'Adam...' I don't know... wrong somehow."

"'Alan Junior?' But I don't much like hanging 'Junior' on a kid. Seems demeaning."

Catherine looked up at him. "Did your mother say anything? She's seen him?"

"She'd love it if we named him after her father."

"Lon?"

"Everyone called him 'Lonnie.'"

"Well, 'Lonny' then, with a *y*." Her eyes closed again.

"We need a middle name."

She rolled her head back and forth on her pillow, as if trying to avoid a fly. "Use *your* middle name, 'Wilson.' Who was that?"

"Mom's maiden name."

She sighed. "Perfect."

"'Lonny Wilson Stuart.'"

"Mmm."

"Kate, I've got to leave tomorrow. Minneapolis, and then Sioux Falls. I'll be back in about a week. Mom will take you home and help out. Everything's ready in the house. You'll be fine."

*　　*　　*

"Shhh. Shh, shh."

Baby Lonny's tiny hands reached up toward the bottle as Catherine tipped the nipple to his mouth. Beginning to suck, he stopped crying.

"That's the boy. Nobody can eat and cry at the same time." With the child on her arm, Catherine paced the kitchen floor in her soft slippers. She held the formula bottle with her free hand. "I'll do the crying for you, Lonny. I do plenty for myself, anyway.

"You were hungry this time, weren't you, little guy? Yes. Last time you weren't hungry at all." She glanced at the clock over the back door. It's 'the dead of night,' little guy. You just get lonely sometimes, don't you? Or scared." She paced more slowly. "I wish my mother were here. That's your other grandmother. She'd have loved you, Lonny, as much as Grandma Lena does. But she's gone. My father, too... your other grandfather."

Remembering her father, she stopped moving. "He had black hair, Lonny. Jet black. I was just a girl when he died." She saw him sitting on the running board of his car, smiling, holding out his arms to her.

"Black hair," she said, moving about the room again. "But *you* are a little blondie, like Alan."

The baby squirmed on her arm.

"You've had enough, little man?"

She put the bottle on the counter, lifted the baby to her shoulder and patted his back till he burped.

"That was a good one, but someday we'll have to teach you better manners. Your father shouldn't have left us alone again. Home a week and then off on the road he goes, as far as Boise, he said. Even your grandmother wondered about that. But would your daddy dare ask for a couple of weeks off the road just because he's got a new baby at home? Oh no, he couldn't do that."

Still holding the baby against her shoulder, Catherine reached down a glass from the cupboard above the counter and filled it under the cold faucet in the sink. She took a sip. "Ahh. We do have a good well here." She set her glass on the counter and lowered the baby onto her arm. "You're asleep already. Let's go back to bed." She took up her water glass to keep on her night stand, crossed the room and switched off the ceiling light.

The new darkness revealed a glow from the kitchen window over the sink. She moved to the window to look out: moonlight lay like a dusting of snow on the apple tree and the budding rose bushes. "Oh, Lonny," she whispered, "you should see this. It's so beautiful. Let's go outside and take a peek at the moon."

Still carrying the glass in her free hand, she started for the back door, forgetting the pail of mop water she had left in the hall. She cried out as her right foot struck the pail, splashing soapy water over the floor. Hobbling about with the pain of her stubbed toe, she dropped the water glass. Its shattering impact on the floor made her jump and slip on the soapy wet linoleum and she fell forward, landing hard on her right shoulder. Lonny's head hit the floor and he screamed wildly, obliterating the darkness. Catherine lay stunned, until the second scream brought her up onto her knees. She took the baby into her arms and hugged him close. With great care she got to her feet and made her way to the wall switch. The sudden light sparkled in the shards of broken glass, and it revealed a redness spreading out in the water on the floor. She peeled the screaming infant from her shoulder to look at him, caught her breath. She dashed to the sink, grabbed the dish towel from the counter and wiped at the blood. She rinsed the towel in cold water, squeezed it out with one hand, and wiped at the blood again, gently, cooing now, as well to herself as to the infant gasping for breath between screams. But the blood kept oozing from the gash that curved upward from the baby's lip to the cheekbone under his left eye.

*   *   *

Holding her little boy by the hand, Catherine walked up Plane Street to visit his grandmother three doors up the hill. They found her sitting on the porch swing reading. Her long graying brown hair, recently washed and still drying, hung down over the towel covering her shoulders. Why her mother-in-law kept her hair so long was a mystery to Catherine. At least she usually kept it up in a bun.

Lena put down her book when she saw her visitors enter the driveway. She took off her glasses.

"Hello, you two."

Lonny ran up to get his hug and a kiss, then saw the yellow cat under the swing and dropped to the floor to pick it up.

"I need to talk," Catherine said.

"Yes?"

"Can we go inside?" With a look and turn of her head Catherine indicated a conversation out of the boy's hearing. "Lonny, You can play with Patches out here on the porch, okay?"

The women went inside.

"Catherine, just give me a minute to put my hair up. Then you can tell me what's on your mind."

Full of her purpose held in abeyance, Catherine moved around the living room, glancing at the familiar photographs on small tables and on the walls. When Lena returned they sat down and Catherine began immediately: "It's about Lonny. I took him to a specialist yesterday and he said there was nothing he or anyone else could do now about the scar. He said there's nothing to worry about, there's no harm to the boy, it's just a scar. But Lena, it's the first thing you notice about him, and it affects his speech."

"*You* notice, Catherine, not me. And I doubt other people, do, either. Not the way you do. You worry about it far too much. First thing I see is a sweet little boy with bright blue eyes. Try to see *that*. You don't have to try, either. He *is* a sweet little boy with bright blue eyes. Just love him. The more you worry about the scar the more *he* will, and he'll be self-conscious about it. And that will hurt him."

"And I've hurt him enough already. Point taken."

"That's not what I meant."

"I hope I never have another child. Sometimes when I look at Lonny I just want to shrivel up."

Shocked, Lena could find no words.

Catherine went on, oblivious. "But I want to tell you, Lena, I'm not going to be useless. I want to find a job. With so many men gone off to war now they're hiring women for all kinds of work. I did very well in school. I'm especially good with figures." She paused. "Could you look after Lonny tomorrow afternoon? I want to go downtown and start with the banks."

Lena found her voice, but there was no force in it. "Have you written to Alan? Would he want you to work?"

"I'll see if I can get a job, first. You know how long it takes to get a letter to England, if it gets there at all. And then to get a reply. It could take months. If he objects I promise I'll quit."

"So you want me to take care of Lonny while you're working?"

"Oh Lena, do you really think you could? He loves you so much. He's always happiest when he's with his Gammy. And goodness knows we could use the money. I mean all of us. While Alan's away in this awful war."

"A child needs his mother, Catherine."

"Not so much now. And he's a sturdy little guy." She smiled, like a proud mother.

Lena looked at the ceiling, saying nothing. Catherine also fell silent, but her fingers worked at the folds of her dress. It was three years old. What could she wear tomorrow? First impressions are important. She sat up straight in her chair, practicing, her hands folded in her lap, her gaze fixed on a photograph beside Lena's chair. Yes, Mr. Peabody, I can type and file. I can add long columns without an error and do it quickly, too. 'Mr. Peabody." What movie was that from? Ages since Alan had taken her to movies. Would he ever come home? The war just goes on and on...

Finally Lena spoke: "Though I want the best for Lonny, Catherine, I can see this is something you really want to do, and I've got to admire your spunk. So, all right. Bring him over tomorrow. We'll have a nice afternoon together."

Back at home Catherine picked up her little boy, held him in her arms and looked in his face. His eyes looked back at her, wide open, taking her in whole, all of her, as if devouring her with his eyes. She pressed him closer to herself, loving him, hating the scar, feeling the life of his small body, the ceaseless small movements. A stifled cry burned in her throat; it came out with her breath, squeezing through clenched teeth, a low keening whine.

Catherine asked for the day off to meet her soldier husband returning from the war in Europe.

"There are several very important loans you're reviewing. It's not a good time to be away from your responsibilities, Mrs. Stuart."

"He's my husband, Mr. Cole. He's returning from the war. He's been gone over three years."

"Yes... Yes. Well. We're not unpatriotic. Go on then, go welcome your soldier home."

"His train arrives at one-fifteen, sir. I can stay through lunch."

"No, no. I've decided. You go now. You couldn't possibly keep your mind on your work this morning, and we don't want any mistakes, do we? Take a walk. Maybe there's some last minute shopping. Have a nice lunch. Go meet your husband, Mrs. Stuart. We'll see you tomorrow. And then you'll have the weekend."

"You're a dear, Mr. Cole." She thought to kiss his cheek, as in the movies, but decided against it. "Thank you."

She tidied her desk top, wrote herself a few notes for the next day, picked up her handbag and sweater, and left the bank. The big clock over the sidewalk said ten-twenty-five. It was early June and still quite cool. A brisk walk suddenly seemed like an excellent idea. It would bring a little color into her cheeks and settle her nerves. And then lunch at Max's. Maybe. She didn't think she could eat. She could barely eat a piece of toast at breakfast. Lena also had wanted to meet Alan, drive down to the station and bring Lonny along to see his dad. But Catherine wanted him to herself when he arrived. She promised to bring Alan up the hill to see his mother and son as soon as she got him home.

She started north on Superior Street, away from the train station. There's a little park – Leif Erikson – she'd head for that.

A window displaying the new summer fashions caught her eye as she passed Glass Block department store. She stopped for a more careful appraisal. She thought the pink dress absurdly fussy. The blue wasn't bad. But the black cocktail dress had possibilities – with just the right shoes.

What a luxury! Two free hours on a weekday to shop! To enjoy herself, take her time. But the black dress was a silly idea. She bought a satin nightgown, and for her husband soft flannel pajamas. No, she could not take her purchases with her. They'll have to be delivered. She was meeting her husband, you see. At one-fifteen. He's coming home from the war. He's been gone three years.

Alan looked handsome in his dress uniform. He had hardly changed at all. He was still tall, the line of his jaw only a little softer than when he left, and in the sunlight his sandy hair still pleased her eye when he took off his cap. He wasn't maimed.

7

There was no sign of the battle fatigue that she'd read about in a Sunday paper a while ago. He had a ribbon on his chest. Only one.

They sat in the back seat of a Yellow Cab heading home. "You've grown a little paunch, honey," Catherine said, patting his stomach.

"I'm one of the lucky ones, Kate. A desk job in the Quartermasters, and the bombs never hit closer than two blocks away."

"What did you do to get the ribbon?" She touched it, then ran her finger the length of it.

"I showed up. It just means I was there. But I never had to be a hero, or find out I'm a coward."

"Oh."

"Kate, don't be *too* disappointed. Some of the heroes with medals and ribbons who are alive enough to come home are coming home without much left of them, and they know they're not going to be much use to anyone, or to themselves." He pulled her closer against his side. "I plan on being very useful, Mrs. Stuart." He kissed her smooth cheek, and then her lips.

"Alan," she said, reaching her arm around him, "I'm glad you're home."

The little house three doors down the hill from his mother's place – his childhood home – was newly painted inside and out. The furniture was new. Catherine had bought complete suites for the living room and their bedroom. His six-year old son slept in a bed with maple foot- and headboards. "The kitchen refrigerator was the finest available from Sears Roebuck," said Catherine proudly.

"I tried to give Lena a new refrigerator, too, Alan," she explained, "but she refused it. She said she was satisfied 'with the old box.' She said I should spend my money on my own home and husband and growing boy. She's been wonderful, Alan, taking care of Lonny every day I went to work."

Catherine held her husband's hand and led him around to see all the improvements she'd made, explaining the quality of each item, how she'd bargained for the best prices. "Except for Sears & Roebuck. You can't bargain with them. They have their prices, and that's that."

Alan's fixed smile was beginning to hurt his face. "This is all fine, Kate, but how much do we owe for all this?"

"Nothing! Honey, it's all paid for!"

"How...?"

"It must be one of my letters you didn't get. I got promoted, to loan officer. I'm on salary! They love me at old Duluth National."

"I had no idea."

They had returned to the living room. Alan looked around – at the cherry wood writing table, the sofa and chair. "You hardly needed the little stipend the Army sent you every month."

"Oh it helped, Alan." She patted his arm. "It paid for groceries and odds and ends."

*   *   *

Five years after V-E Day Catherine found herself pregnant again. An accident. There had been a rare romantic evening after an especially successful sales trip that earned Alan a promotion, a raise, and a few days off. He'd been happy, working outside the house cleaning and putting up storm windows and glancing in at his wife now and then through the window in the kitchen where she was making tuna sandwiches for a picnic lunch in the backyard. And there was a cake in the oven

Later that afternoon Alan took Lonny to a Duke's game. In the evening he told Catherine how Lonny had at first shown little interest, but as the game went on and the Dukes built up a four-run lead he had started to cheer.

"Amazing how little he knew about baseball. I explained things to him at first, but then he started asking questions, and he caught on pretty quick. But how could an American kid not know everything about baseball? I know I've not been around to teach him, but kids pick it up by themselves and from other kids."

"He spends a lot of time in the woods."

"Doing what?"

"I don't know. Tracking rabbits? Shooting birds? He takes his BB gun with him sometimes."

"What BB gun?"

"We gave him one for his last birthday. That must be another letter you didn't get."

"I sure didn't. Anyway, I guess we've got a young Daniel Boone. Maybe he'll be an explorer when he grows up."

"There's not a lot left to explore, honey."

Alan put his arm around her. He nuzzled her ear and touched his lips to her neck. "Kate. Let's you and me do a little exploring. How about dinner out tomorrow night, some fancy place. We'll get all dressed up."

"We can't leave Lonny alone."

"He can sleep over at his Gammy's."

Catherine snuggled into his shoulder. "They're great friends, those two. When he's not in the woods he's at Lena's."

"So do I have a date with my lovely wife?"

*   *   *

Alan was away again when the doctor confirmed what Catherine already knew. Two months later she resigned from the bank, and, she thought, from her life. But the girl she eventually gave birth to was perfect – and beautiful. Alan was sitting by his wife's bed all smiles when she awoke. A nurse brought in the baby girl and Catherine named her Rebecca, after her mother's sister, Catherine's favorite of the three Morgan sisters – "the pretty one."

Chapter 2 Fire and Ice

"Lonny, go see who's pounding on the front door. Nobody I know would be out this early the day after Christmas."

"Okay Ma." The boy scooted his chair back from the table.

"And don't call me 'Ma.' Where did you learn that?"

Lonny picked up his jam-laden toast, went out the kitchen door and started down the hall.

"Lonny, close the door! I want to keep heat in the kitchen."

He stopped, closed the door, and shoved a last bit of toast into his mouth. Chewing fast, he went along the hall, then swallowed before he opened the front door.

"Stiggy! Hi." His friend stood on the porch bundled up in parka, scarf, wool cap, chopper mitts, and high-top leather boots. A pair of hockey skates hung by their laces around his neck, the toes layered with strips of scuffed-up white adhesive tape.

"Get your skates and c'mon out. The ponds in the old gravel pit are frozen over and they're smooth enough for skating."

"Who said?"

"Phil. My brother's friend. He came by yesterday and said him and Scharnot had been out there."

"I'll get ready." He called to his mother: "It's my friend Stiggy. We're going skating." He ran upstairs leaving his friend to wait in the hall.

Using his teeth, Stiggy pulled off one of his chopper mitts, then with his bared fingers pulled off the other one. He stuffed the mitts into the deep pockets of his parka as he took in his surroundings. At the end of the hall was a closed door. The walls on either side of him were bare except for a single framed photograph of some people facing the camera, and one little kid standing next to a man, probably his dad, and holding on to the man's fingers, one finger in each hand. Stiggy thought it might be Lonny when he was little, but the face was turned away so he couldn't tell.

Bored, he wandered through an archway into the living room, his hands hanging onto the blades of the skates still slung from his neck. Then he remembered his boots. He looked behind him and saw he'd left small clumps of melting snow on the hall carpet. He examined his bootsoles. They were clear of snow now, so he continued exploring. Other people's houses were strange. The furniture was different, more or less the same sorts of things but different from the furniture in his own house. And other people's houses smelled funny. His own didn't smell at all, except when Ma was frying bacon.

Through another arch he saw a big dining room table with four chairs around it and a candle stick sitting in the middle of it. The top looked real shiny and he went up to the table to touch it.

"Aah!" came a startled voice to his left.

Stiggy jerked around and found himself looking through a partially open doorway at a woman holding a spoon in front of a baby in a highchair.

"Hi," he said, embarrassed, feeling he'd been caught doing something bad. "Mrs. Stuart?"

"You must be Stiggy."

"Yeah, that's me."

"Well if you're through snooping around come in here and meet Lonny's baby sister."

Stiggy shoved his hands into his coat pockets with his mitts and entered the warm kitchen.

"This little lady having her breakfast is Rebecca. She's seven months old and she just loves her baby rice cereal."

"Hi Rebecca." Stiggy bent forward to see her face, but as he did so his skates swung out, one barely missing Catherine's nose. He jumped back. "Sorry, Mrs. Stuart! I'm really sorry."

"Watch what you're doing! Good Lord, be careful! Those are dangerous weapons you're wearing, young man. Please, take off those skates!"

"Yes, Ma'am." He ducked his head and lifted the skates from his shoulders.

"Thank you. Goodness! Accidents can happen so quickly! You have to be especially careful around a baby." She put a hand to her chest and took a deep breath. Stig stood frozen by her chair.

Finally Catherine said, "Well, I expect Lonny will be a while, and I see you're dressed for the Arctic. Why don't you take off your hat and coat?"

"Yeah. It's pretty hot in here."

"You can pile everything on that chair over there and then sit here by the table with Becky and me. Is Stiggy your real name?"

"No. It's Stig."

"St*eeg*. And your last name?"

"Panelius."

"Panelius!" She laughed. "What kind of name is that?"

"It's Swedish," he said, annoyed. Divested of his outer garments, he sat down.

"I suppose it's not an unusual name in Sweden."

"I don't know."

"Well, now that you're disarmed you may have a closer look." Stiggy leaned forward to see. "Rebecca Stuart, this is Stig Panelius. He's Lonny's friend. You'll forgive her, Stig, if she doesn't say hello. She's very hungry this morning."

"Hi Rebecca," Stiggy said, looking in her face. "Lonny calls her Becky."

"Yes, he does."

"She sure is little."

"She's just about right for seven months."

"I've got a brother," Stiggy said, sitting back in his chair. "He's older'n me, by a couple years."

"It would be very different to have a sister."

"Yeah? I guess."

Stiggy looked around the kitchen, then back at the baby, and then at Mrs. Stuart. She didn't really look like a mother. She was thin. All the mothers he knew were fat – "pleasingly plump," his father said. Stiggy liked that his own mother was fat and soft to snuggle up to.

"So, how old are you, Stig?"

"Same as Lonny. I'm eleven going on twelve."

He watched Mrs. Stuart open another little jar that said "Apple Sauce" on it under a picture of a baby's face.

"Well, you'd *have* to be going on twelve if you're eleven now, wouldn't you?

"Yeah..."

"Unless you died." Catherine held a spoonful of apple sauce to Becky's mouth.

"What?"

The mouth opened and Catherine tipped up the spoon then pulled it out against Becky's upper lip so that the contents slid in. "You're 'going on twelve' because you're alive and so you're getting older all the time. But if you died you'd stay eleven. You'd stay eleven forever."

Stiggy saw himself lying on the ground, stiff and stretched out.

Catherine noticed his staring eyes. "Did I frighten you? Oh dear. I have ideas popping into my head all the time. When I was in school I planned to become an author. I had such wonderful ideas for stories and all my English teachers said I was a good writer. I was good at geometry, too, by the way. In fact I got good grades in everything. Good enough that I could have gone to college. But then I met *Al*an, that's Lonny's father, and I got *mar*ried."

Stiggy thought she sounded angry, the way she said that. "Whiney," his mother would say. He had an aunt who sounded like that all the time.

"Were you born in Sweden?"

"Huh?"

"I asked if you were born in Sweden.'"

"No. I was born here in Duluth. Mrs. Stuart, can I have a glass of milk?"

"Yes you *may* have a glass of milk. Help yourself. You'll find a glass on the dish rack."

They heard Lonny trotting down the stairs and then the sound of skates dropping onto the hall rug. He shouted, "I'll be there in a minute." Then they heard his feet pounding back up the stairs. Stiggy wished he would hurry.

"So you weren't born in Sweden. How about your parents?"

"Yeah, *they* were."

"Did you know that Lonny's ancestors, *my* people, have been in this country for over two hundred years?"

"No." Stiggy poured his glass half full and drank it down standing. Then he put the glass in the sink and the milk bottle back in the refrigerator. "My dad came over in 1924," he said. "Ma came about the same time."

"So *you're* the one who taught Lonny to say 'Ma'!"

"Huh?"

"Never mind. So was it hard for them, your parents, when they came to this country?"

"I don't know. Ma says they had a lot of fun." He took his seat at the table again facing Mrs. Stuart and the baby.

"Were they very young?"

"No. Ma says she was nineteen." He tilted his chair back, balancing on two legs.

"That's *young*." Catherine put down the spoon and wiped Becky's mouth with the bib. "Have you and Lonny been friends long?"

"Yeah." He thought about it. "Since last year. He sat next to me in fourth grade."

"That long?" Catherine looked up. "Stig, don't lean your chair back like that."

"Sorry." He rode the chair down with a bump.

"I'm surprised I haven't met you before. Tell me, do you hate school as much as Lonny does?"

"Sometimes. I hate music class when we have to sing just the notes in a song. That's so dumb. But I like arithmetic." He brightened: "And recess!"

"Lonny doesn't even like recess, I believe." She looked at Stiggy appraisingly. "Does your mother have curly hair like yours?"

Automatically he ran a hand through his hair. "Yeah, I guess. She gets permanents. She and her friend Gladys give each other a *Toni* sometimes. It really stinks when they do it at our house."

They heard a door slam overhead, followed by a thundering down the stairs and "Stiggy, lets go!" shouted from the hall.

The boy jumped up from his chair and grabbed his clothes and skates. "Bye Mrs. Stuart. Thanks for the milk. Oh, and g'bye Becky." He ran from the room and joined Lonny in the hall where they began to wrestle into their outdoor clothes.

"Lonny," Catherine called. "Come here and close this kitchen door."

With one boot on he hobbled down the hall then stood in the doorway and waved to Becky, who responded with a smile and food dribbling down her chin. He turned to his mother: "I'll be back for lunch."

"Yes. And make it no later than twelve-thirty. I've decided to go shopping this afternoon and I want you to watch Rebecca."

The boys hurried along the snow-packed road toward the abandoned gravel pit.

"You sure took a long time, Lonny."

"Whaddaya mean? Ten minutes, maybe."

"Seemed like an hour. What did you get for Christmas?"

"Some clothes and stuff. This knife." Lonny opened his coat and pulled the new hunting knife out of its sheath on his belt. He held it out lying flat on his hand so Stiggy could admire the full shape of it.

"Wow. That's neat." Stiggy took off a mitt and picked the knife off his friend's hand. He hefted it, felt the handle's fit in his hand, ran his thumb across the blade. "It's sharp," he said.

"It'll cut paper," Lonny said. He took the knife back, slid it into its sheath and snapped the retaining strap around it. "I got these boots for Christmas." Stiggy took a few running steps then slid as far as he could, holding the skates that hung around his neck to keep them from banging into his face. Lonny followed suit, but didn't slide so far.

"Hard-soled boots beat packs any day," Stiggy said, his nose running from the cold. He wiped it on the back of his chopper mitt.

"Packs are made not to slip. So I don't fall down like you do in those boots."

"I never fall down."

"Yes you do." Lonny pushed him and Stiggy slipped backwards, did a little dance, threw out his arms and regained his balance.

"See? I never go down." He returned the push but Lonny put one foot back and just stood there.

"See? See? I didn't slip at all."

"But you can't slide." Stiggy ran and slid then waited for Lonny to catch up.

"Your ma gave me the third degree."

"She did? What for?"

"Asked me a bunch of questions. She's sure different from my ma. She's like a movie star."

"*Your* mom's nice."

"She gives you cookies when you come over."

"Yeah. She's nice."

Lonny ran and slid on a patch of glare ice but quickly hit packed snow and staggered forward. He hung on to his skates, his elbows out and flapping up and down. But he didn't fall.

Stiggy laughed. He ran and slid to catch up.

"There's a car coming." Lonny pulled his friend to the side of the road. A black Hudson coupe came up behind them, honked its horn and passed by, the chains on its rear tires beating on the packed snow.

"That's old man Linkvist," said Lonny. "He never goes more'n fifteen miles an hour, even in the summer."

They turned off the road and onto a path dimly visible as an indentation in the new snow. It crossed a field dotted with brush and a few young poplars and birch trees. The bare upper branches of the birches looked to Stiggy like ink drawings he'd seen in a book.

At the edge of the gravel pit they stopped and looked down at the ponds separated by mounds of tailings and spurs of land bearing brush and saplings.

"They're clear!" said Lonny. "The wind's blown all the snow off the ice. I've never seen it all clear like that!"

"Let's get down there." Stiggy jumped off the edge and slid and fell feet first down the wall of the pit, landing in a snowbank. He scrambled out of the bank onto frozen ground swept clean of snow. Lonny came down by the path and was the first to arrive at the nearest pond. He put his skates down and looked around.

"What are you looking for?" Stiggy said as he came up, beating snow off the legs of his Roebuck jeans.

"Something to make a fire with."

"Yeah! Great!" Stiggy dropped his skates and started scouring the clear areas for sticks and dead brush.

"Let's make the fire on the ice," Stiggy said. "It'll be safer and it'll be fun to see if it melts the ice."

"And falls through and goes CUSH!"

They gathered what looked like an adequate stack of fuel then decided to skate first and light the fire later. They skated all around the little pond, exploring the irregular edges, the coves and fingers reaching out between tailing piles and stands of young trees. Lonny found the surface was not so smooth as it had appeared from a distance, especially where the water had frozen in ripples. It sure wasn't glassy like the ice of the rink down at Quincy Adams School. Hjälmar Ekman did that. He flooded the school playground every winter before Christmas and kept the ice in good condition, re-flooding it every now and then. Lonny watched him once from his classroom window. He'd been gazing out the window, day-dreaming about Jeannie Oaks, who sat on the other side of the classroom, when suddenly there was Ekman dragging a big black hose gushing water across the rink. Everybody liked Ol' Ekman. He kept the pot-bellied stove in the rink's warming shack stoked with coal and blazing in the afternoons and Friday and Saturday nights. What a great job to have, Lonny thought. You could skate all you want, and it would always be great to come in out of the cold into the warm shack and stump across the plank floor in your skates. He wondered if polishing the shiny brass rail around the stove was part of Ekman's job, too. He must be paid pretty well to do all that. Maybe it was the school that paid him.

"Hey Lonny, come over here!" Stiggy skated out from behind some little trees and waved to him. "This connects to the next pond!"

Lonny followed Stiggy up the narrow passage. They had to weave carefully around some rocks sticking up out of the ice and around a high pile of tailings. Then the clear ice opened out and they were on the next pond.

"I wonder if we could skate from pond to pond all the way over to the creek," Lonny said. "The water here comes from that creek."

"Let's find out."

They scoured the edges until they found a passage winding among hillocks of dead cattails and finally leading them into Dinghy's Pond where in the summertime they went swimming.

"Let's stay near the edges," Lonny said. "Dinghy's is deep."

"Yeah. Probably thin ice."

"Yeah."

Both remembered Lonny's near drowning there the previous summer when he'd waded out to where the bottom dropped away. Their friend Wendell who was with them and could swim really well managed to get him out but almost got drowned himself under Lonny's struggling. Wendell still hated Lonny for that.

They explored the edges but could find no further outlet.

"I don't get it," said Lonny. "How does the creek water get here?"

"Maybe it goes underground."

"Yeah! An underground river."

"Or maybe it just oozes through the dirt and gravel."

"Nah. Must be an underground river."

"There could be springs," Stiggy said.

"Yeah? What *are* springs, anyway? Where's the water come from?"

"Maybe when it oozes through the ground, it just comes up in a low place."

"Hey, I know," Lonny said. "In the spring the creek gets real high. And that's when it floods over to these ponds."

"Maybe." Stiggy stood still, thinking. "No. That's not it because then the ponds would dry up in the summer and they don't dry up."

"Why don't you dry up?"

"I'm too cold to dry up. Let's go make a fire!"

Without thinking they skated directly across the pond. As they passed over the middle they heard the ice cracking beneath their blades. "Yeeoww!" they yelled and skated as fast as they could till they swooshed to a stop at the opposite shore, spraying flakes of ice up onto the bank.

"Cheese and crackers!" Stiggy said. "Lucky it's a *little* pond!"

Lonny stood panting, one mitted hand on his friend's shoulder. "Dinghy's trying to kill me."

They went on, both a little shaken. Taking no chances, they kept to the edges of the next pond and then the next, and Lonny wondered aloud if Dinghy's Pond really could be some kind of evil thing trying to kill him.

"Maybe it's haunted," Stiggy said as they approached the bank where they'd left their stash of firewood.

"That's what I was thinking."

"I wonder who this guy Dinghy was?"

"Some mean son of a bitch," Lonny said.

"I wish you wouldn't swear," Stiggy said.

"'Bitch' ain't swearing. It's a female dog. Besides, what did you say back there? 'Cheese and crackers.' That's stupid. Everybody knows you're saying 'Jesus Christ.'"

"No I'm not. I'm saying 'cheese and crackers.' And I wish we had some."

"Yeah. I'm getting hungry."

They set to building their fire. Eventually Stiggy was down to his last three matches. His fingers were numb with cold. "I wish we had some paper."

Lonny stood up and looked around, as if he'd be able to see paper somewhere caught in a bush somewhere. But he did see a dead spruce sapling. "Hold on a minute." He skated to the sapling and with the new hunting knife he was going to carry on his belt from now on – except to school, some teacher would take it away – he cut a couple of twigs that still bore some brown needles.

"Here's kindling," he said and dropped it in front of Stiggy where he knelt by their little tent of sticks. Stiggy pulled his hands from his armpits where he'd been warming them and carefully worked the spruce twigs under the sticks then struck a precious match. Smoke rose from the needles, and then a flame. With great care Stiggy added more of the kindling, the sap in it burning hotter and hotter and finally igniting the sticks tented over it. Lonny skated off and came back with larger cuttings of spruce. Stiggy kept feeding the little fire, carefully encouraging it to grow until it was burning on its own, consuming sticks as big as their wrists and warming their faces.

"This is great!" said Stiggy.

"We need something to sit on." Lonny skated off again and came back after a few minutes with an armload of tamarack boughs. "I had to walk up into the woods a ways to find them."

"I wondered if you'd gone home to get chairs."

"Very funny. It's hard to walk in deep snow with skates on."

They shared out the boughs and made themselves comfortable there on the ice beside the healthy little fire.

"This is fun. It's like camping," said Stiggy.

"It *is* camping. If we had a tent we could stay here."

"And if we had food."

Then both realized they were very, very hungry.

"We should have at least brought sandwiches," Stiggy said.

"And some of your mom's cookies."

"Yeah."

They stared hungrily at the fire.

"They do a lot of camping in Boy Scouts," Stiggy said. I think I might join. How about you?"

"You can camp without the Boy Scouts. Just go out in the woods and camp. Pitch a tent and crawl in."

"There's a lot more to it than that."

"Like what?"

"The Scouts go places to camp."

"Woods are woods. Don't matter where."

"You don't know anything about it."

"Well, what would you get out of it?"

"Lots of things."

"Like what?"

Stiggy thought a while. "Okay. Instead of Scouts let's get up a baseball team this summer and join a league."

Lonny poked a stick at the fire. "I'd rather build a shack in the woods. In those woods up there." He pointed with the smoking stick toward where he'd gathered the tamarack boughs. "There's a real nice spot up there. A little clearing, but the trees are real close together around it and probably no one would ever find it. We could hang around there in the summer and go down to the ponds and swim and over to the creek and fish and we could come back and fry and eat the fish. And we could explore all over and follow DeAmity up to those apple trees we found last summer. And if it rained we'd be dry in the shack and we could sit inside and listen to the rain."

"Yeah. That'd be fun. But I'd sure like to play baseball on a real team, maybe even get jerseys with the team name on them."

"I don't like baseball much. Hey look. The fire's melting the ice."

Lonny poked his stick in the puddle that had formed under the fire. Steam hissed from the bottom sticks.

"The water will put out the fire," Stiggy said. He thought a second. "Though maybe... Which do you think will happen first? The fire goes out or it falls through the ice?"

Lonny checked their fuel supply. He jabbed his stick down into the puddle. "I guess we could keep adding more dry wood on top of the wet stuff."

"Let's just pile on all we got and see what happens."

"Okay. When the fire goes out we head for home. I'm really getting hungry." He looked up at the grey overcast sky. "I can't tell where the sun is. What time do you think it is?"

Stiggy looked up. "Must be about noon. I can't see the sun, either. I see two light spots but they could just be thin places in the clouds."

The fire was now hissing loudly. The boys heaped on the remaining fuel and sat back to watch. The flames rose up high making them scoot back from the heat. They took off their skates and tied the laces together. Lonny pulled on his packs and Stiggy his boots.

The fire was dying. They stood by it with their skates slung around their necks and watched. Charred wood chunks floated under two burning branches that bridged the puddle and supported the rest of the fire.

"I'm going to see how deep it is and then let's go," Lonny said. He still had his stick and he poked it into the puddle. It kept going down till Lonny's hand got too close to the fire and he pulled it back. "It's melted through!"

"And the fire's still burning. We've gotta wait."

"Yeah."

Stiggy's feet started to freeze in his boots. He held his skates and jogged in place.

"You shoulda got packs," Lonny said.

Then the bridge broke and the burning pile fell into the water.

"It went *CUSH!*" Lonny said. "Did you hear that?"

Chapter 3 The Amity

The creek was important to Lonny, mainly because it fed Dinghy's Pond in the gravel pit where he went swimming in the summer with Stig Panelius and sometimes with a couple of other kids from the neighborhood. The water in the pond sat still and warmed up in the sun. The creek was much colder than the pond, and there was only one time that Lonny swam in it.

It was a hot July day between fifth and sixth grade. Lonny and Stig were riding their bikes toward the creek by way of the dirt track along the west side of the gravel pit. The two-rut track ran though weeds higher than their heads. Cicadas in the weeds seemed to love the heat, and their ringing swarmed down around their heads like a million bees. It reminded Lonny of the sound he got in his head when he was sick and had a high fever. He pedaled faster, leaving Stig behind, and finally got out of the weeds and across a little open space and into the woods lining the creek. It was cooler there, out of the hot sun.

"What's your cotton-pickin' hurry?" Stig said when he came up. He dropped his bike in the brush beside Lonny's.

"Hot," Lonny said. "Let's get to the creek."

"You get even hotter pedaling hard like that." Stig was wearing the green plaid jack-shirt he always wore. Today he wore it unbuttoned. They followed the narrow path through the brush and trees. When they got to the creek the boys dropped to the ground and Lonny pulled off his sneakers and socks and Stig unlaced his boots, the black Chippewas, new last Christmas, but getting a little small for his feet now, and getting a little worn. He stuffed his socks into the boots and waded out in the cold dark water. The creek flowed rapidly over rocks there. It was shallow and maybe twenty feet wide.

"Aren't you coming in?" Stig said.

"In a minute." Lonny sat on a rock beside a little eddy with his feet in the water. He had picked up a stick and was poking the water skippers. "They skate on little bubbles," he said. Stig waded over to have a look.

"They look like bubbles, "Stig said. "Must be a reflection or something. It looks like each foot dents the water a little. That's really strange."

"You can't dent water," Lonny said. "That makes no sense."

"Yes, you can. If you push your finger just a tiny ways into water you dent it. Sometimes your finger doesn't even get wet, not unless you break the surface. And if you don't break the surface, you just dent it."

"That's crazy," Lonny said, and went on poking at the water skippers.

Stig's feet were getting numb. He came out of the creek, picked up his boots and found a flat rock to sit on while his feet dried in a patch of sunlight that came through the canopy of branches overhead.

"Do you know where this creek comes from?" Lonny said. He had unsheathed his hunting knife and was whittling down his stick to a point.

"No. Never thought about it. Do you?"

"Uh uh. I guess at the other end it runs into Lake Superior but I've never followed it downstream very far."

Lake Superior lay maybe five or six miles downhill to the south of them. The boys lived in a neighborhood just beyond the east city limits of Duluth, which extended along a hillside on the north shore of Lake Superior. At the creek they were about a mile east of their neighborhood.

"Let's follow it the other way," Stig said.

"Yeah, let's find out where it comes from."

The boys pulled on their socks and boots and laced up. Lonny stabbed his sharpened stick at a frog but missed and left his stick stuck in the eddy.

"I've gotta be home by five for chores, " Lonny said.

"I don't have to be home till supper at six," Stig said.

"You don't have chores?"

"Nope. I help out with the dishes sometimes, if we're talking. Ma washes and I dry. She tells me stories about when she was a little girl in Sweden. Sometimes when she's tired she asks me to do the dishes."

"She asks you! Boy, you're lucky. My mother just yells at me if I don't do them. How come you don't have chores.?"

"I don't know. What do you have to do at five?"

"Gather eggs, and I feed and water the chickens and rabbits, and sweep out the back hall if it's gotten dirty. And then there's always something else Ma thinks up for me to do before supper, like peel potatoes and put 'em in a pot to boil."

"My mom does all the cooking. She loves to cook."

"My mom cooks okay." Lonny said. "But sometimes she leaves my little sister at Grandma Lena's and goes and does something in town. Then she leaves me a note to start cooking. My dad always cooks when he's home and we kill a rabbit or a chicken."

"I have to do *some* things," Stig said. "Like cut the grass and take out the garbage. And shovel snow in the winter. Last winter it took me a whole morning to shovel out the car after that big blizzard. The one we had a couple days after Christmas."

After a while it was hard going right alongside the creek. Brush came right down to the edge. Eventually it got so thick the boys had to cut into the woods to go around. They came out in a big empty field. They figured it was sometimes a pasture because there were lots of big cow pies around. So they stayed out there in the field, following the tree line north. After climbing a fence they passed near a little apple orchard that seemed abandoned. There was high grass all through it and some branches had broken off, but the trees were loaded.

"We should come back later when the apples are ripe," Lonny said.

"Yeah, before summer's over." Stig said.

"I hate school," Lonny said.

"You and me both."

They came to the end of the field. Nothing but woods in front of them – popple mostly, some birch and maple. "So where's the creek?" Stig said. "Do you hear it?"

They stood still and listened. "Yeah," Lonny said. "And I smell it, too. It's to the right somewhere. Not far. Can you smell water? There's this old guy who lives on our street, he says deer can smell it from miles away."

"I can smell rain coming," Stig said.

"Everybody can smell rain."

"And I can smell a lake if it's not far away. I can hear the creek now, but I don't smell it."

"You should train your nose," Lonny said.

That reminded Stig of Lonny's scar. Sometimes it made him talk funny, like he had a cold. And since the near drowning Wendell made fun of it. "Hniff hniff hniff," he'd say. He did that one evening when a few of the neighborhood kids were playing hide n seek out by the streetlight and he and Lonny had gotten into an argument. Lonny could have come back at him and made fun of the big brown birthmark below Wendell's right ear, but he just called him a couple of names and went home.

The boys had to scramble through the woods quite a way before they got back to the creek.

"It doesn't look much smaller," Stig said, "so we haven't gotten much closer to where it starts. I wonder where we are. Do you think this creek comes all the way from Woodland?"

"I don't know."

"I smell rain."

"That's the creek." Lonny sniffed the air. "No, you're right. It's a different smell from the creek." He looked at the bit of sky he could see through the treetops. "No clouds yet, but the light feels yellow, like it does before a thunderstorm."

"What do you mean, 'feels yellow'?"

"The air just *feels* yellow. I don't know. As if it would look yellow if you could see it."

Stig looked at him, irritated. "Maybe you see the light change somehow. The atmosphere changes and that changes the light. But it doesn't make sense to say you can *feel* it."

"I do, though... What's that?"

"What's what?"

"I heard something over there." He pointed where the creek was slow and quiet behind a fallen log. He moved toward it slowly, Stig following behind.

"There," he whispered, pointing. Stig saw the back legs of a frog. The rest of it was in the mouth of a garter snake.

"Ugh. I hate that," Stig whispered. "Should we kill the snake?"

"Yeah."

Lonny picked up a rock. "Or maybe we shouldn't," he whispered. "It's natural. Animals eat other animals."

"And so do we," Stig said. "So what?"

"I don't know. I hate snakes, though." Lonny raised his rock to throw it when suddenly a doe crashed out of the woods in front of them, crossed the shallow creek in two bounds and disappeared crashing into the woods behind them. And then a dog came tearing after it. A black mutt of some kind, but the water slowed him down. Lonny threw his rock at the dog and hit its behind. It yelped and stopped in mid-stream and only then noticed the boys.

"ROWRRRR!" Lonny growled, and the dog spun around and took off the way it had come. Stig threw a rock after it and must have just nicked its back leg because it yelped again and jogged sideways for a jump or two before it disappeared in the brush.

The boys stood there and laughed and laughed and then started pushing and punching each other until Stig almost fell in the creek. He had to step into it to catch himself and the water went over his boot top.

"Shit," Stig said, and sat down on the ground to unlace his boot. "I hate wet socks." He wrung out the sock then got up and hobbled with one boot on and one boot off to a tree and hung the sock over a twig. "Hey, I'm Peg Leg Pete," he said.

Lonny took off his sneakers and socks and waded out in the creek. "Hey Stig, the water looks really deep in front of this log. There's a *bunch* of logs jammed up here. Beaver, maybe."

"Could be," said Stig. "Do you see teeth marks?"

"Can't tell." Lonny waded back to the shore. "I'm going swimming." He stripped, then waded back in and glided out into the pool in front of the logs. "Ohhh, this is great! Really cold, but you get used to it. Come on in!"

"Uh uh."

Lonny splashed him.

"Cut that out." Stig backed away from the creek.

"Come on in, it's great. It's not muddy like the dang gravel pit."

"I don't feel like it. I'm not hot anymore, anyway."

"It's not too deep, either. Look." He let his feet touch the bottom and stood up. The water came only to his chest.

"We were going to find out where this creek comes from," Stig said. "Let's get going."

Lonny paddled around some more. He liked how his body looked under water, kind of coppery around the edges. Sort of glowing, like the amber beads his mother wore sometimes. But then he came out and squeegeed most of the water off his body with his hands and put his clothes back on. Stig said his sock was still damp, but he put it on anyway and they started off.

The trees and brush didn't crowd the banks there so they could walk along beside the creek. Eventually a fence came right down into the water and blocked their way. They climbed over the fence and continued along the creek through a big pasture that had been eaten bare of grass, leaving just a few rocks sticking up here and there and cow pies all over. The sunshine here in the open field felt good to Lonny, but he could tell it was weaker and said so. And now the air not only felt yellow to him but it looked yellow, too.

"You see how yellow it's all getting?" he said.

"Yeah, sure. It's like I said, the light changes before a storm and you *see* that, you don't *feel* it."

"My grandma says, 'feels like a storm's coming.' We might move up to her house and live with her 'cause she's alone now since Grandpa died."

"We should turn back," Stig said.

"Yeah, I guess."

But they kept going, Lonny in the lead. "Watch out for the cow pies."

They'd been hearing thunder in the distance ahead of them for maybe fifteen minutes when they felt the first rush of a cool wind, and it stirred the branches all around them. The creek had narrowed quite a bit after they crossed another little creek that ran into it.

"I can smell that storm now," Lonny said.

"I don't know, Lonny. I think it's something rotten. Like old garbage or something."

"Yeah, *that's* what I smell. Garbage. Look!"

He pointed upstream. The rusted hulk of an old car was sitting in the middle of the creek. In fact, half the creek ran in at the passenger side and out the driver's side.

"A dump!" Lonny said.

They hurried up to the old car. It was one of those funny-faced things like they made before the war, with horns that went "ooogah." There was trash all around, and up both sides of the creek – old tires, paper scraps, milk bottles, oil cans, all kinds of cans, mostly rusted, some fresh with their labels still on them, lots of Campbell Soup cans and coffee cans. A road crossed over the creek just beyond the old car. It was obvious that people driving by threw trash from the bridge down to the creek.

Lonny thought it was a real pretty bridge. There were spaces between the top stones along the road edge like the top of a castle wall. He remembered Bergy telling him that a lot of the bridges in the county were built of quarried stone. That was somehow important. Bergy was one of the older kids in the neighborhood. He said that the bridges were built by the government during the Depression to make jobs for men out of work. Lonny explained all that to Stig now, and they looked until they found the stone with a date carved into it: "1935."

The water in the creek was low enough that the boys could walk through the tunnel under the road. There was even more trash on the other side. They wondered about that.

"Cars would be coming from town on the downstream side," Stig said, "and on the upper side they'd be heading *to* town."

"Yeah, so?"

"Well, you wouldn't throw away stuff you've just bought, would you? You'd throw away old stuff on your way to town to buy new stuff."

Lonny laughed. "Yeah, I guess you're right!"

"And look!" Lonny said, pointing, "there's an old radio somebody tossed on his way to buy a new one."

They climbed over trash to get to it. "So," Stig said, "we'll find the new radio on the other side of the bridge, right?" Lonny didn't answer. The heap they were climbing over was springy. He kicked some trash aside until he could see that down underneath all of it was an old bedsprings. That struck him as funny somehow.

Stig got to the radio and said that half the tubes in it were broken. But they thought it was a neat find, anyway.

"Maybe it would work if we got new tubes for it," Stig said.

And then the rain hit. It came with a big gust of wind and the boys dove for shelter under the bridge. There was a strip of dry ground about two feet wide between the water and the tunnel wall. The rain poured down outside. Then a flash of lightning lit up the whole tunnel and a second or two later, "BOOM!" The blast of thunder almost knocked them down.

Stig said something Lonny couldn't hear over the roar of the pounding rain.

"What'd you say?" he shouted, and Stig shouted back, "I said, 'I guess we're safe in here.'"

The swirling, gusting wind carried rain in from both ends of the tunnel. They moved to the exact center but the cold mist got to them anyway. They could talk without shouting but at first they just stood and shivered and listened to the storm and stared at the rising water. After a while Stig said, "Lonny, this creek feeds the ponds in the gravel pit, right?"

"Yeah, so?"

"And it flows through this dump. So all this old trash probably poisons the water you were swimming in."

Lonny thought a minute. "Nah. If water runs a hundred feet in open sunshine it gets purified."

"Who says?"

"I don't know. That's what they say. Bergy said that."

"I don't believe it. Maybe if it was a real little creek that's real shallow."

"What's the difference?"

"More of the water would get shined on by the sun."

"Yeah..." Lonny wasn't convinced. "But with a big creek like DeAmity, you wouldn't even notice a little poison. Say somebody throws an old car battery down here. The acid in it runs out in the creek. If it's a little creek there's a lot of acid in the water where it landed. But if it's a big creek, it just gets lost in all that water."

"You know what's worse?" said Stig.

"What?"

"We followed this creek through a cow pasture."

"Yeah... Yuck! I've been swimming in shitty water!" He punched Stig in the shoulder. Then Stig hit Lonny in the shoulder and Lonny hit him back and they punched each other for a while, laughing, and the rain was pouring down at either end of the tunnel and they were having a great time.

The fighting warmed them up and after a while the rain quit and there was bright sunshine again. The creek had risen so there was barely a foot of dry ground to stand on. The boys stepped out from the tunnel – "like a couple of ground hogs," Stig said, blinking in the light.

"What's a ground hog look like?" Lonny said. "I've never seen one."

"Me neither."

They looked around. The old tires now were a shiny wet black. A chrome bumper gleamed in the bright sunlight. There were sparkles in the wet green grass climbing up the banks, and a white steam rose in the heat of the sun from all the newly soaked trash. Lonny thought it was all real pretty.

Chapter 4 Alan

"Where's Mommy?" Becky held a big spoon in her fist. It hovered in mid-air, full of soggy corn puffs, inches from her face.

"She had to go somewhere real early, honey." Alan Stuart sat slouched in his chair, his fingers toying with the ear of his coffee mug. The spoon of corn puffs resumed their trajectory to Becky's mouth.

Alan drank off the last of his coffee. It was cold now, and bitter. He sat up. "Let's go visit Grandma, Becky. We'll surprise her."

"Okay!" Becky's broad grin revealed a missing tooth and a bit of cereal mush on her gums. "Is it Saturday? Where's Lonny?"

"It's not Saturday, honey, it's Thursday. Lonny's gone to school as usual, but I decided not to go to work today. I'm going to be home with you, so today you won't have to go to Mrs. Solheim's."

"Mrs. Solheim lets me and Gracie fingerpaint."

"Let's make it a special day. You finish breakfast and we'll clean up in here and then go visit Grandma."

Becky ate the last of the mush in her bowl and took a big gulp of milk, holding the glass in both hands. "I'm done!" She set down the glass and jumped off her chair.

Alan caught her arm. "Tell you what. You go pick some daisies for Grandma Lena while I clean up the kitchen."

"Mommy's daisies?"

"Yes, by the back door. What's wrong?"

"She'll get mad."

"No she won't. It's okay. I'll take the blame for it, but I know she won't mind at all. You go wash the milk off your face and pick a handful of daisies for Grandma."

Becky held the flowers in one hand and her father's hand in the other. They walked up the steep road past the Hershels' big white house and the Linkvists' house with the green shutters. Then they crossed the road and turned into the long driveway of Lena Stuart's house which, in summer, when the trees were fully leafed out, would be almost hidden. The first spring buds peeked out from among the leaves of the rose bushes along the front of the porch. Alan had to knock three times before they finally heard Lena's footsteps scuffing toward them.

"Alan! she said, opening the door. "Becky! My goodness. Are those for me?"

Becky gave her the daisies.

"Why thank you, honey. What a surprise! Come in. I'd better put these in water." They followed her through the living room. "What brings you two out on a weekday morning? Don't you work today, Alan?"

Father and daughter stood in the kitchen doorway as Lena filled a small vase at the sink. She cut off the broken stems and arranged the flowers in the vase, glancing at Alan as she worked, and again she glanced at him quizzically when she passed by into the living room carrying the flowers. She set them on a side table. "There. That brightens the room, doesn't it Becky?"

"Where's Kitty?" Becky said.

"Why don't you go find him? He's probably in the backyard waiting for a bird to say hello."

Becky ran from the room calling "Kitty! Kitty!"and heading for the back door.

Lena sat down in the overstuffed chair beside the daisies. "Alan, sit. Tell me what's going on."

She picked up the pack of Chesterfields lying on the table and began to tap out a cigarette, but stopped herself and opened her hand, letting the pack drop back onto the table. "Phooey. I've already had my morning smoke. Alan. Speak."

He sat down on the sofa opposite his mother. "Kate's gone."

"'Gone.'" She studied her son's face. "When?"

"Last night."

"So *tell* me."

He began reluctantly: "After the kids were asleep. I was getting ready for bed. In the bathroom brushing my teeth. I was in my pajamas. She came to the door holding a suitcase I'd never seen before. She was dressed to go out – black dress and jacket, ny-lons." Alan warmed to his story, remembering. "She says 'Alan' and I turned around, my mouth full of toothpaste. She says 'Alan, I'm leaving you. And the kids. I left a Post Office address on the bedside table. You can send divorce papers there. And I won't fight you for custody.' I just stared at her, holding my damn toothbrush. I barely had a chance to spit and she's halfway down the stairs. I caught up to her at the front door and grabbed her shoulder but she twisted away. 'Alan,' she says, 'You can't stop me, and why would you want to?' She says 'It doesn't work anymore. I can't stand it.' I said 'Why? What's so goddamn wrong?' 'Never mind,' she says. 'I don't want to hurt you,' and she walks out the door. 'You don't want to *hurt* me?' I said. There's a car waiting for her on the road. It was dark out and I don't think I'd ever seen it before. It wasn't a taxi. She's almost to the car and the engine starts up. She puts her suitcase in the backseat, gets in the front, and the car drives off. The driver was on the other side, so I couldn't see who it was."

After the rush of words Alan stood up, put his hands in his pockets. He looked at the floor, the ceiling, took his hands out of his pockets. Sat down again.

"Oh Alan," Lena said, finally. "I'm so sorry. You had no idea?"

He looked away, toward the front door. "Maybe it wasn't so good between us. But not terrible. We hadn't been... together... for a long time. I'm away so much. That's what it is to be a salesman. Kate was always at home with Becky, and she kept the house, and looked after Lonny, too, though he doesn't seem to need much looking after. I don't know what else she did. It seems we didn't know each other very well anymore. When I'd come home she'd tell me about the kids and then we didn't have much else to talk about. I guess I thought that's how marriages go. Just ordinary life."

"You make it sound dull, Alan. Didn't you even fight?"

"We never fought. That was one good thing, anyway."

"Maybe. Maybe not."

"Do you think she was bored? I always figured she was happy with Becky, at least. Do you think maybe she wanted to go back to work?"

"Did she ever mention it?"

"A couple of times, but I didn't think she was serious about it. She never pushed the idea."

"She left with another man?"

"Looks like it. There were signs, now that I think about it. I guess I didn't want to see them."

"Maybe you wanted her to go."

"Did I?" He thought about it. "Maybe. Maybe I wanted to leave, myself. Never thought that directly. Pushed it away, I guess, the thought."

"What are you going to do?"

"I don't know. Think I should try to get her back?"

"For the kids, yes, for Becky especially. Catherine's their mother, whatever else she is. But how will you find her?"

"The police should be able to. She left that Post Office address."

"That's right, she did... Well she sure made it easy for you."

"*Easy* for me? You think this is easy?"

"Think, my boy. Use your noodle, *she* did. She left the PO address so she could be found, if you wanted to make the effort. And if not she at least made herself easily served with legal papers. I've never liked Catherine particularly. She seemed vain and selfish to me. But I knew she was smart. Looks like she found a way to get you off your fanny. I'd say you could probably get her back if you wanted to. But I think you'd have to court her all over again."

Alan slouched down in the sofa, shoving his hands deep in his pockets. Lena saw his lips tighten. "You don't want her back, do you? Tell the truth, now. If she came in that door right now, crying, saying she was sorry and asking you to take her back, would you be glad to see her?"

"Yes!" Alan sat up and looked hard in his mother's eyes. But her even expression did not change, and the air went out of him through puffed out lips. He took a deep breath and sighed again. "No, I wouldn't be glad to see her, though I would at first. Because it feels like such a mess without her. And it's going to be hell on the kids." He paused. "But in fact, I'd be really sorry to see her. Not that I don't love her anymore. The thing is, she doesn't love me. I think she stopped loving me a long time ago. What I don't understand is how she could just run off from the kids."

A few weeks later Alan Stuart, his fourteen year old son Lonny and five year old Rebecca left their rented house three doors down the hill from Grandma Lena's to board a train for Seattle. Lena drove them to the station downtown.

"A new start, a new city," Alan said. Lena wished him well, kissed the children goodbye. As she drove home she wondered about herself, how she could pretend such coolness. It was good for Alan to go, but the children – she ached for them, seeing them walking away from her down the platform, past the engine and then along that long line of coaches, little Becky holding onto Lonny's hand, and Lonny's shoulders looking a little stooped.

On the third day of the long train ride the little family had just finished lunch. Lonny, sitting opposite his father and sister, watched the drizzling rain make horizontal tracks in the dirt on the window beside him. Becky was holding a quiet conversation with the rag doll on her lap, speaking in a low voice for herself and a squeaky little voice for the doll. Alan sipped a second cup of coffee and entertained himself with furtive glances down the aisle of the restaurant car at a brunette he found extremely attractive. She was chatting with someone across the table from her – man or woman he couldn't quite tell, his view blocked by two large men at an intervening table.

Becky bouncing her doll on his leg brought him out of his fantasy. "Daddy, Annie wants to ask you something."

"What? What does she want to ask me?"

"She wants to know where we're going."

"You can tell her, honey. You know where we're going."

"But Annie wants *you* to tell her."

"Annie," he said, bending down to the doll. "We're going to Seattle, just as Becky said. You should believe what Becky tells you." He straightened up. "By the way, kids... Lonny? Hey, daydreamer."

"Huh?"

"There's something I'd like to tell you two. Rebecca, I'd like you to listen, too."

"And Annie. She wants to listen."

"Lonny, listen up."

"Mmm."

"Okay, then. You know how my job takes me all over the north. I go to Fargo, Boise, Cœur d'Alene, Spokane, Seattle. I've sent you postcards from all those places."

Lonny barely nodded. Becky started moving one arm of her doll, up and down. Alan glanced out the dirty window at the aspens rushing by in their new leaves. The rhythmic clacking of the rails helped slow and steady his thoughts. He had to say this right to head off a lot of upset.

"Well, I've made friends in all those places. Some good friends. It's really a salesman's job to cultivate friendships all over, partly because sometimes those friendships get him contacts with potential customers, and partly because he'd get awfully lonely otherwise, having to be away from home so much. Becky, I'm sure you miss your friend Gracie, don't you?"

He paused, but she didn't answer.

"Anyway, I made a friend in Seattle who happens to be in the real estate business. She helps people sell their houses when they want to move away, and helps other people who need a house to find one. That's her job. She gets paid for doing that. This lady has found us a nice house in a neighborhood that's close to schools – close enough that you can both walk to school. You're going to be in first grade, Becky. A real school girl." He gave her a hug. "And there's a junior high, Lonny. It's a good school. It even has shop classes. I had the lady check." He paused, took a breath. "So. She's going to meet us at the train and go with us to the house. She's really nice and she'll probably have dinner with us. Her name is Clare."

Chapter 5 Clare

Seattle

"Alan, Becky's been in my make-up again. See, this jar lid's not on right. And look at that! Damn it! It's a smudge of mascara in my face cream! I can't stand this! Why can't she leave my stuff alone?"

"I wish you wouldn't swear. It's ugly."

"Oh golly gee! What about my things?"

"Look, Clare, I'm sorry about this. I'll talk to her again. And maybe it wouldn't hurt if you talked to her yourself once in a while."

"I'll talk to her, all right."

"*After* you've calmed down. Clare, she's a little kid. I think she's just curious about you. Wants to know you. It might really help if you talk to her, really talk, and listen, like a friend. Get acquainted."

"So this mess is all my fault?"

"We've all been together, what, three months? I'll bet you haven't spent an hour alone with her, just connecting a little bit."

"Your kid messes with my things and it's my fault for not playing mommy. I told you I'm not a mommy type. God, I can't stand it! Look here, in my underwear drawer. That's cold cream! Alan, I want a key lock on the door. I've got to have something here that's mine or I'll go nuts."

Clare dropped onto the bed, wadding the smeared panties in her hand. Alan sat down and put his arm around her.

"Yeah, okay. You should have some private space. I'll put a lock on the door. But I really wish you'd make a little effort to connect with the kids. Especially with Becky. She's lost her mother, Clare. Try to imagine what that's like for her."

She wriggled free of his arm: "I didn't drive her mother away. You said she didn't know anything about us. She took off on her own with some guy. Is that right, Alan? Or did she know about us? Did you tell her? Or did she figure it out? You told me you tried to avoid sleeping with her. That would make any woman suspicious."

"Clare, good Lord, it's not your fault. I'm only asking for the kid's sake – and for yours. You might even like the little girl. She thinks you're pretty. You know, maybe she thought she could find the secret of your beauty. I don't know. I don't know how kids think."

"Well I sure as hell don't." Her voice had softened. Alan put his arm around her again. He felt her shoulders relax, and she leaned against him, rested her hand on his thigh.

"I hope you're not getting cold cream on my pants," Alan said. "That'd raise some eyebrows when I visit buyers today."

"They'll just envy you. All your women grabbing at you."

"Tomorrow's Saturday," Alan said. "I'll get a lock at Sudwin's and install it. Two keys. One for you and one for me. Unless you want to lock me out too."

"Oh, I might let you in now and then."

"How about now?"

"Opportunist! No! Get away from me. I'm not done being mad at you."

"Me? You were mad at Becky."

"The whole package. You, Becky, Lonny. One package. It's a big one for a girl like me."

"Yeah," Alan sighed. "I guess it is."

"Now get out of here and let me get dressed. I'm going to take a long shower and try to calm down."

"I'll get the kids off to school. Want to meet at Casey's for lunch?"

"If I can. I might have a client. If I don't show, that's why."

"You found a buyer for the Mitchell place?"

"Maybe."

"Atta girl! Good luck."

Alan went downstairs and found his son and daughter at the kitchen table. Becky had a half-full bowl of cereal before her but she'd stopped eating. Lonny was reading aloud from the corn flakes box. The white formica of the table top bore splashes of milk, and the juice pitcher sat in an orange puddle. There were drawings Scotch-taped to the wall beside Becky's chair. Alan had put them up the day before but had barely noticed their content. Now they caught his eye. One showed a bold yellow sun disk and flat green lawn bearing stick figures of Daddy (the tall figure wearing a hat), little Becky (in the red triangular dress), and middle-sized Lonny holding something in his hand that might have been a baseball bat or just a stick. In the picture above it a little box house with smoke curling up from a chimney sat sandwiched between two big brown curved lines, representing hills, Alan surmised, but why were they brown? The house was an outline in red and the smoke was a curling black line. Down in the left hand corner was a tiny pink triangle and two stick legs while the corner opposite bore a messy scribble of what looked like all the colors from a two-bit box of crayons.

"Morning, kids. It's about time to leave. Lonny, wipe up that mess on the table. Becky, eat up, honey, you've got to leave in just few minutes."

"Dad, listen to this: 'Two box tops and fifty cents to Kellogg's blah blah blah Battle Creek, Michigan.'" He looked up. "Where's Battle Creek? Is that Northern Michigan?"

"I don't think so. They wouldn't put a grain mill in the middle of the woods. What's the offer this time?"

"It's for a spy something," Becky said. "What's a spy?"

"You tell her, Lonny. You're more up on that stuff than I am."

"Come on, Squirt. Go wash the milk off your face and I'll tell you on the way to school."

"And you wipe that mess off the table, Lonny. You know how Clare is."

"I know how Clare is."

"Don't scare Becky with your spy story."

Becky saw a robin pulling a worm out of the freshly dug flower bed beside the front walk.

"Come on, Squirt, you're going to be late."

She ran to catch up. "Lonny, are worms alive?"

"Yeah. Sure."

"The robin was eating a worm."

"That's what they do."

"Are worms alive like us?"

"That's a hard question. Look out, now. Look both ways."

They crossed the wide street.

"I wouldn't want to be a worm."

"Then be sure to look both ways before you cross the street." Lonny looked up through the budding boulevard trees, squinted at the bright sun. "It's going to be warm today. Really feels like spring. I guess it gets to be spring in Seattle long before Duluth."

"Do you like Clare?" Becky said.

"Umm."

"I think she's pretty."

"Yeah."

"Does she like us?"

"Becky, I was going to tell you about spies. A spy is someone who works for a government – like the US, or the Russians. And he watches what goes on in another or country. Or the spy could be a woman, you know. Lots of spies are women. Anyway the spy does this spying in secret and tells his government what he's seen. It's real dangerous because if a spy gets caught by the country he's spying on they torture him and pull out his tongue and then they kill him."

They walked on in silence to the next cross walk. Becky hit her brother in the leg and said, "Watch." She turned her head to the left and then to the right.

"Good girl."

They started across. "I wouldn't want to be a spy," Becky said.

"Or a worm, either, right?"

"Uh huh."

A robin flew up from a lawn and crossed in front of them. "I'd like to be a robin, or *like* a robin," Lonny said.

"And eat worms?

"Fly! Dumbhead."

"Do robins ever fall down?"

"There's your friend Karen," Lonny said. "I'll see you at three." They had arrived in front of the red brick elementary school. A yellow bus parked at the curb was disgorging children who, in spite of a lot of running around, moved in the general direction of the school's double front doors.

"Bye Lonny."

He turned away, crossed the road and hurried down four blocks and across the Great Northern tracks to his own school and Miss Van Cleave's English class. He hated to come in late because her face would take on an expression of terrible pain, and she'd press her palm to her stomach as though the pain were in there and it hurt like a swallowed razor blade. Lonny was fifteen, only in the eighth grade, having had to repeat seventh, and he hated school. Usually he tried not to complain about it in front of Becky, so as not to sour *her* on school. All through the lower grades at Quincy Adams School in Duluth "C" was the best mark he could ever get, and that didn't happen often except for "Deportment," but why only a "C"in Deportment he could never understand. He'd never been in trouble, never passed notes or whispered in class. Stiggy, his only friend at that school, was always seated at least three rows away, and the last year they hadn't even been in the same class.

When he slipped into his seat just before the bell rang Lonny was thinking about Stig, wondering if he still lived in Chicago where he'd moved with his family just after sixth grade. He'd come over to say goodbye, and they promised to write to each other. Stig was real unhappy about moving and so were his mom and brother, he said, and his dad didn't like it either. But his dad had a chance for a good job in Chicago because of belonging to a union there. In Duluth there was never was enough work for people. Stig did write to him once but Lonny hadn't answered. He wasn't good at writing, and he couldn't think of what to say anyway.

"You just made it," whispered the boy across the aisle.

Lonny grinned and nodded.

"Mister Stuart." The teacher addressed him from the front of the classroom. "Technically you were in your seat before the bell rang. However, as you are talking to your neighbor you are not yet ready for lessons. Can you think of a reason I should not mark you tardy?"

"I wasn't talking."

"He *can't* talk" came a stage whisper from the back of the room, followed by muffled laughter.

Miss Van Cleave shot a dark look toward the offenders but said nothing.

And now Lonny was remembering how his father had come to supper one night and announced that they were moving to Seattle the next day. Grandma Lena wouldn't be coming with them because she owned the house she lived in. And that was it. That night Lonny packed his clothes and a few things he liked. His hunting knife, his pocket knife – a gift from his mother, who had run off one morning "with some guy," his father said, and hadn't come back – some fishing gear, and two figures he'd carved out of dried yellow pine. One was a chipmunk with only one ear and only the beginnings of a tail. He'd carved the body too big for the piece of wood he had, but Lonny felt it looked pretty much like a chipmunk anyway. And the other was a loon, the way it looks when it's floating on a lake. It had been a lot easier to carve than the chipmunk.

The next morning Lena had driven them downtown to the Great Northern station. Three days later they were in Seattle, and meeting Clare.

Lonny came out of his daydream and saw that Miss VanCleave had finished taking roll and now held *The Red Badge of Courage* open in front of her. She was young and pretty and Lonny wished she liked him.

"I assume you've all read the assigned chapters," she said. "I have some questions I want you to write down and then I want you to think silently about your answers. The first question asks a simple fact and won't require any thinking: When did the Civil War begin?"

Lonny opened his notebook and pulled his pencil out of the holder in the back. The lead was broken. He worked at it with his thumbnail to scrape away enough wood fibers so it would write. Then came the next question.

"How much older than you was Henry Fleming when he enlisted in the Union Army?"

Lonny wrote "Civil War? Henry's age?"

"And the third question, When he ran from the battle was he a coward?"

Lonny wrote "Coward?" He had read the chapters. He liked the book better than any book he'd ever read. He felt sorry for Henry. Who could blame him for running? And he wasn't the only one who ran, either. But that didn't change anything, really. He ran... because he was afraid? Lonny picked up his copy and started searching for the place where Henry turned and ran, listening with half an ear to the class discussion.

"Vicki Sims, when did the war begin?"

Lonny found the place and started to read.

"Wasn't it at Harper's Ferry?"

"No, and that's not when but where. Anyone?"

"Fort Sumter" – from the windows side of the room.

"I asked '*When*.'"

"1860."

"No."

"1861."

47

"You're all just guessing. April 21, 1861." She turned and wrote the date on the blackboard. "Remember that," she said. "Now tell me *why* the war started."

"That's not one of your questions" – shouted from the back of the room.

"We can branch out a little. Does anyone know?"

Lonny found what he was looking for and stopped listening. Eventually he put down the book and looked up. He never decided to run. Henry never decided. He just ran. He was standing there shooting and then he was running. It doesn't say he was afraid. In his mind he saw Henry running through the woods, running and running, sunlight splashing off the leaves. Lonny loved the woods in Minnesota. He'd run after a partridge once, in the snow. That was hard going.

"How old are you, Michael Purvis?"

Lonny remembered the partridge tracks in the snow...

"Thirteen."

...Henry was the partridge...

"Can you see yourself enlisting to fight in a war next year?"

"I'd get out of school."

... Probably seemed to him like the whole rebel army was shooting at him...

"Lonny Stuart? Yoo hoo! Lonny Stuart!"

His eyes snapped away from the windows – the trees outside, their dark green leaves shiny in the sunlight – and focused on the teacher.

"Was Henry Fleming a coward?"

"Oh, ah..."

"Yes?"

"I... I don't know... I mean it's hard to say. He did run, I guess, but..."

"And you did read the assignment?"

"Yes. It's the best book I've ever read."

"The only book," someone said. "He can't read" – came the back-of-the-room whisper.

"Cornell, what do you think?"

48

"Chicken, Ma'am. Yellow in the belly. You could hear him squawking like he'd laid an egg."

"That's not in the book, Cornell."

"You asked me what I thought."

A teacher's meeting that afternoon required an early dismissal of classes. That left Lonny a free hour before meeting Becky to walk her home. It had occurred to him that the boy next to him in English class seemed to want to be friends, and now he found this Dickie Tolliver, and another kid he didn't know, shooting baskets in the school playground.

"Lonny," Dickie said, "come on and play. This is Royce."

Lonny had never cared for sports and was slow on his feet. He was a little heavier than Dickie and the same height, but they were both at least an inch shorter than Royce. Dickie did a lot of dribbling whenever he got a rebound and it wasn't hard for Royce or even Lonny to slap the ball away from him. Lonny made a lucky basket once just by throwing it up like a baseball from near the free throw line. Royce left then and eventually the custodian came out to retrieve the school's ball and lock it away.

Lonny and Dickie sat down on the concrete walk beside the school and leaned back against the brick wall. Dickie started telling about his family, about his older brother in the Army in Korea and another older brother who was 4F because of asthma. He said his father was a deacon in their church and his mother was in some ladies' aid circle sewing things for poor people when she wasn't visiting her sister who was often sick.

"That's my Aunt Elizabeth and you know what? She has a scar on her forehead. It looks a lot like yours. I guess that's why it's not such a weird thing for me like it is for Ray Morris and those other bastards that tease you in class. Aunt Elizabeth, she's not married. My mother says nobody ever expected anyone would ask her. But she's really nice. Never forgets my birthday, or Christmas. She plays the piano in church, when she's not sick. How did you get that scar, anyway? Did you fall or something?"

Lonny looked at his feet. "Yeah. Sort of."

"What do you mean, 'sort of'?"

"Look, I don't want to talk about it."

"Did you do something stupid?"

"No. Just drop it, okay?"

"You don't have to get mad."

"I'm not mad."

"So what's the big deal?"

"I told you to drop it!"

"Okay, okay. Jeez, take it easy. I'm just curious, you know?"

Neither boy said anything for while. Then Dickie said, "So tell me about your family. What church do you go to?"

"I don't."

"I mean your family."

"My dad never goes to church. I don't remember him ever mentioning church. In Duluth I had a friend who got out of school to go to religious education. Every Wednesday he went."

"You didn't say about your mother."

"What about her?"

"Well does *she* go to church?"

"No! I mean I don't know, I mean it's none of your business what she does!"

"Now what are you getting mad about? What's wrong with your mother?"

Lonny jumped up and shouted down at him. "There's nothing wrong with my mother! Why don't you just shut up!"

Dickie got up slowly, eyeing Lonny suspiciously, his back against the wall. "So there *is* something wrong with her. Or wait! You don't *have* a mother, do you? That's why you don't know..."

"Shut up!" Lonny swung at him. Dickie turned and took the blow on his shoulder. He spun around and hit Lonny in the stomach, but delivered off balance the punch had no effect. Lonny swung wildly, lefts and rights, most of them blocked by Dickie's raised arms but enough landing to make him keep backing away and barely able to fight back. A right caught Dickie on the mouth and he staggered backwards.

"Hey! You boys stop that fighting! Stop it! Stop it now!"

Lonny turned his head toward the male voice and Dickie hit him on the side of the face but again he was off balance when he swung and both of them fell to the sidewalk just as the big man arrived and locked each boy by an arm in a steel grip. He pulled them to their feet and shook them.

"What the hell do you think you're doing fighting on the school grounds? If I report this you'll both be expelled!"

"Please don't report me Mr. Lohmeier," said Dickie. "This jerk just started hitting me for no reason. I wasn't fighting. I had to protect myself."

"Don't give me that shit!" His voice boomed. "Don't you ever, either of you, fight on the school grounds again! Is that clear?"

Both boys nodded.

"I said," the man thundered, 'Is that clear?'"

"Yeah."

"Yes sir."

"Good. Now, is anybody hurt?

He dropped Dickie's arm and grabbed him by the jaw. "That's a cut on your lip, but it's not serious. What's your name?"

"Dickie Tolliver, sir."

"And you?" He jerked Lonny around to face him.

"A little scrape on the jaw there. What's your name?"

"Lonny Stuart," he said, his voice was shaky. He could feel tears in his eyes and his whole body vibrating.

"Well, you're neither much the worse for wear. Now both of you, Dickie, Lonny" – he was memorizing their names – "you get out of here now. Go home. No more fighting."

He let go of them. Lonny rubbed his bicep where the teacher had squeezed it.

"Thank you, Mr. Lohmeier," said Dickie. "And I won't go anywhere near that bastard again."

"Go on, get out of here," said the big man, waving his arm.

There were other teachers coming out of the building now, and Lonny headed in the direction of Becky's school. After a few steps he looked over his shoulder to see where Dickie was going. He saw him just then stop and turn around in the empty schoolyard, and he heard him yell, "You're so damn ugly your mother ran off!"

Lonny had to wait at the railroad crossing for the last few cars of a long freight train to pass by. A brakeman standing on the rear platform of the caboose waved to him. When the crossing gates rose Lonny stopped on the tracks and watched the train going away. He remembered Becky then and checked his watch: she'd be out of school already, waiting for him on the sidewalk.

When he finally met up with her he could see she'd been crying.

"Where have you been?" she said. "I've been waiting a long time. Angie's mother picked her up in a big car and she wanted to give me a ride home but I said I had to wait for my brother. What happened to your face?"

"Nothing. I guess I ran into a tree. I wasn't looking where I was going."

"How could you run into a tree? I don't believe you."

"Just never mind. Forget it. Let's go home."

They had gone a block when Becky started to giggle. "That's funny," she said. "You running into a tree."

"Yeah. Real funny. Look, Squirt. I'm glad you waited for me. I wouldn't have known what to do if you weren't there."

"Lonny! Have you been fighting?"

"He ran into a tree, Daddy," said Becky.

"My foot he ran into a tree. Where were you fighting? What happened to the other guy?"

"He had a cut lip, I guess. He's okay."

"You *were* fighting!" Becky said. "You lied to me."

"Becky, shut up. Lonny, where was this, at school? Are you getting expelled?"

"It was after school. There's no problem, Dad. It wasn't reported."

"Well you better wash off that scrape. Put some iodine on it."

In the bathroom Lonny saw his face in the mirror. He started to cry and he hated himself for crying and for being so ugly and for not having a mother and *maybe she did leave to get away from me,* he thought, *I sure would.* He soaped a washcloth and scrubbed the scrape on his cheek. It hurt and he stopped crying. He rinsed off the soap and then patted the abrasion dry with toilet paper. When he touched the iodine to it the stinging felt good. It was clear and sharp. He thought about school Monday. He wouldn't have one friend there. And now he had an enemy.

They had begun eating dinner when Clare clinked her water glass with a fork, smiled at everyone when they looked up and said, "I have an announcement to make. Escrow closed on a house today, a house I sold. It was a big house, worth lots of money. So I earned a pretty nice commission on that sale." She smiled at Lonny and Becky: "So I'm sharing some of that commission with you kids." She passed each of them a white envelope. "Consider it a little bonus to your allowance this month."

"What do you say, kids?" said their father.

"Thank you, Clare," they said in unison, looking stupidly at their envelopes.

"What's an ess crow?" said Becky.

"Oh," said Clare. "It's not a bird. It's a neutral party account that holds the money in a business transaction until all the papers are signed."

Becky stared at her. Lonny opened his envelope. It contained as much as an entire month's allowance. He looked up at Clare. "Thanks," he said.

"You're welcome." She peered at him across the table. "Lonny, what happened to your face?"

"Go ask my mother."

"Lonny! Don't be smart!" said his father. Then to Clare, "He got in a fight after school."

"Oh God!" Clare said. "Are you one of these street toughs that beats up on other kids?"

Lonny looked at Clare, then at his father, bewildered. He scooted back his chair, jumped up cramming the money in his pants pocket, and left the room.

"Come back here, Lonny!" his father shouted, but the boy ignored him. They heard him running up the stairs and then a door slamming shut.

"He's gone to his room," Clare said. "Just as well. Does he get in fights often?" She looked at Alan, then Becky.

"Not that I know of," said Alan. "Becky?"

She started to cry and then fled from the table and followed Lonny up the stairs. The white envelope lay unopened beside her plate.

"Well for Christ's sake," said Clare. "I try to do something nice for them and what do I get?"

Saturday morning Lonny was up early. He wolfed down a bowl of cereal and then set the bowl carefully in the sink. He walked quietly along the hall and out the front door then ran two blocks to "the Greek's" grocery store. Outside it there was a pay phone and a phone book. He opened to the white pages and found a listing for Great Northern Railway followed by several numbers. He found the one he wanted, put a nickel in the box and dialed.

When he got back to the house he opened the front door as quietly as he could, stepped inside and listened. He heard his father's voice in the kitchen and then Becky's. And then he heard the shower running. Amazed by his luck he took off his shoes and carried them up the stairs. At the door to his father's and Clare's room he stopped and listened. The showering continued full force. One thing he knew about Clare, she loved long showers. He opened the door to their room and stepped inside. Beside a lamp on her dresser Clare's purse stood upright. Still carrying his shoes, Lonny opened it with his free hand, undoing the clasp with thumb and forefinger. Inside it he found a long white envelope, unsealed. He lifted the flap with one finger. The envelope was full of twenty-dollar bills. He took two and put them in his pocket, closed the envelope, nudged the purse to exactly the spot where he'd found it, and left the room, closing the door carefully behind him.

He stepped quietly to the stairs then stopped, thinking. He turned around and went into his room. There he put his shoes down on the rug, found his gym bag and tossed the contents into a corner of the closet. He replaced the gym clothes with a pair of under-pants, an undershirt, one pair of socks, and a flannel shirt – not much: it wouldn't be missed. He got his hunting knife out of the drawer of the little student desk and dropped that in too, then thought better of it and put it back. He looked around, saw the chipmunk and loon, wanted to take them but decided it was unwise. Then holding the gym bag under his arm he picked up his shoes and went out of the room. The shower was still running in the bathroom and he went quietly down the stairs. From the kitchen he heard the clink of a spoon against a dish and the sound of a chair sliding on the floor. Quickly he slipped out the front door and down the porch steps. He crammed his feet in his shoes and without tying them took off running.

The next day, from his window seat in a Great Northern passenger car, Lonny admired the now yellowed aspen leaves passing by on the Great Divide. He knew Grandma Lena would be glad to see him and that she'd probably let him stay. But he felt rotten for leaving Becky, and for not even saying goodbye to her. He thought he'd feel better getting away, heading back home to Duluth. But what he felt was something like sickness in his stomach. "Chicken," the kid had said. "Yellow in the belly."

Chapter 6 Sixteen

Duluth

Jeter Provich was pimply, skinny, tow-headed, and, as he liked to boast, a whiz at math and a zero at everything else. In woodshop he had shared a bench with Lonny their first semester at East Junior High. The shop teacher had called the first project a "sample," a 9-inch chunk of 1x6 dry yellow pine that a student was to plane to 5¾ x 8¾ inches, keeping three corners square and rounding one corner to a 1½ inch radius using a coping saw and a file. Provich's sample was down to almost 4 x 8 and still not quite square. Mr.Duff gave him a "D" and set him to the next task on the syllabus, a magazine rack. Provich came back to his side of the bench carrying four sticks of walnut stock.

"Hey Stuart," he said, "do *you* have any use for a magazine rack?"

Lonny, planing away the dried excess glue from a panel he'd glued up, stopped and thought for a second.

"Nope. My grandmother might."

"I've got a stack of comic books, but this thing we're supposed to make could only hold maybe a handful of them. I could give it to my mother, I guess."

He picked up one of the pieces and sighted down its length. Directions were to cut the pieces to length, then plane the edges square so as to glue the pieces together into a 15 x 20 inch panel. Then plane and glue up a shorter panel to set in front of the first one in order to hold magazines between them.

"Only, my mother doesn't *have* magazines. Too cheap to buy them. She reads them at the beauty parlor."

"Maybe you can sell the rack," Lonny said.

Provich laughed.

Eventually it worked out that Lonny was helping Provich in woodshop – doing his planing for him, which Mr. Duff saw but ignored – and Provich helping Lonny with the arithmetic he had failed to learn in grammar school.

As arranged, on a Tuesday in late May Lonny met Jeter at the gym just after their first period classes. They worked their way into the locker room through the crowd of boys coming and going, all of them banging lockers – either shutting or opening them – talking and laughing and yelling across the room.

Over the noise Jeter said, "I'd hate to have P.E. first thing in the morning."

They stopped when they got to the service door beside the equipment cage and tried to look inconspicuous, waiting until there was no one nearby to see them. On Tuesdays just after first period the normally locked door would be unlocked to let in a laundry service that delivered fresh towels and picked up dirty ones. Eventually there was only one boy left among the lockers near the door. He finished buttoning up his shirt, banged his locker shut and started to leave, but then noticed Lonny and Jeter watching him.

"What are you queers looking at?"

"Nothing," Jeter said. "How's the team shaping up?"

"We're fantastic." He looked at his watch. "Jesus." He took his gym bag and left in a hurry.

"What team is that, Jeter?"

"Basketball, Junior Varsity. That's Getty Krause. He's starting forward, I think."

Lonny pushed open the door and they slipped out. The laundry's panel truck was already moving away up the service drive between the back of the school and the playing field. They ran to catch up then trotted along beside it, keeping their heads down and staying between the truck and the brick wall of the school. When they reached the street they turned onto the sidewalk where a line of spruce trees shielded them from the view of anyone at the school. They walked quickly up to the Wallace Street intersection at the top of the hill then continued down to the next cross street and turned left to get off the main thoroughfare.

At Third Street they turned right, then slowed to a comfortable stroll, heading for downtown, maybe a movie.

"Lonny, do you know what's showing?"

"No, how would I know?"

Jeter took a couple of swings around a sign post, hanging out arm's length, his feet planted at the base. Then he trotted to catch up. "Your birthday's in June, right?"

"No. May."

"Mine's June sixth. Pearl Harbor!" He took a deep breath and intoned, "'A day that will live in infamy.'"

"No. It's D-Day. The Allied Invasion of Normandy."

"That's right. I was just testing you."

"Sure you were."

"The liberation of France, then all of Europe. Oh hey." Jeter paused. "It's also the liberation of Lonny Stuart from the prison of East Junior High."

"Yeah, almost. It'll only take a few more days to finish out the semester. I think it'll be easier for my grandmother that way. She'll get used to me not going off to school all summer, and in the fall I'll just keep doing whatever I'm doing. Going to work, probably."

"Boy, not me, man. If I was sixteen I wouldn't hang around Duluth. I've got a whole damn year to go." They crossed a street without looking. Off the main drag there was almost no traffic.

"I don't get it, Jeter. You get *A*'s in math and *F*'s and *D*'s in everything else."

"What's to get? I don't give a shit about all that other stuff. But math's fun. It's like a game."

"I wish I was good at something. The old farmer I work for on weekends thinks I could be a good farmer."

"Too bad they don't teach farming at East."

"I'd probably flunk it. It'd be full of assholes screwing around like in any other class."

"I ignore those guys. I do math problems in my head."

"That's what I mean. School's a complete waste of time. I was drawing a canoe in English this morning, wishing I was in a canoe on some lake up north."

Jeter swung around another sign post and Lonny's daydream came back to him. The lake was blue and still, pine and spruce trees all around the shores, a slight breeze making the water shimmer a little, nobody around for miles. But now the dream changed. He was paddling toward an island in the lake. He'd caught a big walleye and it was lying in the bottom of the canoe. He was bringing it to camp for dinner... Helen Billingham is waiting for him – she's there and she's got a fire going and she's put potatoes around the edge to roast. She sees him now and waves. And then he sees only her face, her lips are a little bit apart, and he leans toward her and her eyes close and she breathes "love you" and waits for him. She waits for him to kiss her... waits for him...

Lonny shook his head. No Helen Billingham was ever going let him kiss her.

"My dad says if I want to quit school I'll have to pay rent or move out."

Lonny didn't answer.

"He's such a prick," Jeter said.

"Just get a job."

"Work for some dumb farmer, like you?"

Lonny looked Jeter up and down and laughed. "You wouldn't last a day on a farm."

"My dad says I should try a bank. He'd 'put a word in for me' he said. He's got friends in banks."

"You gonna do it?"

"Shit, I don't know. I want to go to Chicago or at least Minneapolis. The bank seems worse than school. I'd get paid, though. Be nice to have some money."

"Yeah."

Then Jeter was saying something more about banks but Lonny was thinking about Helen Billingham. She sat two seats up from him in the row next to his in Social Studies. She had brown hair and liked to wear white button-up sweaters unbuttoned over her blouse. She always scooped her hand down her behind to smooth her skirt when she sat. Lonny liked that she wasn't part of the in-crowd, though he figured she was pretty enough for them. She hung out with the same three girls in the cafeteria every day. He'd never seen her with a boy.

"Hey hey hey! It's Scarface and his little buddy Sticks! Cutting school, are we?"

Courtney Bolger had his head out of the driver's side window of the black '51 Ford rolling along beside them on the wrong side of the street.

"Fuck you, Bolger," Jeter said.

They heard Elvis on the car radio. *"Don't be cruel, to a heart that's true,"* Bolger mouthing the words at them. He said, "Jeter baby, don't be nasty now."

He leaned over to say something to the guy beside him – Lonny saw it was the boy from the locker room, Getty Krause, and in the back seat he recognized Hokan Borg fron English class huddled forward with the guys in front.

Jeter whispered, "That's three-fifths of J.V. basketball. And Bolger's president of our class."

"I know who he is," Lonny said.

"He's on the debating team, too."

"So?"

"Look my friends," Bolger said, "there's a gathering of young people like ourselves out at Rice Lake. Some people from Central High. Cass told me about it. We're picking her up on the way. Would you like to come? We could use a stronger East High presence there. It's just that you must have money for beer. If you do, we'd be pleased if you'd be kind enough to join us."

"Cass" was Cass Constant. Lonny had heard she'd been suspended the week before, some said for smoking in the girl's john, some said for drinking, some said for screwing Bolger in the boy's john.

Jeter poked him. "Let's go with them!"

Lonny turned his back to the car. "I don't trust these assholes."

"Why? What do you think'll happen? It'll be fun."

"You haven't got any money."

"You do."

"I'm not going. They just want money for beer."

"So what? Come on, let's go!"

"You guys coming or what?" Bolger said.

"Lend me five bucks, then," Jeter whispered.

"These guys ain't your friends, Jeter."

"C'mon Lonny." He had his hand out. "Lend me five bucks."

"No."

"Damn you, Lonny." Jeter crossed the narrow boulevard to the car and leaned over Bolger's open window. He had one hand in his pocket. "Bolgy, I've got almost enough for a six-pack."

"He called you 'Bolgy,'" said Krause, laughing.

"Shove your pennies up your ass, Little Shit. And if you ever call me 'Bolgy' again I'll break your face." He gave him a big fake smile, then put the Ford in gear and revved the engine. "Bye bye, girls," he said. He wiggled his fingers at them and pulled away from the curb. Jeter stood there and watched the car go on down the street.

Lonny and Jeter took a bus downtown and arrived too early for the first show at the Granada. They walked the four blocks down to the Strand, discovered that its first show wasn't till evening, then walked back to Coney Island Hot Dogs next to the Granada. They picked a booth, Lonny taking the side facing the storefront window. He bought them each an orange soda and a hot dog smothered in onions and chili.

"This is a lot better than cafeteria slop," Jeter said, his mouth full.

"Mmhm. They do something special with onions here. You smell them when you come in the door. Maybe they steam them or something. Best hot dogs anywhere."

"So what do we do now?" Jeter said. "Show doesn't start for another hour. It's a dumb movie, too."

"Well, Jeat, I guess we could sit here and wish we were back at school."

"Very funny. We shoulda gone with Bolger."

"Looks like you've got another chance." Lonny nodded toward the window and Jeter turned to look. Between "Coney" and "Island" painted in an arc on the glass they saw Hokan Borg's head. Then Borg was joined by Bolger, Cass Constant, and Krause.

"I've paid for these," Lonny said suddenly. "I'm getting out of here. You coming?"

Lonny stuffed his mouth full of hot dog and led the way to the back of the café, down a hall past the johns, through a storeroom, and finally out a back door that opened on the alley behind the café and theater.

"Were they coming in?" said Jeter.

"I think so."

"I wonder what happened to the party at Rice Lake?"

"It was bullshit. They've got plenty of money, those guys. They just wanted to shake us down for the hell of it."

Lonny and Jeter walked down the alley to the cross street.

"Look, there's Bolger's car," said Jeter. It was parked on the other side of the street.

"Wait here," Lonny said. He went down to Superior Street and peeked around the edge of the building on the corner. There was an old man under the theater marquee studying the posters and a woman in a flowered dress and a big hat coming toward him on the sidewalk carrying a shopping bag. Bolger's crowd was gone. Lonny signaled to Jeter, and after traffic cleared they met at Bolger's car.

"Damn, they didn't leave the keys in it," Lonny said.

"You were gonna steal the car?

"I don't know. Maybe just park it somewhere else."

"That'd be great! Man, he'd kill you if he found out it was you."

"You'd tell him?" Lonny looked at him hard.

"No, man. I wouldn't tell him."

"Yeah?"

"Why the hell would I tell him?"

"Yeah, why would you?"

"Jesus, Lonny."

They walked along Superior Street, drifting in the direction of the train station and the center of town, looking in store windows, fooling around. They saw a Lionel train in one window running around the feet of a couple of dressed-up dummies.

Jeter said, "Let's jump a train! We can take a bus out to the switch yard and jump a train going up the grade."

"They're just ore cars, Jeat. You can't ride in them."

"Yeah. But we could hang on a side ladder for while. It'd be fun... Hey look, someone left his keys in this Merc." Jeter had been glancing into parked cars as they walked along. "Should we take it for a ride?"

"Whose car is it?"

"How should I know? Why?"

"I don't want to steal a car. We'd get caught and go to jail."

"What about Bolger's car? You were gonna steal that."

"I wasn't going to steal it. Just move it around the block. We wouldn't have had it long enough to get caught."

"You don't always make a lot of sense, Lonny."

They took a bus out to Park Point at the end of the long narrow peninsula that cuts St. Louis Bay off from the western tip of Lake Superior.

"There's hardly anyone here," Jeter said. "We should come on a weekend."

They walked around among the rides and concessions. Finally, Lonny bought tickets and they drove the bumper cars, ramming each other head-on over and over until the operator made them quit. They bought ice cream bars then walked over the low hill to the beach. The sun was warm, about as high overhead as it would get that day.

Lonny dipped a finger in the water. "It was ice this morning," he said, and stood up, looking out across the lake. "I wonder what it would be like to live in Florida and swim in the ocean all year round."

"I've got an uncle in Florida," Jeter said.

Lonny sat down on the sand. Then he leaned back on one elbow and started digging in the sand with the wooden stick from his ice cream bar. "I'm going to build myself a house someday," he said.

Jeter sat down with his elbows on his knees. He was watching an ore boat steaming out into Lake Superior, low in the water, loaded with iron ore for the mills in Indiana or Ohio. "I might ship out on an ore boat," Jeter said.

"How would you get a job like that?"

"I don't know. I could ask my dad."

Chapter 7 Education

Early in May Bengt and Signe Olafson sold their farm and moved to town. The new owners, Mark and Tess Nowicke, hired Lonny full-time the day after his school year ended. He had told no one but Jeter it would be his last. The Nowickes came from Pennsylvania, Lonny wasn't sure where. They seemed to have plenty of money to spend turning the farm into a riding stable, building fancy new stalls in the old barn, adding a corral and white-painted fencing, besides fixing up the house and building an office onto the side of it. All that before opening up for business. By mid-August they offered trail rides, hourly horse rentals, and boarding. At first the Nowickes used Lonny for odd jobs and clean up, but soon he was helping the old carpenter Hjälmar Ekman with the rough carpentry and discovering that he enjoyed learning the new skills. Ekman, it turned out, also lived on Plane Street like Lonny and his grandmother, but way up near the top of the hill.

Lonny also worked with the horses. It was Tess who bought them. She'd show up after she'd been gone for a couple of days, driving the big Dodge Power Wagon and hauling the trailer home loaded with one or two new saddle horses. Once it was a mare and colt. Mark stayed home and supervised the construction while building the corral and fencing himself. He said Tess went to auction sales as far south as Minneapolis and east into Wisconsin.

Ekman, the carpenter, remarked to Lonny that Mark was a fool to let his pretty wife traipse around the country for days alone. "Trust is a good thing but anyone can be tempted."

"My dad went on business trips a lot," Lonny said. "Mom didn't seem to mind."

"Uh huh. Does he still go on these trips?"

"I don't know. Maybe."

"You don't know. Your pa doesn't live with you. Is that right?"

Lonny didn't answer. His father was in Seattle, he knew that. He didn't know where his mother was, and he was never sure why she left. That was a long time ago.

Ekman went on nailing studs into the wall section they were building. Lonny held the studs in place and the old man drove in the nails, two or three blows each. Lonny liked him. His whole face wrinkled up when he smiled, and he smiled a lot. He had even white teeth and his blue eyes looked right into you and seemed to like what he saw.

"Okay, let's tilt this up," Ekman said. "I'll hold it and you nail the plate to the floor. Two sixteen-pennys between every other stud."

Lonny used an old hammer Ekman had given him. He only bent one nail. The old man made him pull it and start another. Then Ekman nailed two-by-four props at each end while Lonny held the section steady and plumb with the help of a long level against one of the studs. When the section was up securely Ekman looked at his bare wrist and announced, "It's time for coffee."

They sat by the creek on a bark-stripped log that was one of a pair destined to span the creek and support a footbridge.

"Dad's in Seattle," Lonny said. "When I was fourteen he packed up me and Becky and we moved to Seattle."

Ekman grinned at him. "But you're here." He looked around at the new construction and the trees across the creek. "I don't think this here's Seattle, leastwise it wasn't last time I checked." He filled a tin cup from his thermos and handed it to Lonny. Then he filled one for himself. "Where's your ma, by the way? She didn't go with you?"

"It's a long story."

"Sounds like it. You're a very young man to have a long story already."

Lonny held the cup in both hands. His stomach seemed to press up against his chest.

"My mother went away somewhere. I don't know where she is."

"I'm sorry to hear than, son."

Lonny wanted to cry suddenly. But he wasn't going to let that happen. He said, "There was this woman – Clare – there in Seattle, and I guess they got married, my dad and her, and she didn't like me much. She liked Becky okay I think, but she didn't like me and I didn't like her either. She thought she was so high class and I was this dumb kid from the back woods. And I hated going to school in Seattle. I didn't know any of the kids and they were all a bunch of assholes anyway... sorry, I mean jerks."

His voice was shaking. He took a sip of coffee and stared at the creek. The water went over a boulder in a glossy black curve. He was remembering Dickie Tolliver in Seattle, the fight they got into after school and the teacher coming by and separating them. And then Dickie yelling, "You're so ugly your mother ran off!" Yelling it across the whole schoolyard.

"I never knew my mother," said the carpenter. "She died in childbirth. That happened a lot in the old days. I killed my own mother coming into the world. Isn't that something? Of course I didn't know a thing about it at the time. An aunt told me – when I was a little younger than you, probably. My stepmother was the only mother I knew, and I didn't know she was a stepmother until that aunt told me. I don't know why I had to know about killing my mother. She was a mean one, that aunt."

They sat on the log, watching the water.

"So how is it you're here in Duluth and your pa's in Seattle?"

"I ran away."

"Well, gee whiz! How'd you do that?"

"I paid it back. Every penny. I worked for Olafson, you know, the farmer that owned this place before the Nowickes. I paid her back every penny."

"Paid who back? Why?"

Lonny dug his boot heel in the dirt. "I stole money from Clare's purse and took the Great Northern back here, to my grandmother. She made a long distance call and told my dad where I was." He looked up and smiled. "And then Becky wanted to come, and Gram said she'd take her, too. Becky's a good kid. And she's smart, not like me. I'm dumb as a popple tree."

"Well, what do you know," said Ekman. "But look, a tree, even a popple, ain't so terrible dumb. Most trees got the good sense to stay in one place." He finished his coffee and turned the cup over, letting the last drops fall to the ground. "Lonny, I expect you'd make a good carpenter."

"Do you like horses?" Lonny said.

"Horses? Gee, I don't know. These skinny things Tess brings home seem kind of useless to me." His face brightened: "You know," he said, "I used to drive a pair of 'em, years ago, to plow up the garden and the potato field. I borrowed that team. Big geldings, Percherons, I guess. Deal was I had to pay some bushels of potatoes to the farmer that owned the horses."

He paused, remembering.

"One of that pair I liked, a no-nonsense black mountain of a horse. But the other guy was young and gave me all kinds of grief – like any kid does, I guess – always jumping around, scared of a dirt clod or nothing at all, getting the harness tangled. The black mountain and me, we had to wait till the young guy settled down, then go on with the plowing."

In late October some mornings Lonny had to break through a thin layer of ice on the creek in order to let the horses drink. "You could break that ice yourself, Benny." Lonny tangled his fingers in the gelding's mane while the horse drank at the cold stream. "Your hoof's harder'n my boot heel. What if you was a wild horse?

You'd die of thirst waiting for some dope like me to come along and break the ice for you."

A twig snapped somewhere across the creek and the horse jerked his head up and stared in the direction of the sound, ears forward, nostrils flared.

"Ooo, boy! What d'you think? Bear?"

The horse snorted and stamped his foot. But there were no more twig-snappings. He snorted again, shook his mane, then lowered his nose back to the dark water. It was so quiet in the early morning that Lonny could hear the occasional hissing sound Benny made when he sucked in a little air with the water. Finished, the horse backed up then butted his nose into Lonny's stomach.

"Okay. Back we go to your nice warm stall." They started off, Lonny leading him by the halter rope. But on an impulse he stopped and looped the rope over the horse's neck and tied it with a granny knot in the halter ring under the chin. Then he grabbed hold of the mane with both hands and jumped and swung himself up onto the broad back. The horse crow-hopped sideways, snorted, pranced, tried to put his head down to buck, but Lonny held it up with the halter rope. He gripped the warm back with his knees and headed the horse crow-hopping, prancing, snorting, back toward the barn.

"You like the cold, don't you Benny-boy?"

Lonny took the other horses – eight of them – two at a time down the slope to the creek Three of them he brought back to their stalls. The others he snubbed to fence posts in the corral then set to saddling them. Tess had scheduled a trail ride that morning for two couples, tourists from Chicago. Most of the tourists Lonny had seen came from Chicago, most of them in August, and they'd said how wonderful it was to escape the heat and humidity and ragweed pollen and come to the "air conditioned city" at the head of Lake Superior. Lonny felt proud of his hometown when people said things like that, but then they complained about the horse flies that got busy when the sun got hot. And if they didn't get back from their rides before dusk they complained about the mosquitoes. Lonny didn't like the mosquitoes, either, but he felt proud of them, too. They were big mosquitoes, special to Duluth, like how cold it got in the winter. Thirty below sometimes.

But Lonny wondered what Chicago was like. He figured it must be very different from Seattle, which was a big city, too, but he thought it hadn't seemed so different from Duluth. Just a lot more of it.

After Tess left with the Chicago people, Lonny went up to the house to ask Mark what he wanted him to do that day. A side door opened directly into Mark's office. Lonny knocked and waited. No response. He knocked again, looked in the window, saw the office was unoccupied. He opened the door and called – "Mark? It's Lonny." There was no answer. He went inside and closed the door. In the summer Lonny had helped Ekman build this office onto the side of the old farmhouse. He looked around now and thought how he could build his own house some day. Then he heard footsteps coming up the basement stairs. He called again so Mark would know he was there.

"Lonny," Mark said, ducking his head – unnecessarily – as he came into the room, probably a habit, Lonny thought. Maybe they had low doorways in Pennsylvania. His boss was tall, but not *that* tall.

"Here, I want to show you something," Mark said. He elbowed aside a book and some papers on his desk and set down a metal box, about the size of the typewriter beside it, but not so high. Rust had blistered the blue enamel of the box and flaked it completely off the corners.

"I found this on the floor way in the back under Olafson's old workbench. Have you seen it before? When you worked for him?"

"No, I never seen it." Lonny grinned: "Do you think it's full of money?"

"Well let's just find out. It's rusted shut. I was looking for something to open it with when I heard you up here. There should be a screwdriver in the junk drawer in the kitchen." He went to get it.

Lonny looked at the box and thought about Bengt Olafson who had given him his car when he sold the farm. Lonny hadn't seen him since helping with the move. Now he wondered if maybe there was something important in the box that the old guy had forgotten.

Mark returned with a screwdriver. "Let's see if this will open it."

"Olafson must have forgotten about this box when he moved."

"And maybe it was there when *he* bought the place." Mark forced the blade of the screwdriver down into the seam between the top and bottom and then pried up. He succeeded in bending the metal slightly but the halves wouldn't separate.

"I don't know," Lonny said. "I think Olafson built the house. Why don't we call and ask him about it?"

"I want to see what's in it first." Mark's tone was hard. There'd be no more discussion. He studied the latch. "I can drill out these two rivets... No, I only need to drill out one of them. That'll do it. Anyway, Lonny, you've finished with the horses, right?"

"Yeah. They really like the cold weather, they're all snorty and frisky."

"Good. I've got a job for you today. We should have done it last month. You gas up the tractor while I take the loader and fill the manure spreader. I'll spread the first load and you watch, see how I do it. Then you do the rest of it. Probably you'll finish before noon. After that I won't need you till morning."

Lonny rode behind the tractor on the tongue of the manure spreader till they got to the hay field then jumped off and watched while Mark made one full lap. Lonny resumed his perch on the wagon tongue and they drove back to the stable yard.

Mark shut off the tractor and turned around in the seat. "Any questions?"

"No."

"I'll leave you to it, then. I've got business in town so I won't see you till tomorrow." He got off the tractor and started up toward the house. Suddenly he spun around and walking backwards he said, "Be sure to hose off the equipment when you're done." Then with a wave he turned around and strode away.

Lonny made up his mind that he also had business in town.

"You smell like horse shit," said Lena Stuart when Lonny came in the back door. "You've been rolling in it now, like a dog?"

"Spreading it, Grandma. I've been hauling a manure spreader. It makes the shit fly and any little wind blows the dry stuff around."

"You better have a shower, young man. But strip those clothes off outside. Lunch can wait."

Lena decided to ride to town with him, do a couple of errands. "We've got to be back before Becky gets home." She settled into the front seat of Lonny's Chevrolet. When he started the car she shifted around to inspect the back seat.

"You keep this jalopy rather tidy, for a young man. That's something young ladies will appreciate."

"I don't know any young ladies." He backed the car out of the drive.

"You will."

"How do you know that?" He headed the car down the hill past the rental house where he used to live... with Mom, Dad, and Becky.

"It's inevitable. Nature's decree."

"You sure use big words."

"'Decree' is a little word, and you should read more."

"I quit school, Grandma."

"So that you could get on with your education. It doesn't stop with public school, you know."

"'School of Hard Knocks?'"

"That's not quite what I had in mind. I was thinking more along the lines of..." She thought for a moment. "Maybe a school of mental pleasures. If I get you a book will you promise to read it?"

"The whole thing?"

"Promise to read at least the first twenty pages. After that you're on your own."

"You don't need to go buying books for me."

"I'll get it from the library."

Lonny dropped off his grandmother by the Granada Theater. They agreed to meet later in front of Wahl's Department Store on Second Street, two blocks up the hill.

"Two o'clock. Don't be late." Lena gave the car door a pat on the frame of the rolled-down window.

Lonny drove up to Third Street, then east a few blocks till he came to the Olafson's red brick house on the upper side of the street. He parked and climbed the concrete steps to the front lawn then up the steps to the porch. He rang the bell and waited. After a minute he rang again. Through the partially curtained window of the door he could see the old farmer frowning as he approached. The door opened and the frown left his face.

"Lonny! Come in, come in. I'm working in the basement. I got coffee on a hot plate. We get you a cup from the kitchen and go down. Nice to see you. Not working today? Just a minute." He went to the kitchen and came back with a cup.

"I wanted to talk to you," Lonny said.

Olafson led the way down to the basement. "Motor burned out in the wife's washer. I re-wired it and now I have to solder all the wires to the what-you-call-it... the communta-ter."

"Commutator, I think."

"Yah, that's it."

"Wife's out shopping. She loves it in town. Shopping all the time. She says 'shopping' but she never buys nothing. Almost never. Here's coffee." He gave Lonny the full cup then rested his hand on the newly wired armature. It was held in a bench vise between two wooden blocks. "Not so hard to do, just remember how it all goes when you take it apart."

"I hope I don't have to do one of these," Lonny said, taking a close look.

"Not so hard as it looks. But maybe I do something wrong. Find out when I finish."

"Mr. Olafson, I need to ask you something."

"Yah, what's that?" He wiped the hot tip of his soldering iron with a steel wool pad.

Lonny told about the blue enameled box Mark found under the workbench in the farmhouse basement. Olafson put down the soldering iron in its cradle and thought, staring at the concrete wall in front of him. "Yoo...*nu kommer det. Ja, jag vet...*I know what that was. Forgot all about it. *Små saker. Brött.* Junk, from the old country. I bring some little tools with me when I come. Sewing things. *Sax.* Scissors. File, I think. Knife, maybe. Oh *ja! En sten, okså!* from *min* papa's farm."

"*Sten?*"

"Stone. A little stone. All junk. I carried in my pockets from Sweden. I was a boy like you, maybe little older. Twenty. Hah! *Många år sen...* Many year ago. Was going to throw it all away but I had a box I found in the dump, so I put all the crap in the box probably to throw away later. Must have got kicked under the bench."

He picked up the soldering iron and wiped the tip again. "So you thought maybe buried treasure, hah?" He grinned at Lonny, crowsfeet wrinkling at the corners of his eyes.

"I think Mark thinks so – Mr. Nowicke. He was trying to open it this morning. He likes money a lot. But I thought it might be something you wanted."

"Nah. Let him play with it. Best thing in it is the stone and I don't need that no more." He held a wire end against one of the lugs of the commutator with the hot tip of his soldering iron, then touched the end of a coil of solder to the lug and wire. When the solder ran he set the coil down, picked up a pair of needlenose pliers and used them to continue holding the wire against the lug while he put the iron down. He blew on the joint to cool it then let go of the wire.

"Didn't you miss your parents when you came to this country?"

"Ya, sure. But here I met Signe. And I got my own farm. In Sweden I didn't have nothing."

A block from Wahl's Lonny found a parking place, and he found his grandmother waiting beside the revolving glass doors.

She held a shopping bag in one hand and two books in the other. The books she extended to Lonny as he came up.

"Not fair. That's two books, Grandma. I promised to try one. And I didn't really promise, either."

"If you don't like one you can try the other."

They started back toward the car.

"This one – " she pecked it with her forefinger – *"Huckleberry Finn,* it's an adventure story about a boy, younger than you but similar in some ways." She thought for a moment. "Yes, maybe a lot like you. And this other one, *Diary of Anne Frank*, is about a Jewish girl who hid from the Nazis in an attic with her family. And I guess she was about as different from you as anyone could possibly be. It's a true story, her actual diary."

Lonny looked at the books in his hands. "I guess I'll try this one about the girl first. It's shorter."

"Give it twenty pages, at least."

Chapter 8 Lonny

Lonny studied the beaver board ceiling above his bed. It seemed to have sagged a little more during the night. He felt his face, ran his fingers over his cheek, chin, upper lip, decided he could shave again. He made a fist suddenly and pounded the edge of it against the wall. One blow. Two. Started a third, stopped, let his arm fall.

He threw back the covers, sat up, reached for his Wranglers hanging over the back of a chair and pulled them on. As he buttoned up his shirt he inspected the saddle he'd been working on the last few evenings. The stitching and the leather lashings. It was all soaped and oiled now. Finished.

He stuck his head out the open window. The false dawn washed everything grey, erasing the hard lines between one thing and another. His grandmother's old Plymouth was one more bush among the others by the driveway. Even in daylight, he thought, the car looked like a brown bush going down the road.

Breakfast was Cheerios and Kellogg's Pep mixed in a bowl with a handful of raspberries on top. He had picked the berries after leaving the stables yesterday afternoon. A good patch of them grew tall beside the trail a ways back behind the hay barn where the path to his favorite place turned off and crossed the creek. Lonny thought about that spot as he ate. Great place to build a little cabin for himself. The ground's rocky there; foundation girders could rest on rocks stacked right on the ground, no digging required. And with the creek right there he wouldn't need a well.

His grandmother shuffled into the kitchen in her no-heel slippers and terry cloth robe. Her white hair hung unbrushed down past her shoulders. She pushed it away from her face.

"You eat the same damn thing every morning," she said, leaning toward him over the table.

"Mmhmm," Lonny grunted and tried to smile up at her with his full mouth closed. She looked him in the face. Then smiled slowly. An odd smile he thought, sort of pained. His hand went to his face again, brushed over his cheek and the long curved scar. "What do you think, Gram? Do I need a shave?"

"Not yet." She sighed, turned to the refrigerator and opened it. "Don't you ever want eggs or bacon?"

"I like this."

She stood looking in the refrigerator, then closed it. "I don't feel so good this morning. Don't get old, Lonny. You want coffee? I'm making a pot, no instant."

"Sure."

She loaded the percolator with water and coffee, plugged it in, then took a slice of bread from the breadbox and dropped it in the toaster. "It's Sunday," she said. "You're not going to the stables today, are you?"

"I thought I would."

"They don't pay you for Sunday."

"I finished the saddle Mark gave me. I want to try it out today."

"You've been working over a year now, for this Mark. With the Polish name."

"Nowicke."

"I might want you for something this afternoon."

"Okay. I'll be back. Becky up yet?"

"I heard her go out. She's feeding the hens, probably."

Lena settled into a chair at the table. "Lonny, get me the paper, would you?"

He smelled the coffee when he came back with the Sunday *Tribune*. "This time I found it in that old rose bush by the road. Some of the front page got torn."

He had just finished the funnies when the back screen door complained then banged to. The utility porch door opened and his little sister entered with an egg basket over her arm.

"What's that in your hand?" Lonny said.

"Look." She held it out to him.

"That's a mighty old egg," he said. A little yellow fluff ball sat unmoving in her hand. Lonny poked it with his finger. The chick's eyes opened.

"He's so cute!"

"Well, Becky, what'll it be," said her grandmother, "fried eggs or fried chick?"

"Eggs. I'll take this little guy back to his ma. She's the Banty hen that disappeared."

"Where'd you find that hen?" said Lonny.

"In a corner of the shed. I don't know how she got out of the coop."

Becky left and they heard the screen door squeal and bang again. Lonny finished his coffee and stood up.

"Hope you feel better, Grandma."

"Ah. I'm just old."

Lonny set the saddle down in the trunk of his car. He was proud of it, the '46 Chevy. It was over ten years old now, and the engine burned too much oil. But it ran, and the body wasn't bad. He got it two days after he turned sixteen and quit school. He couldn't decide whether he was happier the day he walked out of East High for the last time or two days later when Bengt Olafson handed him the keys and said he hoped he'd accept the car in place of the wages owed him. It was really a birthday present. Olafson didn't owe him nearly as much as the car was worth.

"I've been trying to sell the place, you know," the farmer had said. "I can't make it any more on what I get for the crops. You see that?" He tilted his head toward the house. Lonny looked and saw the shiny nose of a new car poking out of Olafson's open garage.

"That Oldsmobile is from down payment. The farm sold last week. Remember that big fella was here a while ago? Polish name but looked German. Had his wife with him. He bought it. Signe and me, we're moving to town. She wants Florida, but I can't go where it's so hot. You take the Chevrolet. Maybe help me move next weekend. Okay?"

Lonny turned off the highway onto the drive that followed Poplar Creek up to Arrowhead Stables. He saw four cars in the parking area. Maybe for an early trail ride, led by Tess most likely. He parked, opened the trunk and shouldered his saddle. He carried it to the corral by the barn and was setting it on a top rail when Mark approached, leading the dun mare they called Dusty.

"I was going to exercise this mare, but if you want to try out that saddle I'd be glad for you to do it."

"Okay. Thanks."

"And then give her a good brushing down and curry." Mark looked over the saddle. His face gave Lonny no idea of his thoughts. Mark had never seemed really pleased by anything, but he'd never seemed really mad, either. One morning Lonny forgot to water one of the horses. By noon, the one he'd forgotten started kicking the walls of her stall. Lonny expected a chewing out, but Mark just stood and looked at him. Finally, all he said was, "That's not something you're going to do again." His fourth-grade teacher once said the same thing to him, but she said "is it?" at the end, which made it different.

"That saddle needs a new cinch strap," Mark said. "You can take one from the tack room. If you want to work, Tess' trail group will be back about one. You can see to the horses."

"I can't. Gram wants me at home this afternoon."

"Suit yourself." Mark gave Dusty's haunch a pat and headed up to the house.

Lonny took the trail that left from the corral and followed Poplar Creek upstream and into the woods. Olafson had kept about ten acres of his farm in birch and poplar woods, forty acres in pasture, and the remaining thirty in potatoes and sugar beets. The Nowickes kept the woods and pasture but planted hay on the tilled land. When he reached the woods Lonny turned off the trail onto the faint path that forded the creek. He let Dusty take a sip then pulled up her head and touched his heels to her sides. On the other side of the creek he came into the clearing that he loved. He dismounted and dropped the reins to let the horse graze on the sparse grass then sat on a rock and looked around. He ached to own that spot. It would be his home the rest of his life. Maybe Becky would live with him, for a while at least. She'd eventually find some guy and get married.

He slid off the rock and lay back on the ground to continue his daydream. He fell asleep in his pleasant dream but woke just in time to see Dusty edging back toward the path, toward the barn. A little more distance and she'd trot off. He jumped up and caught the reins. "Let's get some exercise, Dusty, like Mark said." He mounted and re-crossed the creek and followed the main trail. When it emerged from the woods it circled the pasture and hay field and came back to the stables through another part of the woods. But at the far corner of the pasture Lonny opened a gate that let him onto a farm road. It followed property lines between more pastures, plowed fields and woods for two miles or so until it ended at Seven Bridges Road, which followed a creek Lonny called Seven Bridges. He'd never heard any other name for it. The road was graveled but little used. Lonny wondered about that as he rode on. Seemed a waste of money to build a road where it had to keep crossing and re-crossing the same creek. If you weren't in a hurry, though, it was a pretty drive, even prettier from the back of a horse, especially after a rain like yesterday's, which had settled the dust and washed the trees. There were fresh horse droppings on the road, no doubt from the morning trail group.

"Exercise, Dusty." He urged the horse into an easy lope.

As he approached the second bridge he saw the riding group. They had dismounted and were stretching their legs while the horses grazed in the tall grass beside the creek. It was a mixed group, a couple of women, a girl a bit older than Becky, a man, probably her dad, and, standing beside Benny the brown gelding, was a teenage kid in a cowboy hat and white tee shirt. He was wearing tennis shoes, which Tess must have overlooked. They were a danger because the rider's foot could slip through a stirrup and hold him trapped if the horse fell, or worse, he could get dragged by his trapped foot if he fell off and the horse spooked and ran. Lonny thought the kid should be warned to pull his feet out of the stirrups if he starts to fall off. He saw that the horse was standing on his reins and the kid, who was starting to look familiar, was trying to pull them free. The straw hat was neat. He wished he had a hat like that.

Tess called to him. He turned Dusty off the road and let her pick her way down the embankment to the other horses on the flat. "I'm glad you came along," Tess said.

She smiled up at him. She didn't have trouble smiling, as her husband did. In fact she seemed different from Mark in every way – small and quick, and quick to laugh. Strong, though. Lonny had worked with her once loading hay bales.

"Can you give us a little help? I've got to adjust this saddle for Annie here, and that young man's mount over there seems to be favoring his left rear leg. Would you check Benny's hoof? Poor guy probably picked up a rock."

"Okay."

"I'm surprised to see you. It's your day off."

"Trying out the saddle Mark gave me." He dismounted so Tess could admire his work.

"Oh, that ratty old McClellan! It looks great! You really cleaned it up." She ran her hand over the seat. "But is it comfortable – that split seat?" She arched her eyebrows and smiled sideways at him.

"Yeah," he said, feeling his face flush. "You don't feel it. I mean, you don't notice... I fixed the stirrup, too," he said, showing it to her.

"Oh yes, good."

"I'll go check out Benny."

The kid had freed the reins and was patting Benny's neck and talking to him.

"Something wrong with your horse." Lonny said.

"Oh. I guess. Tess wanted to check his back foot." He stared. "Wait a minute. You're Lonny! Remember me? I'm Stig! Stiggy."

Lonny looked at him. Then stepped back, getting it now. But this Stiggy was bigger, older. They'd been friends in fourth and fifth grade... He remembered their skating one Christmas in the gravel pit. Riding bikes to Lakeside. Nearly drowning in Dinghy's pond.

"Stig." Lonny said, glanced again at his face, then turned away. "Lemme check this foot." He pushed a shoulder into Benny's side and tugged at the fetlock. The horse lifted his foot, Lonny caught it and straddled the lifted leg and rested the hoof on his bent knees.

"So that's how you get him to lift his foot. Lonny, it's amazing to find you here! I ran into Bergy downtown yesterday and he said you'd moved to Seattle."

"Came back," Lonny said. He examined the frog of the foot and found a small jagged stone wedged into it.

"I'm up here with my mother, just visiting. We live in Chicago now."

"Give me that little stick there," Lonny said, pointing at the ground.

"This one?"

"Yeah."

Lonny took it and pried out the stone. He scraped the frog clean, decided it was okay now, dropped the foot and straightened up.

"You must be at East High now," Stig said.

"Yeah," Lonny lied, and looked away. He couldn't fit the two together, the friend he tracked rabbits with – and climbed trees with and stole apples – and this soft, pudgy city kid. He turned to the horse again pretending the cinch needed tightening.

"I'm in a vocational high school in Chicago, in electronics. I got real interested in ham radio."

Lonny didn't answer. He untied the cinch strap then kneed Benny in the gut to make him cough and deflate his lungs which let Lonny pull the strap tight.

"You sure know your way around horses. Remember all the stuff we used to do? D'you remember that crystal set we made? We were in fifth grade, I think."

Lonny dropped the stirrup back in place. "You're all set now," he said.

There was a pause. "You work here? For the stables?"

"I'm off today."

"Man, that's neat. ...Hey, what's the matter?"

Lonny was backing up. Then he turned and walked away, almost running. It was hard to breathe near this guy – he *couldn't* be Stiggy. Not the kid he'd stalked partridge with. When they'd pretended to be Indians, trying to move through the woods without making a sound. He got back to his horse, grabbed up the reins and mounted, spinning Dusty around. Out of the corner of his eye he saw that Stig was watching him, a queer look on his face. He heard Tess call his name. He pretended not to hear and kicked Dusty into a gallop.

He slowed Dusty to a walk after a half-mile or so. He'd run like a scared rabbit. It really *was* Stiggy back there, sure as hell. They had been real friends in fourth and fifth grades, and the summers. But not in the sixth. Stig was good at arithmetic and reading and writing – hell, school was easy for him. And then he was put in a different sixth grade class and that was it, they hardly ever saw each other. They sat together on the school bus a couple of times but he was different. He'd gotten to be more like everybody else. There was that time at recess, Stig throwing a football around with one of the Woodland Avenue kids – Charlie Hirsh. Hirsh wasn't the worst, but he was one of them, the rich kids.

Back at the stables Lonny unsaddled the mare and spent the next half hour with the curry comb and brush. Dusty loved it, stretching out her neck as he worked over the withers. If he had turned the horse loose in the corral she would have rolled on her back, scratching all the places that itched from the saddle.

Chapter 9 Lena

How do you tell children you've had enough? "I'm tired," I could say. "I'm going to stop living now. I'll do it neatly in the car in the garage. You can just open the garage door and let out the fumes. Then after an hour or so put some gas in the car – I'll leave a full can of gas for you. Drive my old corpse to the police station in Woodland and let them deal with it."

Oh yes, that would go over real well. Lonny would try to stop me. I'd have to do it when the kids aren't home. Leave a note. But what a mess I'd leave for them. It would be horrible. Poor little Becky, and poor Lonny. He's nearly grown. He's got heart, that boy, he'll manage, but it won't be easy for him.

She sat on her back stoop, an elbow on her knee and her chin in her hand. She didn't feel so very bad this morning. She'd felt worse yesterday, would probably feel bad again tomorrow, or later today. The nausea came in waves sometimes. She knew she was sick, really sick, had been a long time. Lonny had begged her to see a doctor – and she had intended to do it once, took a day a couple of weeks ago and had driven into town.

She'd had lunch at Smyth's restaurant. It was still there, and sinking into shabbiness. Long ago it was quite the fine place when her father took her out for a birthday luncheon. The embossed tin ceiling was yellower now than she remembered. Forty years of cigarette smoke would do that. And forty years of shoes and boots stomping around on the wood floor... and *spinning* around – she remembered that from the birthday luncheon, the waitress spinning away from their table on the balls of her feet and then heading for the kitchen with her pencil stuck in her hair and the order book in her hand. Lena fancied she could see a depression in the floor at the edge of the booth next to her, where generations of waitresses had spun away from the table and headed for the kitchen.

The booths had been re-upholstered. Same black, same shape as before, but new looking. Some of the tables with their chrome edging also looked new. And the very young waitress who now stood before her, pencil in hand, was more evidence of the constant renovation of the world. And a smile so pretty Lena forgot for a moment that she was *not* a little girl with a ribbon in her hair and wearing her best dress to please her father, who was *not* there sitting across from her at the table, deciding what she would eat, what she would have for dessert. She would have to order for herself, for the old woman she was now.

She felt more solitary than she'd ever felt before. Like an *island*, the word coming to mind in company with her fifth grade geography, a big blue book with slick pages that told her *Great* Britain was just an island. But she felt more insular even than an island, rather as though she floated, or hung in the air like a helium balloon just the right weight not to rise or sink.

It was a pink balloon that her father chose for her. It was the red one she wanted, but the pink was nice, too. And she never let it go. It pushed against the ceiling of her room for days. Gradually it sank, a bit more every day, and she forgot about it until she came upon it accidentally in a corner of her room where it lay on the floor, deflated and dusty.

After lunch she left the restaurant and started up toward the hospital and the drop-in clinic. She found Duluth's downtown hillside far more steep than she remembered. She was out of breath in half a block and stopped to rest beside the display window of Henkle's Hobbies and Models, but it wasn't Henkle's anymore, the sign said "Wilson's." It was Henkle's when she brought her son Alan there to buy bulk packages of canceled stamps for his collection. And now he's in Seattle doing who-knows-what and living with a woman who drove his kids away. He sends money for their keep at least.

She started up the hill again, saw ahead of her the little Park Point bus come to a stop on the cross street. When the light changes it'll turn this way, she remembered, stop just up ahead there. She hadn't been out to Park Point in years. In her mind she saw the little Ferris wheel and the bumper cars. Alan loved the bumper cars. She got to the bus stop just as the door started to close. She pulled herself in and plopped down on the unoccupied seat behind the driver. When she'd caught her breath she got out her coin purse, paid the fare, and sat back down. Better an amusement park than a doctor's clinic. Probably do me more good. Satisfied and relieved, she relaxed back in her seat to enjoy the ride.

"It's a nice day!" she said aloud, noticing for the first time the bright sunlight on the streets and reflected in the plate glass storefronts.

"What's that, ma'am?" the driver said, tilting his head back.

"I'm sorry. Nothing. Just an old woman talking to herself. I said it's a nice day."

"It is that, ma'am. When we get out to the end let's all declare a holiday and go for a swim."

"Hah, hah!" wheezed an elderly man on the parallel seat across the aisle. He fell to coughing then, ended with a loud bark, and wiped his mouth with a starched white handkerchief. He was well-dressed, Lena noted, good-looking, with wavy white hair. The man's right hand rested on the crook of a polished cherry wood cane. She smoothed the skirt of her dress, straightened her shoulders. She had put on her best that morning. A lady doesn't go to town in a house dress, she thought, raising her chin slightly.

"I spent all my childhood summers swimming at Park Point," the man said, to the driver apparently, but catching Lena's eye as he turned his head. "Unfortunately today I didn't think to bring my bathing suit."

"Well, nuts. I didn't either," said the driver."We'll just have to spend our holiday driving bumper cars and eating cotton candy." Now they were crossing the bridge. "The World Famous Aerial Lift Bridge," he announced, playing tour guide.

"Provided," the old man said, raising his left hand and holding up one finger, "provided your world doesn't extend much past the borders of Minnesota."

"You're absolutely right, sir. I went to Wisconsin once. The whole time I was afraid I might fall off the earth."

"That's right," said the old man, laughing. "That's why everybody who moves away comes back."

Not everybody, Lena thought. Alan didn't. This man sounds like a professor, this Mr. Wavy White Hair. Or maybe a lawyer.

He caught her looking at him and smiled. She lowered her eyes. He's definitely a lawyer, that one, charms the pants off everybody, keeps crooks out of jail. She sniffed and looked up, fixed her gaze out the front window and folded her hands around the purse on her lap. It's a nice day, I'll enjoy it. Have tea at the tea shop if it's still there in the park, then I'll go to the clinic. There's plenty of time left.

The driver and Wavy White Hair continued their banter the whole trip. It became a contest and they were equally matched. It amused her to listen. Certainly they were both old hands at the game, the driver with his passengers, and Wavy Hair with his judges and opposing attorneys.

At the last stop the lawyer was out the door as soon as it opened. His agility surprised her. And there he stood smiling, hat in hand, his cane hung over his arm, his free hand extended to help her down. What could she do? She took his hand, rewarded his gallantry with a small smile. "Thank you," she said. They nodded to the driver as he closed the door and pulled away. Then she realized Wavy Hair still held her hand.

"I'd like my hand back, if you don't mind."

"Of course, my dear. May I introduce myself? I'm Anthony Tomascini. My friends call me Tony."

And I'm a sick old woman. "Mr. Tomascini," she said, looking him in the eyes and not smiling. "Good day."

"Good day to you, too." He bowed, with an amused expression on his face, and put his hat on his head, the cane now firmly gripped in his left hand.

She started down the walkway which, she remembered, eventually led to a tea shop on the other side of the rides. There were a few mothers and young children picnicking on the grassy area to her right. And the bumper cars ahead of her were groaning and thumping as though this were a weekend. As she approached she saw the patrons were teenage boys happily ignoring the big *No Head-On Collisions!* sign. Their female counterparts, six or seven girls in skirts and bobby socks, loitered outside the arena, sometimes glancing at the boys but mostly chatting among themselves. Suddenly "He DIDn't!" one shrieked, her hand to her mouth. They all shrieked and laughed, glancing at the boys.

It must be a senior hooky day, Lena thought. End of May, term's nearly over. *She* never shrieked like that. Girls had more dignity in her day. And less fun, probably. No, there had been a couple of shriekers. And then she was pregnant, having only just finished her junior year. Luckily little Alan was late so the counters could never be sure about the early wedding.

Lonny missed all that senior class nonsense, too. He hated school. Becky won't miss anything, though. She loves school. Third grade for her next fall. Lena stopped walking. Will I be here for that? She looked around. Where's Mr. Masher? Wavy Hair... Tony Tomato... something or other. She saw him then, over on the grass among the picnickers. He was looking at her, watching her. No luck with the young mothers, then. The old goat. She resumed her quest for the tea shop, and found it where it had always been. Except that now it had transformed itself into a coffee shop. If

Tony Tomato shows up there, she thought, I'll probably talk to him.

But he didn't show up and she relaxed at her little table, sipping coffee since they didn't serve tea and looking out the window across St. Louis Bay toward the industrial shore. Was that the end point of Lake Superior, and was that Wisconsin there, or did Minnesota curve around the point a bit? The coffee was bitter. It soon grew cold in the cup and she pushed it aside.

Time to go. She stepped out into the afternoon sun, closed her eyes and lifted her face gratefully toward the warmth. She would skip the clinic. Didn't need a doctor to tell her what she knew.

On the back steps only a little warmth filtered down to Lena's cheek from the sun now formless and vague behind the high overcast. She watched the ragged sunflower in the garden, trying to see it turn toward the sun. But it's too stiff, like me, she thought. The rest of the little kitchen garden looks okay. There are beet greens for lunch. Hell... and there I go swearing again. I never used to swear so much, even in my head. Hell, goddamn. Shit. That's the word. A good old word. It's all I do now, mostly. Make shit out of pretty red-veined leaves. And carrots, and plucked and gutted chickens.

No, I can't tell the kids. She squinted up at the brightest part of the cloud cover, decided she had about an hour before Becky came home. Why had she told Lonny she needed him this afternoon? She regretted that now. Ughhh... here it comes now. Oh. Oh hell. And I'm going to be sick. Right here on these steps.

Leaning on her right arm she let herself down on her side and vomited over the edge of the steps, onto the marigolds Becky had planted that spring. On a Saturday morning. Sunshine on her hair, yellow gold on a little girl's brown hair.

She retched again. Nothing. Bile in her mouth.

When he came home Lonny found his grandmother lying twisted on the back steps. He closed the screen door quietly behind him, knowing she was dead before the thought formed in his mind. He knelt beside her, touched her arm and looked in her face. The eyes were open, seeing nothing. He heard a wailing sound, as if from far away, and then closer, and then he felt it, gathering from his gut, welling up through his chest, tearing out of his throat. He sat back onto his heels and wailed. The cries seemed to rise into him from the wooden planks of the steps, deeper even, from the earth below them. There was nothing he could do. There was nothing else in the world – there was this dead grandmother and this wailing. No hazy light, no wooden steps, no house, no Lonny. No grandmother.

No grandmother. The words took hold in his mind and the wailing fell to sobs so deep that his shoulders shook when he inhaled. No mother. No father... not much of one. Would he come for a funeral? For Lena?

His mind reeled again. Grandmother. Now *he* was grandmother... father... something, that he wasn't before.

He stood up, his legs unsteady. And through sudden, racking sobs, he stepped around Lena's body, closed her eyes – he'd seen that done in the movies – combed her hair away from her face with his fingers and then managed to lift and slide the body up the stairs and onto the porch floor. He straightened her clothes then retreated to the kitchen and returned with a damp towel that he used it to clean her face. Now it won't be quite so scary for Becky, he thought, and she'll be home any minute. She must be at Lorie's place.

Becky's friend Lorie lived half a mile away in a new house at the lower end of Hill Street. He checked the big clock on the kitchen wall. Twelve-thirty. Becky should be home. He picked up the phone and dialed Lorie's number. The girl's mother answered. No. Becky wasn't there – she'd left an hour ago. Becky was taking her time getting home. She was easily distracted. A grasshopper could do it.

He knew he had to report his grandmother's death to somebody. A coroner? The police? He dialed the police. The desk clerk assured him someone would be out shortly.

As he hung up he looked at the clock. What's happened to Becky? Then it occurred to him that she might have found her grandmother on the steps before he did. Maybe she'd even been home when Lena died. He searched the house then went outside and called her name. He checked the little girl's favorite places – a hollow behind the rosebush by the front door, the hen house, the high weeds at the back of the garden, the loft in the old shed they called the barn.

He found her in the apple tree, sitting on a high branch. He'd never seen her that high in the tree before. Her arms were wrapped around the trunk and Lonny could see that her eyes were shut. He called to her but she didn't answer.

He ran to the shed and came back with a ladder and settled it securely against the trunk. It reached almost to Becky's perch. Her eyes were open now and watched him as he started up, but they betrayed no interest in what they saw.

Standing on the ladder two rungs below the top and leaning against the trunk, Lonny took hold of the girl with both hands and tried to pull her into his arms. He coaxed her gently to let go of the tree. It took a while but she let go finally, and then he was holding her against his side with one arm and gripping the rungs of the ladder with his free hand as they made their descent. He tried to set the girl down but she kept her arms around him as tightly as she had wrapped them around the tree. He carried the silent little girl to the house and into the living room and sat down with her on the sofa and waited.

A uniformed police officer arrived with a young woman who introduced herself as Dr. Hendrikson. Lonny directed them to the back porch. But the doctor seeing the little girl asleep in Lonny's arms felt her forehead and looked in her eyes. She said, "Officer, carry this child out to the car and lay her down on the back seat. You, you're Lonny Stuart, right? You called? Find a blanket and pillow and take them out to the car while I examine your grand-mother."

When Dr. Hendrikson came back to the car Lonny was waiting for her with the white quilt and a pillow from Becky's bed. The doctor took the quilt and wrapped it around the silent girl, took the pillow Lonny passed to her and slid it under Becky's feet. She stepped back and carefully closed the car door.

"She'll be at St. Luke's," she said, sliding into the front seat. "I'll prepare a death certificate. You can pick it up at my office." She closed the door and the police car took them away.

The officer had told Lonny to call a neighbor or some friend of his grandmother's to help him make arrangements with a funeral home. "They'll come and take the body away," he'd said. Lonny thought of Mrs. Björnquist. He'd met her once, one of the times Lena had invited her for coffee. She was much younger than his grandmother. He called her and she said she would come right over, it was a short drive. Lonny sat down on the sofa to wait. He thought he ought to be doing something. He couldn't think what.

Chapter 10 Rebecca

"I still don't see why we can't stay in Grandma Lena's house, Lonny. Just you and me. If it's our house now. You said Grandma gave it to us."

"She did. She put it in her Will. You know what a Will is?"

"No."

"It's a piece of paper that she signed, like a letter, that says what she wants done with what she owns when she's dead."

Becky stared at her older brother.

"You understand, now?" he asked.

The little girl shook her head.

"What don't you understand?"

She just stared, looking bewildered.

"Look, Grandma Lena went to a lawyer and told him to write a Will for her. She told him she wanted you and me to own the house after she's dead and that's what he wrote and she signed it."

Becky's eyes seemed to open wider.

"What? What's the matter?"

"Is Grandma a ghost?"

"No! What are you talking about...?" Then he got it. "*Before* she died, dumbhead! She went to the lawyer *before* she died."

"Oh." Becky looked away, thinking. Lonny watched two girls playing jacks in the middle of the room. It was a big room with a high ceiling, like a gym. There were many windows high up in the walls and he could see the white overcast sky outside. Other children in the room were playing board games at a long folding table. A couple of boys raced around holding model airplanes over their heads. *Little kids*, he thought. A stern-faced woman in a white smock, the morning supervisor, caught each boy firmly by an arm as they raced past her. She bent down and whispered to them. Then she straightened up, smiled, gave each boy a pat on the shoulder, and let them go. They kept sailing their planes but with more arm swoops and without running.

"But how...?" Becky began, and stopped. She gave it up. "I want to go home, Lonny. Let's just go home."

"We can't. *You* can't. You're not old enough."

"Why?"

"It don't make sense to me, either." He took a deep breath. "It's the law. You have to have a guardian and the law says I'm too young to be it."

"I don't want to stay here, Lonny!" She was close to tears, then angry: "I want to go *home*!"

"You can't. People called Dad in Seattle. You can maybe go back there. They said he wasn't sure he could take you."

"Is that Clare still there?"

"I guess so."

"Or," he added, "they can maybe put you in a foster home here in Duluth."

"Does Daddy want us?"

"I don't know. I guess they don't know yet, either."

"*Who* doesn't know?"

"*They*. The State. The Law."

"I wish Grandma wasn't dead. I want to go home."

"Me too."

Brother and sister sat looking down at the floor, neither saying anything. When Lonny looked up he saw the airplane flyers had started running again, and he saw the supervisor eyeing them, then looking at the big clock on the wall. Becky hit Lonny on the knee. "What's a foster home?" she said.

He returned the blow with a light tap. "There's a lady who's going to talk to us this afternoon, after she talks to Dad on the phone. She'll explain it to you."

"But what is it?"

"It's somebody's *home*, Squirt. You live there with the grownups who own it and they take care of you, make sure you go to school and so on. You eat with them... They're like parents, I guess, only they get paid by the State to take care of you."

"Who?"

"'Who' what?"

"What grownups? Do we know them?"

"No." Then a thought occurred to him. "I guess it *could* be somebody we know. Could be anybody who wanted to do it, I guess, wanted to take care of you, who's old enough..." His voice trailed off.

"Lonny?"

He was gazing past her, over her head at the snow flurries outside.

"Lonny!"

"Yeah. Okay, I was just thinking."

"I'm scared."

"Don't be, Squirt. You'll be okay. We're meeting that lady – the social worker – at three o'clock. I'm going to go talk to somebody. I'll be back here by three."

"Oh dear! I don't know! Oh my!" Grey-haired Else Ekman's pale blue eyes seemed to flicker behind her glasses. Lonny couldn't tell if she was smiling or about to cry. Her hands fluttered. She seemed all in motion in her blue-flowered house dress where she sat in her yellow kitchen chair turned away from the table. She faced Lonny who stood before her, still wearing his wool cap and jacket. He had asked her and her husband a big favor, about as big a favor as he could imagine asking anyone. Ekman stood at the stove spooning coffee into the boiling water of a speckled blue and white enameled pot.

"Gee Whiz," he said. He stirred the coffee, then picked up the pot by the handle and moved it off the fire. "Little Becky."

Else turned toward him in her chair: "Ekman, I haven't met the girl, have you?" Then turning to Lonny, "She's eight, you say? Oh dear." And back to her husband, "Hjälmar, *vad tänkar du?*"

"Oh, Else, what I think, is that this is going to be up to you. We're not so young anymore. But not so terrible old either, yet."

Else jumped up. "Lonny, give me your coat and you sit down." She hung his coat on a vacant hook by the back door. "Do you have a picture of her?"

"No. Well, there's one at the house."

"Becky... " Ekman leaned back against the counter, "I met her once. She came with Lonny to the Olafson farm when I was working there. Lonny and me was building stables for those Polish folks that bought the place, turned it into a horse place, riding stables. Lonny works for them, you know, for Mark, he's a big fella, and his cowgirl wife." He winked at the boy, "Lonny's a cowboy."

"Well goodness, Ekman, what did you think of her?" said Else.

"Didn't see much of her. She was always messing with a horse. Pretty woman, though."

"The girl! *Dumskalla!*" Else laughed.

"Oh, you mean Becky! Nice little girl, kinda shy, you know. Wouldn't let go of Lonny's hand, but I got her to laugh."

"You're such a charmer, Ekman. Lonny, all the girls loved Hjälmar. Well what do we do? We have a room. It's full of junk..." She looked around, as if seeing the room in her mind. "Oh dear you know it's going to be cold in there. It will soon be winter, Ekman. You'll have to figure out how to get heat in there. I don't know where we'll put all those things." Abruptly she left the kitchen.

Ekman grinned at Lonny. "Sounds like a 'yes' to me." He set out white cups and saucers on the table and poured steaming black coffee for Lonny and himself.

"Did I ever tell you about our daughter. Ellen? She's all grown up now, teaches school in West Duluth, so she's not so far away. But Else misses her anyway. She'd like to see her every day." He pulled out a chair and sat down. "Y'know we can't let Becky have Ellen's old room."

"Why's that?" Lonny was listening to thumps and sounds of things being dragged on the floor somewhere back in the house.

"Because we don't *have* that room anymore." Ekman hooked his crooked thumb in the ear of his cup. "It disappeared."

Lonny sipped nervously at his coffee. "Disappeared?"

"It's gone."

"Are you really going to be foster parents for Becky?"

"Oh sure. You can see how happy you just made Else."

"That's great!" said Lonny, relieved and standing up. "I'll tell Becky right away. We're seeing the social worker this afternoon so I'll tell her, too, and I guess she'll want to talk to you and Else."

"Sure is a mystery about that room."

"The one that disappeared?" He was putting on his coat.

"Yah. And y'know, at about the same time the living room got bigger. We'll see if Becky can figure it out."

Else prepared a special supper to celebrate the first week of Becky's "coming to live with us." There was fried chicken, sweet potatoes with marshmallows, mashed potatoes and gravy, and for dessert a bowl of *niponsopa* – a cold thickened sauce made from wild rose hips and sugar and eaten with a little milk poured over it. Becky had tasted some with her first breakfast at her new home and loved it. It was too strange a flavor for Lonny. He put down his spoon and sat back in his chair.

"I'm sorry, Else, I can't eat it."

"Mrs. Ekman, I'll eat it for breakfast," Becky said, "if that's okay?"

Else laughed. "Sure, sure. You have it in the morning, honey. But you're family now. I want you should call me Else."

"Elsie."

"Okay. That's good."

"And I'm Hjälmar from now on," said Ekman, leaning over to Becky who was sitting beside him.

"Yelmar?"

"No, *Hjäl*mar."

"Yelmer?"

Lonny laughed.

"Don't laugh at her, Lonny," said Ekman. "She eats like a Swede but that don't mean she can talk like one. Becky," he said, resting his big paw on her shoulder, "why don't you just call me Grandpa?"

"Okay." She smiled up at him. "I never had a grandpa." And then the smile disappeared and she looked down at her empty plate.

The school bus stopped at the intersection where Plane Street ended on Morningside Road. It was a long walk down the hill for Becky. When she and a boy, a sixth grader, got on the bus in the mornings they always found the farm kids taking up the whole back seat. And there they were again after school when Becky and the sixth grader got on the bus every afternoon. The school bus never filled up – there was more bus than there were kids – and Becky noticed that nobody ever sat in the seats right in front of the farm kids.

Becky liked to sit in the front where she could see the road ahead. She saved the seat beside her for her friend Ruthie who got on two stops later where there was a street light on the corner and sidewalks and curbs – like the streets in Seattle where she lived for a while and where Lonny had walked her to first grade before going on to the big kids' school.

"The farm kids get on the bus at the Experimental Farm out on Snively Road," Ruthie said.

"What's 'Spirmental Farm?'" said Becky.

"It's a great big farm. There's a barn with a huge hayloft my brother told me about. He rides his bike out there with his stupid friends and swings on a rope and lets go and lands in the hay."

"Do they get in trouble?"

"I don't know. He never said so. He'd lie about it anyway. All the farm kids are dirty and they smell. Gloria says they shovel manure before breakfast."

"How does she know?" Becky said, and worried that she might have chicken droppings on the bottoms of her shoes. She gathered eggs every morning for Else, just like she did for Grandma Lena before she died.

"She knows," Ruthie said.

"She never talks to me."

"She's the prettiest girl in the whole third grade."

That day – a Monday, the third week of school – Becky hung back when she got off the bus, letting Ruthie go on ahead, while she tried secretly to scrape the soles of her shoes on the edge of the concrete steps that led up to the walkway into the school. Then the farm kids got off the bus and Becky sniffed the air as they passed, but she didn't smell manure or anything other than the spruce trees beside the walkway. They kids weren't very clean though, and they had patches on their knees and elbows. Else had patched Becky's overalls where she tore them on a nail, but her school clothes were new. She recognized one of the boys. He was in her class and sat near the front by the window. Herman. She hadn't realized he was one of the farm kids. He was quiet and looked out the window a lot.

"They don't smell," Becky told Ruthie at recess. "They walked by me and I didn't smell a thing."

"What were you doing? I looked back and saw you still back there on the steps."

"I wanted to see if the farm kids really smelled like Gloria says."

"Well maybe they don't shovel manure every day. Gloria doesn't lie."

Ruthie walked over to where Gloria and another girl were swinging a jump rope for Julie, Gloria's best friend. Becky watched them. They ignored Ruthie. Julie and Gloria didn't ride the school bus because they lived near the school. Probably, Becky thought, in the big old houses on Woodland Avenue that Else called "mansions." Those houses seemed dark, and the yards in front of them seemed to Becky like cemeteries, with huge dark evergreen trees. Even though they didn't have gravestones, they made Becky feel creepy to look at the yards and houses as she rode by on the bus. She noticed that Julie, skipping over the rope as it swung under her feet faster and faster, was wearing red shoes. She wondered what it was like to have different shoes to wear sometimes, like Julie and Gloria. Becky had only one pair for school, and Ruthie wore the same shoes every day, too. The farm kids wore heavy old shoes, even the girls.

"It's reading time, boys and girls," said Miss Turner. This was Becky's favorite time of the school day, just before afternoon recess. Their young teacher let them read anything they wanted – anything on the classroom shelves or something they brought from home. Even comic books were okay. Nobody had believed her when she first said so, but a couple of boys brought comic books and it turned out to be true.

Becky scooted up to the shelf behind Miss Turner's desk and found the little book of short plays she was reading. She had almost finished the second play. It was about a girl who stole candy from a drugstore every day but got caught in the next to the last act. Becky wondered what her punishment would be. She also had the letter from her father in the pocket of her dress. Back at her desk, she took the letter out of her pocket and unfolded it and held it in her open book so that the kids sitting near her wouldn't see she was reading a letter. She knew what it said. She'd read it many times. Her father missed her, he said, and hoped she was happy living with the Ekmans. He asked what she would like for Christmas. He would like to send something but didn't know what she would like. "Clare suggested a baby doll," he wrote, "but I'm not sure."

She carefully folded up the letter and put it back in her pocket. Should she ask for new shoes, or a dress, or a story book? She certainly didn't want a doll. She had Annie, her rag doll. Annie sat on her chest of drawers all day and slept beside her at night. She had gone with her to Seattle and back again to Duluth. Becky didn't ever want another doll. She would like to have a kitty. But still she couldn't decide. Every day she read the letter at school, and then wondered what she wanted.

Lonny had a standing invitation to supper with the Ekmans, and he loved going there, not just to see Becky but also to spend an evening with the old man and Else and to relax in the overheated house filled with the smells of cooking and the constant faint smell of kerosene. The house was unfinished. Only the kitchen, living room and bathroom had electricity. The Ekman's bedroom and Becky's room had kerosene lamps for lighting. The south wall of the house had no siding over the diagonal sheathing, only black tar paper. The social worker made Ekman promise to get electric lighting into Becky's room immediately, and finish covering the walls outside as soon as possible. By October Ekman had wired Becky's room for a bedside lamp and for a space heater that she could use on cold nights and mornings. But in March a year later – when Lonny's draft notice came in the mail – a stack of siding that Ekman had scavenged from an abandoned farm still lay under a tarp covered with snow behind the house. The social worker had not come back after checking up on the wiring, and Becky's father faithfully sent child support every month.

Chapter 11 U.S. Army

He didn't mind getting drafted. In fact, the prospect was exciting, and at first he couldn't say why. He'd be leaving Becky, his job at the stables, Lena's house, and the Ekmans. And what would happen to him in the Army? But he saw himself in uniform, standing at attention as he'd seen in movies... the scar on his face in shadow under a broad-bill cap. He'd send Becky a picture. He imagined a short sergeant yelling up at him, face to face, flecks of spit hitting his cheek – but he'd stand there, stone-faced, not a blink. And all the K.P. he'd heard about, and cleaning latrines, and picking up cigarette butts, it'd be nothing compared to his mucking out stables for the past two years. He was strong from work, too. Stronger than the high school kids he'd see around the neighborhood and goofing off in the back seat of the city bus when he'd take Becky downtown to a movie. And he'd get a leave once in a while, and come back in his uniform and Becky and the Ekmans would make a fuss over him and he'd be still and quiet and they'd be excited and want to know everything he'd been through.

The morning he left in May the sun was shining and all the snow had finally melted away. Lonny waited with Hjälmar and Else Ekman in their car at the bus stop, he and Becky in the back seat, nobody saying much, not even Else. She sat sideways in the front seat and Lonny saw her eyes were moist. He knew she was remembering their son Gus, who had been drafted, and then killed in Korea. The Ekman's never said much when Lonny asked about him. That war was over long ago. He didn't think he'd be in a war. When Becky saw the bus coming that would take him to the train, she hit him on the arm, harder than usual.

"You're always leaving," she said.

Ft. Knox, Kentucky

It was nearly dark and Lonny was so tired from the trip he hardly new where he was. In the barber's mirror he had watched his hair fall away from his head like hay behind a sickle bar. And as the hair disappeared his scar grew larger, seemed to take over his face. It took an effort to keep his hand from flying up to cover it.

He stood outside with the other recruits rubbing their newly bald heads, laughing at each other and themselves. "So why did they have to cut it all off?" said a short recruit, looking at Lonny. He had already asked three or four others. They all stood around waiting for the rest of their group to emerge from the gang of barbers in the barracks.

"I don't know," Lonny said.

"Lice," said the recruit to his left.

"Lice! I don't got no lice! You got lice, kid?"

"It's to make us all alike," said someone behind them.

The short guy spun around. "Whaddaya mean?" He said it as if he'd been punched. He faced a recruit that looked older than the rest of them. Lonny edged away, smelling trouble.

"Your hair on the floor of the barber shop. That was *you*. You're nothing now, like the rest of us."

"What's he saying?" said the short guy, looking around. "That don't make no sense. And who do you think you're calling nothing?"

"It's just how the Army looks at us. Forget it. Nothing personal."

The last of the newly-sheared joined the group, and the corporal in charge marched them to the next station, another long barracks. They entered at one end and walked through the length of it, passing a series of counters manned by clerks in fatigues who demanded shirt size, shoe size, pant waist and inseam. At each counter the duffle bag Lonny dragged along the floor gained bulk and weight. Some of the recruits – just separated from their mothers, Lonny guessed – couldn't answer the questions and had to rely on the clerks' estimates, and he enjoyed a brief feeling of superiority. He pulled his duffle bag up off the floor and onto his shoulder. What he'd packed into it were three different uniforms – dress greens, summer tans, and fatigues – as well as socks, underwear, boots and shoes. By lights out that first day his new clothes were folded more or less in accord with regulations and also arranged in his foot locker at the foot of his bunk in accord with regulations, as interpreted first by their platoon sergeant, then differently by the lieutenant, and finally as interpreted by the captain. After that last change Lonny fell into his bunk dead asleep.

A door slammed and he jerked awake.

"Four o'clock you assholes! Get the fuck up! In ten minutes you WILL be shaved. Dressed. In fatigues. In front of the barracks. In ranks. At attention. MOVE!"

After roll call they learned "Dress right, Dress!" "Stand at ease," and "Attention." Then the sergeant passed slowly through the ranks, minutely inspecting each recruit, finding a patch of unshaved whiskers here, a piece of lint there, a loosely tied boot, an un-centered belt buckle. He dismissed them all with contempt and sent them back into the barracks to shape up. Ten minutes later they were re-mustered and re-inspected. They stood at attention, waiting, while a few were sent back to the barracks to try again. Finally the sergeant relented.

"We haven't got all day just to get you dressed. Since I'm not the bastard you think I am, tomorrow I'll give you an extra half hour to rise and shine. That's three-thirty. But that will mean that I will have to get up a half-hour earlier, too, so I might just be a little cranky. You're in uniform, now, more or less. But you still look like a bunch of civilians. The uniforms can't do it. There ain't no soldiers in 'em. By the end of this eight weeks you'll all look like soldiers. Even when you're naked."

Someone snickered.

"Who made that disgusting noise?" said the sergeant.

No response.

"Fine. The comedian wants you all to enjoy a little extra training this morning. Twenty pushups! Now! All you people! Drop! By my count. One. Two. Three. Four..."

Lonny did the twenty and thought he'd earned praise, or at least immunity.

"What we have here," whined the sergeant, "is a bunch of mama-babies who can't push themselves up off the goddamn dirt. Brush off those fatigues! It's not even daylight and you're already filthy. My name is Sergeant Crew. By the end of the week you will all love me. Atten-hut!"

They did three laps of the parade ground in double time before breakfast. To get to the mess hall door they had to negotiate a length of traveling bars. Lonny thought he was in good shape from hard work, but to swing along these bars required muscles he'd seldom used. He made it half-way and then dropped to the ground. That sent him back to the end of the line to try again. He made it a little further on the second try. After the third he was allowed to walk the rest of the way after he dropped off. He was ashamed of himself. Some made it all the way, but most didn't.

They had ten minutes for breakfast, then waited outside for their sergeant. It was strange to Lonny how much alike they all looked in the pale light of the pre-dawn, with their shaved heads and in their green fatigues. The first rays of sunlight struck them and Lonny saw the trees, all leafed out, all new to him. They'll be training in a forest! And not a popple in sight.

By the end of the first week of basic training he hadn't yet come to love Sergeant Crew, but he didn't hate him, either. Crew's sarcasm, though, at first made Lonny angry, but eventually just bored. "Sergeant Crap" they called him in the barracks. As training continued most recruits acquired nicknames: the short kid who complained about his haircut they called "Ballsy" – for taking a swing at a black kid from St. Paul whose leg muscles, Lonny thought, probably outweighed his attacker and who swept him aside like a mosquito. And Mavrokis was a college graduate so they called him "Professor." A fat kid was "Chubbs." There was "Dutch" from Pennsylvania, "Specs" with his glasses," and "Tiny" the big black kid. But most of Lonny's platoon were called by their surname, sometimes shortened. Ulanowski was Ully. Lonny Stuart became "Stu," and sometimes "Stuie." Not "Funny Face," or "the Scar" or "Scarface" – all of which he'd heard during his two years in high school before he dropped out. And except for one time by a recruit named Poule, no one called him dumb or stupid, not counting the training sergeants who called them all stupid – or pussies or mamas' boys. The Professor explained that they were cutting them down in order to build them up into something else called "soldiers." But Lonny had understood all that, without putting words to it. The Professor reminded him of his childhood friend Stiggy who had to have an explanation for everything even if he had to make one up.

> *February 16, 1959*
> *Dear Becky,*
>
> *How are you? I'm fine, so far I don't mind the Army at all. We have to get up at fore am every day. Everbody complains about it but once I get outside its nice in the dark and cold. This morning the sky was clear and there was a milion stars out. We get into formation for roll call and inspection. The sargent and sometimes with the leutenant he comes by and stops in front of each one of us. I guess theres about 20 in our company and he looks us over to see if we have all our buttons buttoned and so on. Its hard not to laff with his face pushed up right in front of my face. He gets real mad if somethings not exactly right. This one guy Pepper I think his name is something like that anyway had to do 20 pushups because his gig line was crooked, that's an imagenary line down the shirt buttons and the belt buckle. His buckle was out of line!*

*The staff sargent tells some of what we'll be doing
that morning. Then we form columns of two and doubletime (that means trotting), and were wearing these big
black boots so we make a lot of noize, like horses on a
wooden bridge. We doubletime around the parade ground
a few times before breakfast.*

*And then the sun is just coming up after breakfast. I
love that part of the day. Im always going to get up early
like that, even after I get out of the army.*

*We always march to diffrent places on the base for
diffrent training subjects. I like that, espeshly after having
to sit still for an hour listening to somebody explaining
how an M-1 rifle works or how to bandage a wound or
something. Lots of the classes are held outside so its nice
when the lecture is boring and I can watch birds or
squirrels. They have red squirrels here, not like our gray
ones. Whats hard is a boring lecture inside in a classroom. Its hard to stay awake. Just like in school, Whats
funny is theres no homework. But we don't have much free
time to do homework anyway. In fact I should be sleeping
now.*

> *Your big ugly brother,*
> *Lonny*
> *ps say hi to Else and Ekman*

Before falling asleep at night, Lonny usually thought of Tess,
pretty Tess Nowicke, his boss's wife. She had given him a cowboy
belt buckle as a going away present. "Don't mention this to Mark,"
she whispered, as though her husband were hanging around
somewhere near the corral, watching them. Which wasn't likely
since Mark was out with a riding group. "I'll miss you, Lonny, like
all your other girlfriends." She knew he didn't have any girlfriends.
Tess hugged him, then. The top of her head came up to his nose.
Lying now on his bunk he could still smell her hair. She was at
least five years older than he was, but she did seem to like him, and
he couldn't help thinking about her, her quick smile, how it was
when she sat on a horse bareback. "With a saddle you can't really

feel the horse you're riding," she'd said. He'd seen her in a dress once, walking with Mark from the house to their car, and he had watched her all the way. But he knew he was no rival for Mark, who was a full grown man, strong, tall, and good-looking.

And with that memory of Mark Lonny would tear his thoughts away from Tess and think about Becky, how she'd hit him at the train station and said "You're always leaving," but then she'd hugged him quick and hard. And often Else's face would come to mind, the way she looked at Becky when Ekman said to call him "Grandpa," and then Lonny felt again that leaving Becky with Ekman and Else was the best thing he'd ever done.

If he thought about himself it took longer to fall asleep. He'd felt lonely when his mother ran off, but there was a different loneliness when Grandma Lena died, a deep and aching thing, a hollowness that moved into him. It was always there if he thought about himself and he tried not to. He knew it was only a fantasy that he and Becky would share Lena's house some day. Becky was cute and fun to have around, so she'll have boyfriends, get married, and he'll be alone. The future *alone* looked like a dark hole, like the old well he'd uncovered in Lena's backyard. He'd looked down it and couldn't see the bottom. It was fun knowing about that well when Lena was alive. After that it scared him to think about it. Sometimes he dreamed about looking down into it and he'd feel it trying to pull him in. Once his grip on the edge gave way and he fell in and then he saw himself falling, a white figure in the blackness, legs apart, arms reaching out, growing smaller and smaller... but never disappearing.

March 5, 1959
Dear Becky,
Mavrokis, one of the guys in our platoon, they made him company clerk and he typed this letter for me and fixed the spelling. He says spelling is easy if you know a few tricks, like suffixes and prefixes and some regular rules so then you don't have to have every word memorized. He showed me some of that stuff now and it made

sense. I suppose they tried to teach it to me in school but I was probably looking out the window.

I found out there's something I'm pretty good at. I earned a Sharpshooter rating on the firing range. That's the highest rating you can get. I guess I've got a good eye and a steady hand. I hope I don't ever have to shoot anybody

I'm sorry I wasn't able to write for so long. I had KP (that's Kitchen Patrol, dishwashing mostly) for a week. I didn't even have time to get much sleep. This was punishment for getting into a fight. I had been getting along with everybody fine until this one kid started making fun of me during a break after I had answered a question in class. He said out loud to everybody, "Somebody give Stuart a hanky so he can blow his nose." Only one guy laughed. Nobody else did. He kept on with it though and Mavrokis came over and stood between him and me, but he, Poule, the kid's name is, pushed him away and said right in my face, "You're such a dumb shit you can't even blow your damn nose." I hit him in the stomach and we fought for a while before a sergeant broke it up. I got a couple of little cuts but I think Poule ended up with a broken nose so maybe he won't talk so well either for a while. I hope his nose heals okay, though. It made me feel good that only one guy laughed when he made fun of me. It's sure different from school.

Say hi to Ekman and Else.

Lonny

Republic of Korea

"PFC Stuart reporting Sir."

"Sir, PFC Mavrokis reporting."

"At ease, men." Their Commanding Officer, Colonel Hamp, flicked his right hand toward his eyebrow, the officer-to-peon half-salute. He said, "Captain Van Hoff's vehicle broke down up at the DMZ, Charlie Company. I want you to haul it back here to the motor pool. You will go armed even though it's damned unlikely you will need weapons. The North Koreans don't want trouble any more than we do. Corporal Wingham will issue carbines. You will not try to repair the vehicle at "C" Company. You will pick up the vehicle and bring it here immediately for repairs. Any questions?"

"When do we leave, Sir?" said Lonny.

"Now. You'll be back before dark."

As they walked to the motor pool, Mavrokis said, "I hope we'll be back before dark. I want to pay a visit to this coffee shop I heard Kelly and Petit talking about. Seems they have a lot more than coffee on offer."

"Like what?"

"Something like a local gin. And beer. And girls."

"You can get all that at Camptown. Except maybe the local gin."

"True. All true. In spades. But this may be less garish and cutthroat."

"Homey?"

"That's what I'm thinking. Want to come along?"

"I hated Camptown."

"As you so elegantly said at the time. You wouldn't go near the girls. But this village place might be more your style."

"I haven't got a 'style,' Professor. I don't know. Maybe I'll feel like going if we get back in time."

"And if we don't, some other time. Meanwhile, we've got this little job to do. I'll drive and you ride shotgun."

"Why? Maybe I'd like to drive."

"You're the sharpshooter. You can pick off any hostiles sneaking through the DMZ."

Lonny laughed. "Nobody can hit anything with a carbine. The noise might scare 'em, though. So what are your other reasons? Usually you've got at least three for everything."

"I'm trying to cut down. It was too many reasons got me transferred. Col. Hamp called my reasoning 'insubordination.' Otherwise I'd still be at Headquarters typing and staying clean."

"You argued with the Colonel! I thought you *asked* to come to the motor pool."

"I did, after the good colonel made it clear he doesn't appreciate an honest exchange of views. Views go in only one direction where the Colonel's concerned."

"I hope he's always got the right view."

"Hope is all we have, soldier. And a couple of carbines."

"You heard that in an old war movie."

"Possibly. Doesn't make it any less true."

They had been traveling less than an hour when they came around the edge of a mountain where the road was just wide enough for the truck – a steep rise on their left, and a long drop down on their right.

"Great place for an ambush!" Mavrokis had to shout over the noise of the engine and the groaning transmission.

"I haven't heard of any shooting," shouted Lonny.

"No? I saw reports on the Colonel's desk. They're all classified. I shouldn't be telling you."

"You think we might *need* these carbines?" Lonny looked doubtfully at the weapon in his hands. Their Basic Training instructor had called the carbines pop-guns.

"I hope not."

"Why don't they tell us these things?"

"'The cease-fire holds.' That's the official line. Nobody wants to get the hawks in Congress excited."

"You read that on the Colonel's desk?"

"I overheard it. Hamp and somebody else. I didn't see who. They were talking in the hall. Pretty careless. 'Spies everywhere.'"

"Are you a spy, Professor?"

"I'm a patriot. It's a citizen's duty to know what his government is up to."

"I don't believe half of what you say," said Lonny.

"That's wise, Stuart. Apply the same rule to everybody. Hey, looks like 'C' Company on top of that hill."

Lonny checked his watch. "Forty-five minutes. That's forty minutes too long in this bone-grinder. I rode a horse once almost this bad. A mare, trotted like a three-legged fox."

They reported in and a PFC led them to the disabled jeep. Lonny signed for it and put the keys in his pocket.

"There's coffee in the mess tent," said the PFC with the clipboard. "Might be a donut left. We're treated like kings here on the front line. Beneficiaries of a grateful nation."

"Thanks," said Lonny. "Hey, Thornton," he said, reading the name tag on the soldier's field jacket, "has there been any trouble up here with the gooks?"

"Trouble?"

"Skirmishes," said Mavrokis. "Noisy exchanges of goodwill with the North Koreans."

"We're not supposed to talk about it... if there *was* anything to talk about. I didn't say there was. Do you have weapons?"

"We're prepared for hostile rabbits," said Mavrokis. "If there aren't too many of them."

Thornton shoved the clipboard under his arm and turned away. "The coffee's not so bad today. Fresh grounds. Must be Tuesday."

They winched the jeep onto the bed of the truck and secured it, then got their coffee and donuts in the heated mess tent. The cook was more forthcoming than PFC Thornton. "Just last week there was a little thing," he said, "and probably nothing. A night patrol reported being shot at – once. One round of rifle fire. They all heard it. One guy said he saw dirt kick up in the path ahead of him. They hunkered down but nothing else happened. I don't think you've got anything to worry about."

The return trip was mostly a downgrade, following the fast-flowing creek. As they passed between two low hills they heard the sudden crack of rifle fire and the clang of bullets hitting their right front fender.

"They're shooting at us!" yelled Lonny. "Floor it!"

"Return fire, Stuart! Keep your head down! Shoot out the window!"

"Shoot at what, for Christ's sake?"

"Just shoot, man!"

The big truck slowly gained speed as Lonny wound down the window. He stuck out the muzzle of his carbine and pulled the trigger. Nothing happened. The clip. He'd put it in his pocket. He bent down over his weapon below the open window and managed to retrieve and insert the clip. He heard more shooting but it was behind them now. Again he stuck the muzzle out the window but then the road swung them around a bend and put a hill between them and whatever target he might have shot at. He felt let down. He wanted to shoot anyway, but there was no point. Then he was thrown against the door and hit his head on the barrel of his weapon.

"Slow down!" Lonny shouted.

"What?" Mavrokis had his hands clamped on the wheel, his eyes fixed straight ahead. They swung around another turn nearly hitting a tree. A branch from it hit a side-view mirror.

"You idiot, Mavrokis!" Lonny hit him on the shoulder. "Slow down! We're out of range!" A sudden deceleration threw him against the dash.

Mavrokis looked at him. "You never fired a shot!"

"You almost killed us in a wreck!"

"What the hell was that all about?"

"Gooks!"

"God damn!" Shaking his head, Mavrokis turned his attention back to the road. The muscles in his face twitched. Lonny saw that, and then a shiver ran through his own body, pumped full of now useless adrenaline. The truck rolled on.

He sat stiffly in his seat, holding the loaded carbine upright between his knees. He remembered the horse that ran away with him once, the crazy mare with the hard trot. Ran through the damn woods on the Nowickes' place. All he could do was flatten himself to the mare's neck and keep pulling back hard on one rein. Branches slid along his back. It seemed a long time before the head came around and the horse hopped and stumbled and finally stopped. Lonny slid out of the saddle and just stood there by the horse shaking, holding on to the reins. The mare was trembling, too, and the two of them slowly calmed down together.

After some minutes he heard Mavrokis say something but couldn't make it out. The truck came to a stop. Mavrokis turned off the ignition and they both tried to relax in the sudden quiet.

"Those gooks must have had a good laugh," said Mavrokis.

"Bastards," said Lonny.

"They must be bored. I wonder if our guys do that."

"It'd be hard to get away with. We have to account for every round... so at least I won't have to fill out a report."

Mavrokis sighed. "And at least I didn't soil myself, if you'll pardon the expression."

Lonny looked down at himself. He couldn't help it. "I didn't either," he said, and then he found himself laughing.

"So we're not complete assholes," said Mavrokis, laughing. And they kept on laughing.

"Sharpshooter," said Mavrokis.

"Hot rodder," said Lonny.

Eventually the laughing fit passed. Lonny said, "We'd better check the damage."

They spilled out onto the road and came around to the front right fender. There was one hole above and just to the front of the wheel well, and three creases in back of that running parallel to the long axis of the truck.

"I'd say they, or he," Mavrokis said, running his hand over the marks, "– maybe it was just one guy – he tried to shoot out our right front tire, one round straight on, the other three from behind, after we'd passed."

Lonny looked closely. He put his hand on the fender, touched a finger to the bullet hole. That could have been his head. He pushed the thought away. He said, "I wonder if they hit anything in back."

They scoured the rear of the vehicle without finding anything, and Lonny climbed up and looked over the jeep. "Not a mark up here," he said.

"Either whoever shot at us was a terrible marksman," said Mavrokis, "or he was just having fun."

The remaining miles to Headquarters were straight and uneventful. The truck lumbered up to the gate and Lonny and Mavrokis sniggered when they saw the sentry with his carbine at the ready.

He looked in at their faces. "What's with you guys? What's so funny?"

"Rabbits," said Mavrokis.

Ekman sat in the kitchen reading the afternoon *Herald*. He heard Becky come home from school and now she came into the kitchen carrying a letter.

"It's from Lonny, Grampa!"

She dropped the pages of the letter on the table and set about making a sandwich, peanut butter and raspberry jam. She and Else had made the jam last summer after picking berries in the open fields above Indian Head butte. She remembered the hot day and the flies and mosquitoes. But after a while a cool breeze had come up from the lake and the flies and mosquitoes got lazy and left them alone.

Ekman put down his paper. "How's your brother? What's he say?"

"He says hello to you and to Else. He says he feels right at home in Korea. He says it's 'nice and cold, like Duluth.'"

"Oh he says that, does he? Likes the cold!"

"I think he's kidding, don't you? And he says he likes working in the motor pool. He's learning to weld. He says that's a way of connecting steel parts by melting them together."

She sat down at the table with her sandwich on a plate and a tall glass of milk. She picked up the letter. "And he says his friend from basic training, the one he calls 'the Professor,' transferred from Headquarters to the motor pool. So now he's there with Lonny. And he's learning to weld, too." She turned over a page. "And he says the Professor has got him studying for a high school diploma."

"Sounds more like a school than an army," said Ekman. "Maybe I should join the Army, too. I could go to high school and get paid for it. And then get a sitting down job... in a bank, hey? Wear a tie and a white shirt instead of these overalls." He hooked his thumbs under the straps over his shoulders. "*Nej,*" he shuddered and shook his head. "I think we'll let Lonny do the working in a bank."

Becky laughed. "Grampa, Lonny wouldn't work in a bank. And you'd look silly in the Army. You're too old."

"Gee whiz. You think so? I'm always missing my opportunities. Well if Lonny won't work in a bank, who's going to do it? Maybe you would, somebody's got to. We've got to have banks, or else we'll have to stuff all our money in a mattress, like in the funny papers. And it would be lumpy and we wouldn't sleep so good."

"I'm going to be a doctor," said Becky. She took a big bite of her sandwich.

"A doctor? Not a nurse? Our Ellen wanted to be a nurse. Now she's a schoolteacher."

"Maybe I'll be a teacher."

"I never heard of a lady doctor."

"It was a lady who came out when Grandma Lena died. *She* was a doctor."

"You don't say? Well whaddaya know?"

Becky took a big gulp of milk then looked over the letter again. "Here, Grampa, you'll see it's a real army. It isn't just a high school. Lonny says he had to carry a loaded rifle when he went up to the cease-fire line to pick up a jeep to take back to his shop. It's really different up there, he says." She read aloud: "'Up there you see that the war isn't really over. It's only a truce and at the ceasefire line they have to be ready if the North Koreans start shooting again.'"

"Do you think they will, Grampa? Start shooting again?"

"No, I don't think so. But they have to be ready, just in case."

Else appeared suddenly in the doorway. "Becky, I want to... Ekman! What are you doing home drinking coffee? You were building a chicken coop for those people on Hill Street."

"Well, I had to stop. Ran out of chicken wire."

"So get some more, *dumskalla*."

"I was going to do just that, but the truck's got a flat."

Else laughed. "Yah, Hjälmar, so fix the flat."

He grinned. "I was going to do that, too. But I smelled the coffee and couldn't resist."

"There was no coffee left from breakfast. I washed the pot."

"My nose has a good memory. Anyway, there's no big hurry on the chicken coop. They got no chickens yet."

"It's good thing they don't." She turned to Becky, and the low afternoon sunlight through the window over the sink glinted off her glasses. It made her starched white apron shine, brightening the room.

"Becky, stand up, and stand on the chair. I want to measure this against you. It's hard to keep up with how you grow." She held out a red dress. There were pins in the hem.

"Is that for me?" Becky said, pushing back her chair. She climbed up onto it and stood still.

"You're going to Ruthie's birthday party tomorrow, remember? Yes, this looks just about right. Okay, you can get down now."

"It's awfully pretty," said Becky.

"She's going to be a doctor," Ekman said.

"Oh yah? Well, good for her. Good for you, Becky. I'm going to finish this now." And she left the room in a flurry.

Chapter 12 Darling

"You a strong man." The girl squeezed his bicep with her long fingers. She sat close against him on the couch.

"You're pretty," said Lonny. He liked her face, it was open and her skin was clear. She wore red lipstick, but less of it than the others.

"All you boys say I pretty. 'Cause you want to fuck me." She smiled. "But I too thin. I know that."

He felt the blood rush to his face. "No. No, I mean it. I really do think..." Her giggle cut him off.

"You face all red!" She stood up and looked at him, hands on her hips. She wasn't much taller standing than he was sitting. He looked at his hands folded in his lap. He wanted to leave. He glanced over at the door where a few moments ago the Professor had gone out with his arm around the big girl with the heavy makeup.

"Hey, Soldier." Her voice was kind. She slipped onto his lap. He moved his hands out of the way. "You very young," she said.

She took his hands and pulled them around her. He held her then, one hand on her waist, the other lower, the firm softness there.

She touched a slender finger to his face. "You got scar there, Soldier. You a big fighter, hey?"

And then her lips were on his mouth. Soft and moist. He felt her hair fall against his forehead, brush his closed eyes. His arms tightened around her and he strained up into her kiss, inhaling the scent of her. He felt her yielding into him, but then she pulled back, pushing her hands against his shoulders. He opened his eyes.

She was smiling at him. "You not really so young."

A rush of heat swept through him and he pressed his face to the girl's chest and held her tight.

Yielding again, curling her fingers in his hair, the girl said "We go to room now. What you name, Soldier Boy?"

He tried to answer but had to clear his throat first. "Lonny," he said, still pressing his face to her chest.

"Lonny," she said. "Nice name."

He looked at her then, relaxing his grip. "What's your name?" he said.

"Dah-ling. Soldier call me Dah-ling."

"Dah-ling? ...Darling? What's your real name?"

"Soldier call me Dah-ling." She took his hands from around her and stood up. "Come," she said, and tugged. "We go to room now."

Lonny couldn't stand up. The girl looked down at him. "You big man, Lonny. Come, come. She tugged at his arms. Surprised at the girl's strength, Lonny forgot himself enough to stand, a little hunched over, then trail behind her to the door.

Later, he found Mavrokis waiting for him outside. He was leaning against the wall, smoking a cigarette.

"So how was it, Studly? Did you have a good time?"

They started up the gravel road to Battalion.

"Yeah. But I hated when I had to pay her."

"A girl's gotta live."

"Yeah. But it felt crummy. I don't know, she was nice. She seemed to like me. And then with the money... I was just buying her."

"And she was just selling. You did not buy her though. You bought her time, Lonny. You bought her services for an hour. Or less, maybe?" He clapped a hand on Lonny's shoulder. "And she sold those services, like a mechanic, or a kid that cuts your lawn."

"It's different! You know it is. It feels shitty! I'd rather do something nice for her. I gave her money and I left. Like I walk out of a store. She's not a can of beans."

They trudged along in the starlight, the frozen gravel crunching under their boots.

"What did she say when you paid her, Lonny?"

"She said 'Thanks.'"

"Anything else?"

"No."

"She said 'Thanks,' and then you left?"

"No. I didn't leave right then."

"Were you dressed?"

"Yeah."

"And you didn't leave. What did you do?"

"Damn it! What do you want? I sat on the bed."

"And...?"

"I tried to take her hand. She pulled it away. She said, 'You leave now.' She smiled and I tried to kiss her again but she pushed me away. She said 'You go now, Soldier Boy.' She kept pushing me and I had to leave."

"Oh, Lonny." Mavrokis put his arm over Lonny's shoulders but he shook it off.

"She hurt your feelings, didn't she? It's not a romance, Buddy Boy. Maybe she did like you, maybe not. But if she hadn't come on to you, you wouldn't have gone with her and she wouldn't have got your money. She needs that money. She might have a kid to feed. Or parents."

"It's crap. I hate it. I'd rather just give her the money."

"Interesting idea, man. You do that next time – just give her money and not go to bed with her. I'd like to know what she says."

A week later Lonny returned to the coffee shop and passed straight through to the parlor in back. The woman the G.I.s called "Mama-san" sat behind a small desk beside the door.

"Soldier Boy want girl?"

"Darling," He said, looking around. There were four girls in the room. Three of them he recognized from his last visit. The fourth, sitting with her knees drawn up on a sort of low daybed against the opposite wall, was much younger than the others. She wore no make-up that he could see. Her hair was cut short, almost like a boy's, but combed forward. And she wore pajamas, or what seemed like pajamas, while the others wore loose, silky dressing gowns.

The manager followed his gaze. "You like Boy-Girl? She special." The manager gave him a sly smile and rubbed her thumb on her fingertips, the universal sign for money. The girl looked up at Lonny, made eye contact and held him, unblinking. A piercing look, without a smile. It unnerved him.

"No," he said. "I want to see Darling."

"Boy-Girl very young. Do you good."

"No. Darling's not here?" He started to leave.

"You have to wait. Dah-ling busy now. You have coffee. Come back ten minute." She ushered Lonny out into the coffee shop.

He took a stool at the counter, ordered a glass of beer from the barman. It was late afternoon. He was the only American in the place – others would probably come later, get half drunk then go back and visit the girls. He had asked to get off duty early, offered to work late the next day to install the new valve seats and oversize valves and the specially ordered carburetor for the Colonel's hot rod jeep. Mavrokis had said, "He'll break his fool neck and get a Purple Heart. Colonel's too young for his rank."

Two old men from the village sat in the booth behind him, smoking. They were holding the slowest conversation Lonny had ever heard. One would say something slowly, all the words running together in a kind of tune. Then they would both sip from their small cups, a clear liquid, the local "something like gin," probably. After a while the second man would say something just as slowly, and Lonny couldn't tell if he were responding to what the other guy had said or just talking to himself. When he finished they would both just sit there looking at their cigarettes, taking long drags, squinting through the smoke. Lonny thought they might fall asleep that way but eventually the first guy would speak again. Time seemed to pass more and more slowly. Lonny began to feel as though he could be there listening forever to words that had no meaning. The sound of their speech was soothing and he felt a deep peacefulness in his body, as though he'd lain down on a soft bed.

Suddenly the back room door banged open knocking him out of his revery and almost off his stool. Corky – Corporal Corcoran – came through, spotted Lonny at the bar and slapped him on the back. "Here for some afternoon cho, eh Sport?" His hand felt like a claw on his back; Lonny shrugged it off and turned on his stool.

"Hey Cork," he said, concealing his annoyance.

"I heard you went with Darling last week. I just took her for a spin. She hadn't had anything like me before. I'd tell you all about it, kid, but I better get back before they miss me. See ya, Sport."

Lonny watched him go. The old men in the booth were jabbering now, talking over each other. Lonny paid for his beer and went into the back room.

"Dah-ling ready soon," said the manager.

Lonny sat on a couch and waited. Finally the girl appeared at the side door, her eyes lowered. He went to her. Without looking up she took his hand and they went down the short hall to her room. There was a towel spread out flat on the bed. Lonny took off his jacket and the girl started to unbutton his shirt. He noticed her fingers trembling. And then he saw tears moving down her cheeks. No sobs, no shudders, just tears.

Lonny held her arms, gently, to stop them.

"He hurt you."

"We fuck now," she said. A small voice.

"No." He looked at the towel on the bed, reached over and peeled it off. There was blood on the sheet, not quite dry.

She took the towel from him and put it back on the bed. Then she tried again to unbutton his shirt.

"No," he said, and moved her hands away. He pulled his wallet from his back pocket, took out two bills and gave them to her. Then he lay down on the bed. "I've paid for an hour," he said. "You come lie down. Rest."

She hesitated, then lay down beside him, with her head on his arm.

Eventually she fell asleep. Lonny lay there looking at the ceiling, trying to make out what he was doing, where in the world he was. He thought of his grandmother, mornings in her kitchen, she in her old robe standing by the stove sipping coffee from her World's Fair mug, her long white hair still uncombed. She kept it gathered in a bun all day, but at night she let it down when she went to bed. It was odd, he realized. Other women didn't have long hair. And she swore sometimes; he had never heard other women swear, not until he met Clare. He thought of Seattle, the house, and the dining room, and he felt again how he didn't like being there. His thoughts returned to Lena's kitchen in the morning. Becky would be there clumsily eating cereal with a spoon that looked too big for her mouth. She managed, though. She refused to use a smaller spoon. And she held her milk glass with both hands to drink.

He heard music from the parlor – American rock n roll – and looked at his watch. He must have dozed off. His hour was up a while ago. There was a knock on the door and Mama-san came in.

"Time up!" she said. Darling jerked awake.

"You sleeping!"

"Mama-san." He got up from the bed. "I'll pay for the night. That Corcoran hurt Darling. I'll pay for the night so she can rest, get better."

"Fi...ten dollar." She held out her hand. Short fingers, thick.

"Ten!"

"Ten dollar."

"Six."

She squinted. "Eight."

"Too much. Seven."

"Okay, seven." Her hand was still out.

Lonny gave her a five-dollar bill.

"Two more."

"I already gave Darling two."

The girl had got up from the bed. She took the two dollars from the pocket of her gown and held them out.

The manager snatched them from her hand. She squinted at Lonny again. "Smart cooky,"she said, winked, and left the room.

"You go now?" the girl said.

"Will you be okay?"

She nodded.

"Mama-san won't make you work?"

She shook her head.

"You sure?"

"Yes."

"Tell me your real name."

"Dah-ling."

"No. Your real name."

She whispered, "Iseul."

Next morning at breakfast Lonny overheard Corcoran at the end of the table telling about Darling's "skinny shanks" and how he'd taken her for a "spin she'll never forget." Lonny pushed back his chair, moved down to the corporal and grabbed his shoulder.

"You're a son of a bitch, Cork!"

Without answering, Cork drove his elbow straight back into Lonny's groin. He went down on one knee, doubled over, gasping for breath.

Cork stood up. "What the fuck, Stuie!"

Lonny panted, shaking his head. Slowly the nausea receded. "Darling. You prick. You hurt that girl."

"She's a whore! Besides, she loved it. She really did. Wise up, kid."

Later that week Lonny got an afternoon off. He went to the coffee shop and asked for Darling.

"She not here now. She come later. Nobody here now. You horny so early?" The Mama-san's red lips pulled back in a wide smile.

"When? When does she come in?"

"'Bout t'ree. You come back 'bout t'ree. Be first one."

That gave him an hour to kill. He left the shop and started back to Battalion.

The weather had changed that morning. The freezing cold of the past few weeks had given way to milder temperatures and a sky that showed patches of real sunlight. Pot holes in the road were filled with water instead of ice, though they would probably freeze over again at night. "A false spring" said the old-timers on their second and third tours of duty in Korea. "Winter ain't done yet."

Suddenly he stopped and headed back into the village. It had occurred to him that he might see Iseul coming to work. *Work*. He hated it, that it was work for her, what she did with him, earning a living. Mavrokis kept saying, "Don't kid yourself, Bucky." But Iseul was glad when she saw it was him last time, that it wasn't someone else.

He passed by the coffee shop and glanced down the narrow passage between the shop and the rice seller next door. He saw someone – it *looked* like a woman – emerging from a path that came straight across the field behind the shops. It could be Iseul – the slight figure, head down, approaching quickly with short steps. He hurried down the passage to meet her, passing a back door to the coffee shop on his way. Closer now, he saw it *was* a woman. Iseul! She saw him and stopped. Then she came on, slowly at first, then quickening her pace. He held out his hand to her.

"Iseul," he said.

"Soldier Boy." She smiled but didn't stop, didn't touch his hand. She glanced behind her as she moved past him toward the back door.

"Iseul," he said again. She reached the door, opened it, and went inside.

Why did she look behind her?

He surveyed the field she had come across, looking for someone, or for something like a house or a hut, but there was nothing except a line of brush at some distance, maybe a hundred yards away, suggesting that a road or track came across there. Beyond that the field continued. She must have come a long way.

He went back around and entered the coffee shop from the front and Mama-san led him into the parlor. When Iseul come in from the back, wearing the same red robe she'd worn on his every visit, he held out his hand to her again. This time she took it. She smiled and said his name. She led him into her little room and he closed the door. Then he took her in his arms.

He said, "Is it bad for you to be seen with me outside? Why?"

She looked in his eyes, a long moment, then hugged him, pressing her face to his chest.

"Iseul...," he began, but she pushed against his chest then reached her hand up and touched his face.

"We fuck now," she said. He saw her eyes were moist. "I know you *ready.*" She began to undo his pants.

"Don't," Lonny said. "I'll do that."

"No." She pushed away his hands. "You let me. I be very good to you."

In the following week Lonny managed to visit Iseul twice. "You're one horny G.I.," said Mavrokis. Then Lonny got stuck at Battalion for a couple of weeks. They had to work days and nights preparing for a General Inspection, finishing repair and maintenance jobs, cleaning tools and setting them out in order, scrubbing down the concrete, re-painting scuffed surfaces. And after the inspection, Lonny drew several shifts of guard duty. When he finally got an evening free he walked back alone to the coffee shop at the edge of the village. It was early and he found the Mama-san behind the bar. He ordered a cup of the drink they called coffee and told the woman he wanted to see Iseul.

"Iseul? How you know her name? Dah-ling. She not here." The woman peered at his face. "I know you. You go with Dah-ling all time. You like her."

"Yes. I want to see her."

"Dah-ling mama sick. She stay with Mama. I have other girl for you."

"Tell me where she lives. Maybe I can help her."

The woman's eyes narrowed. "Other girl here. Take you pick." She waved her arm toward three women of various ages sitting together in a booth.

He ignored them. "I want to help Iseul if I can."

"Give her money?"

"If she needs it."

"You give to me. I give to her." The woman held out her hand.

"Please, just tell me where she lives."

The woman's look softened. For a second it seemed she pitied him.

"You sit. Enjoy you coffee. I get small girl like Dah-ling for you. She busy now. Come out in few minutes."

"No! Mama-san, I don't want another girl! Just tell me where I can find Iseul."

"You make trouble? Go 'way, Soldier Boy. No trouble here. You go now." She stepped out from behind the counter waving her thick hands at him, shooing him toward the door.

Outside, the sudden cold made his eyes tear. Through the blur he looked down the road through the village. It was dark now except for a faint silvering of moonlight and the occasional glow from a window in the passageways between dwellings. The shops were all closed up. A cold wind stung his face with fine flakes of snow. He wanted Iseul, the girl who'd come to him, pulled his arms around her so that he held her, felt her warm body, and the smooth fabric of her gown. "You big fighter, hey?" she'd said, and touched his face.

He started down the passageway beside the coffee shop. When he reached the back he hunted around in the dark until he found the path Iseul had taken, where he'd seen her coming toward him across the field. He stepped onto the path, went a little way, then stopped. It was dark. There were no lights ahead. He had no idea how to find Iseul.

"You dope," he said quietly. "Falling in love with a whore." He turned around and walked slowly back up the passageway beside the shop then onto the road to Battalion. His eyes had grown accustomed to the cold, but as he came out from the village his vision blurred over again. He saw ahead of him the gauzy glow of a nearly-full moon low in the overcast sky. Its light falling on drifted snow had a bluish hue. It looked the same here as it did at home or anywhere.

Chapter 13   *Denver*

Dear Becky,

I thought spring would come earlier in Korea than in Duluth but I was wrong. It's April and yesterday when I walked back from the village it was snowing and a cold wind. There's still snow on the ground, too.

I've got news. Me and Mavrokis are both shipping out soon. Our tour of duty is almost over. I thought about reenlisting because they pay a big bonus to do that. But I decided not to.

I like Korea. It's very pretty what wasn't tore up by the war. I'm glad I wasn't here then (during the war).

I hope you are fine and are doing good in school. That reminds me. I am now a high school graduate, thanks to lots of help from Mavrokis, that's the Professor. I don't call him that anymore. Also I don't have him fix my writing anymore either. Though maybe I should.

*Say hi to the Ekmans. I don't know when I'll get home
exactly. It's a long boat ride, and then it takes a while to
get processed out of active duty. That's what I've been
told.*

Lonny

*PS. The picture is of me and Mavrokis in front of the
coffee shop in the village. Another guy who was there with
us took it.*

The day he processed out of active duty Lonny caught a hop on
a military transport flying to Denver from Travis AFB. In the plane
he sat by a window and next to an Army sergeant. The next leg
would be Denver to St. Louis. Then he could take a Greyhound
home by way of Minneapolis. It would be good to see his sister
again, and the Ekmans, but he was in no hurry. He was still in
uniform because he'd given away his old civilian clothes the last
week of basic training. In his new freedom he kept stretching and
taking deep breaths, as though he were just waking up, freed from
two long years of following rules and taking orders that often made
no sense. When he walked out of Oakland Army Terminal early
that morning carrying his duffle bag over his shoulder and his
discharge papers in a big brown envelope under his arm, it was like
walking into the woods back home, early in the morning in the fall
with the sun just coming up, and the sky clear, and there's frost on
the dead leaves in the path and you can see your breath and you
can *see* everything, every twig, the patterns of tree bark and how
rough it is and different colors on a rock. It's like seeing for the
first time. And standing still you hear little things, like a chipmunk
running over a log, or dried leaves that haven't fallen yet making
little ticking sounds when the air moves them against each other.

But as he looked out now at the clouds they were flying
through and under and over he thought of Iseul. She was his first
time. And she was a whore. The other guys had joked about the
whores and he'd listened, and laughed with them a little. But then
Cork had made that crack about Iseul's "skinny haunches" and
Lonny never laughed about the whores again. When he was with
her after that, it was always on his mind that she had to let bullies

like Cork screw her. It bothered him more and more what her life was like as a whore, and the last time he saw her he had just lain on the bed beside her and didn't feel like making love though she kissed him and kept stroking his hair. After a while she told him he had to leave and he got up from the bed and paid her, and the next time he came to see her she was gone and he never saw her again.

From his seat by the window he was looking down on a mountain range but what he was seeing was Iseul's pretty face. There was something else now, about her eyes, a faraway look. Eventually he focused on the land far below him.

"What mountains are those down there?" He spoke to his seatmate, a sergeant with three stripes on his shoulder who looked to be a few years older than himself. The man had quarter-inch pale blond hair, was lean, square-shouldered, and sat a couple of inches taller in the seat than Lonny.

"Utah mountains," he said, without looking up. He was reading a training manual. "We're over Utah about now."

"That's their name?"

"The mountains? Fuck, I don't know their *name*. Haven't got a name, probably." He stretched his neck to look out the window over Lonny's head. "Fuckin Utah. Nothin there worth a goddamn name, Soldier." He snorted happily at his joke and went back to his manual.

"Where do we hit the Rockies?"

"Hope to hell we don't *hit* the sonsobitches." He did his snorting chuckle again. "In Colorado, Soldier, just before we land." He closed the manual on his thumb to hold his place and glanced at Lonny's name tag. "Where're you from, Stuart?" He held out his hand. "Gabe Williams."

"Lonny." He'd almost said *Stuie*, but that was Army. Now he was Lonny again. They shook hands. "I'm from Minnesota."

"No mountains in Minnesota, are there? I'm from Texas. No mountains there either. "You regular Army or draftee?"

"Draftee. But I just got out." Lonny stretched his arms as he said it, high above his head.

"You didn't re-up? Why not? Man, there's rank to be made. There's a war heating up in Vietnam. You hear about that?"

"Yeah. Lieutenant in my outfit in Korea was all excited about it. He put in for a transfer."

"Smart man. So what's Lonny Stuart the civilian going to do?"

"I don't know yet. I worked as a wrangler before I was drafted."

"In *Minnesota*?"

"Riding stable."

"Oh. No future in that. You were maybe a fool getting out of the Army."

"Do you know Denver?"

"Yeah, I know Denver. That's where my folks live now. My Harley's in their garage. And after a couple days I'm going to ride off cross-country. I've been transferred to Washington – D.C., that is – before going to Vietnam, and I got this two-week leave. I'll look up an old buddy of mine in Fort Worth and then wander all over hell till I end up in D.C. And then I'll sell the bike, because, man, I mean to stay in Vietnam a long time. Till I make E-7 anyway, maybe even E-8. Master Sergeant Gabriel Williams, how's that sound?"

"Hope you make it." Lonny looked out the window again. They were flying over high desert now. And back in the far distance behind them he could just make out the mountains he'd been looking down on. The sun was sinking, turning high streaks of cloud a bright gold.

It was a girl he wanted, not a job. He wasn't worried about finding work. He was sure he could find something.

Gabe Williams had gone back to his manual but now he closed it again. "It bothers me, your having no idea what you're going to do."

"Well, I have *some* ideas. The stables, maybe. And I've done a little carpentry." His gaze went back to the window. "Or maybe auto mechanic, I could do that. I was in a motor pool in Korea." He looked back at Williams. "Have you been to Korea? Lots of mountains there..."

"How old are you, man, twenty-two, three?"

"Twenty-one in June."

Williams shook his head. "You'd better do some serious thinking about your future. You're a pretty rough-looking character but you must have had it pretty easy all your life not to be planning a career."

Lonny laughed, more to himself than out loud. He said, "Well, I never went to bed hungry till I joined the Army."

"Hah! Basic training, right?"

When they landed and Lonny saw the snow-peaked Rockies looming west of the city he decided to find a hotel and stay overnight. Williams gave him his parents' phone number and said to call him if he was going to stay longer, said he would show him around on his motorcycle.

Lonny stowed his duffle bag in a locker and caught a bus into the city. He found a hotel, and he noticed some posters on the wall behind the desk as he checked in. One was for a rodeo, in a town called Edith.

In Duluth, so far as he knew, there'd never been a rodeo. Maybe here in the West every little town had a rodeo. The desk clerk told him Edith was in the mountains, just past the foothills.

He had dinner that evening in a Chinese restaurant down the street from the hotel. Then he used the pay phone in the hotel lobby to call Gabe Williams.

"A rodeo up in Edith? Well, I don't know, Lonny. I haven't been to one since I left Texas. Might be fun, though. Saturday's day after tomorrow.... Well Hell, Wrangler, sure, let's go. You're not fixin to ride in it are you?"

"No! I haven't even *seen* a rodeo." But then he considered the idea. "I guess I could ride a bucking horse... But I'd hate to get banged up this far from home."

"And no Uncle Sam to pay your bills. You should'a re-upped, Soldier."

In the morning Lonny went shopping for jeans and a shirt and a wide leather belt. He thought of buying a pair of cowboy boots, but it seemed a dumb expense just for going to a rodeo, and he had a good pair stored with some other things in the Ekmans' attic.

That afternoon he explored the city, mostly on foot but once he took a bus to the end of its run and then back again. In the evening he sat in the lobby of the hotel and wrote a postcard to Becky. It felt good to relax in civies in a big soft chair and watch the few people who came into the hotel, or went out, and to think about home, and about the Army, and wonder what Mavrokis was getting up to in Florida, whether he would go to college again and become a teacher as he'd said. When he finished the card to Becky, he thought of writing to his father, also. He had sent him a card when he went into the Army; and now that he was out he could send him another. But he hadn't heard from his father since basic training, a short note that began with "Congratulations," which Mavrokis had thought was funny when Lonny showed it to him: Getting drafted's no great achievement, he'd said. Is your old man trying too hard to be nice or doesn't he expect much of you? Well fuck you, Lonny'd said but instead of getting angry Mavrokis had just kept talking and listening and after a while Lonny had admitted that he'd felt put down when he first read that "congratulations." Mavrokis and he became friends after that. The note had gone on with a hope that Lonny would get along well in the Army and learn some useful skills.

As he wondered whether his high school diploma would count as a "useful skill," Lonny watched a lean elderly man come in and make his way toward the elevator. He had a white mustache and white chin whiskers and wore a dark suit and shiny black shoes with narrow toes. He walked slowly, unsteadily, leaning on a cane. The desk clerk was watching, too. He called to him: "Mr. Sanchez, sir, your key..."

The man stopped and looked back at the clerk. Lonny jumped up from his chair, put his pen and postcards on the table beside him, and went over to the desk. "I'll give it to him," he said. He took the key and brought it to the old man, who looked at it, confused. He smelled of whisky. Lonny took his arm. "I'll go up with you." The man let Lonny help him to the elevator then stabbed the up button with the end of his cane.

"Bull's eye," Lonny said.

"Damn right," said the old man.

Lonny checked the room number on the key and pushed the third floor button.

In the elevator Mr. Sanchez suddenly straightened up and said in a strong voice, "If you think you can roll me for money you're mistaken, young man." He gave him a fierce look.

"I don't want your money, sir."

"I've got a lot of money..." His voice weakened as he spoke and he leaned against the side of the elevator.

It stopped at the third floor and the door opened. "Here we go, sir," said Lonny. They made their way down the hall, Lonny counting off the room numbers till they got to 312. He put the key in the lock, swung the door open and helped Mr. Sanchez to his bed. The old man sat down heavily, with a big sigh. Lonny put the key on the dresser and started to leave. "Goodnight, Mr. Sanchez."

The old man looked up, and his eyes, though watery, caught and held him. They were a pale, piercing blue, and strange. And then the eyes softened but without leaving Lonny's face: "You're a good man." Then he bent over and began studiously untying his shoes. "Damn lot of money."

Lonny left the room then and closed the door quietly behind him.

Chapter 14 Rodeo

Lonny's Army field jacket and the watch cap borrowed from
Gabe kept the edge off the cold wind that rushed by his ears and
rippled his cheeks. Lonny enjoyed the ride, his body pulled one
way and then the other as they followed the tight curves of the
mountain road. He tried to guide the bike with his knees as he
would a horse until Gabe yelled over his shoulder to stop it.
Eventually he gave in, relaxed, let the machine take him over, lean
with it, watch the scenery.

He loved the high mountain air, the freshness, the clarity it
gave to everything. He was higher up here than in Korea, and he
felt free and even farther from Duluth. He didn't have to go back.
It seemed to be carried on the wind: *you don't have to go back.* He
could find a job in these "hills," as Gabe called them. In some little
town. Set up on his own. Becky could have Lena's house when she
grows up... That thought put him in Duluth, where he didn't want
to be right now. He brought his mind back to where he was, on the

back of a motorcycle, flying along a mountain road, following a river upstream higher and higher.

They came to a valley, all in pasture to the foot of the pine-forested hills all around, ranch buildings far off at the north end, a few white-faced Herefords grazing on the spring grass. They sped on through the valley and rose into the forest on the other side.

In the next valley they slowed as they passed a welcome sign: "Edith, population 1683." The highway became Edith Street, according to a sign, and split the town.

"Who's this Edith?" Lonny said over Gabe's shoulder.

"Damned if I know. Founder's lady love, probably."

Edith Street took them to the fairgrounds on the west side of town. Gabe pulled into the parking lot by the grandstand and stopped the bike under a blue spruce. At the box office a posted schedule showed a parade at 10:00 followed by Welcoming Remarks, Dance Demonstration by The Edith Squares, followed by Henton County Award-Winning Bulls. The rodeo didn't start till 11:00.

"It's only 9:30," said Gabe, "and I'm not watching that local crap."

"Me, neither," said Lonny, though he had a feeling the parade might be fun.

They bought tickets and agreed to meet at the box office just before eleven. Gabe headed for a café they'd passed as they came into town and Lonny decided to take a walk and maybe check out the stables. The air was still cool but the sun was hot and shining down hard. It seemed closer to the earth here than anywhere else he'd ever been, a more direct shot right at his head. He ran his hand over his pale blond hair, still G.I. short. He'd noticed in Denver that a lot of the young guys had long hair, much longer than the ducktails and sideburns on some of the draftees when they'd arrived at basic training. Girls in Denver had even longer hair, and just hanging straight without even a wave.

He walked around the grandstand, his field jacket slung over his shoulder. It was a bulky thing and he wished he could stow it somewhere for a while. He came to a gate with a sign saying "Contestants Only Beyond This Point." The gate was open. He walked through looking straight ahead as though he knew where he was going. His shirt and Levi's qualified but he lacked the authentic hat, and if anyone looked they'd see his round-toed black G.I. boots. He came around a little grove of pine trees with picnic tables in among them and then he saw the stables and a familiar scene that made him smile. In front of a long row of stalls it was almost all girls who had led the horses out for a last-minute grooming. They were currying, brushing, combing snags out of manes and tails, washing fetlocks. The riders, boys and men, the few who had shown up so far, stood around smoking, leaning against stalls, sitting on the rails. One of them, about Lonny's age, wearing a black cowboy hat, was carefully curling a rope. It looked very stiff. Brand new, probably. Or maybe it had been soaked and let dry in the sun.

Just beyond Black Hat a girl with a long pony tail and wearing jeans was combing out the mane of a red quarterhorse with massive haunches and a broad chest. Annoyed, the gelding's ears were back and he kept swinging his head around to her as if warning her to stop. Lonny saw him nip at her leg.

"Barney! Damn you, stop that!" The girl slapped his muzzle and the horse jerked his head away. She rubbed her thigh, then saw Lonny standing a few yards away watching her.

"And what are *you* looking at?"

"Did he hurt you?"

"Not bad. Why aren't you laughing?"

"Nothing funny about a bite."

She looked at him, as if expecting more, but he just stood there.

"Well, now that you've had your little entertainment you can do something useful. Come here and hold his damn head, would you?"

"Sure." He approached and took hold of the halter and put his other hand on the horse's neck. "What's the matter, Barney?" he said. "Something hurting you? Combing your mane shouldn't hurt." He turned to the girl, "Is there a sore or something under his mane?"

"I'm looking." She was carefully lifting sections of the mane, parting it, checking the roots. "Oh, here it is. Poor Barney. I must have scraped off a scab. Looks like someone took a little chomp out of him. I'll put some baby oil on it."

She went to open the locker just inside the stall and came back with a little bottle of Johnson & Johnson. She put some on her fingertips and gently touched it to the open wound. The horse jerked his head but Lonny held him firmly.

"You're not a contestant, are you?" she said, eyeing his round-toed boots and army jacket.

"No."

"You're not supposed to be back here."

"I wanted to see the horses."

"Barney's a roping horse, just for a while, for my little brother till his colt grows up. But Barney's my baby." She cupped his soft muzzle in her hand. "He's really a barrel racer. We're gonna show 'em all this fall, aren't we Barney?" She looked at Lonny. "You're not from around here. You come for our little rodeo?"

"Yeah."

"'Yeah' what? I asked two questions."

"I only heard one question. But yes I'm not from around here and yes I came for the rodeo."

"Where'd you get boots like that?"

"Army. They're good boots." He scuffed his toe in the dirt.

"They wouldn't fit in stirrups."

He laughed. "Nope."

The girl looked at him, waiting. Then she turned back to combing the mane, very carefully.

"I just got out of the Army," he said to her back.

"Oh! It talks. So maybe you were a cowboy before the Army, a real one maybe? Not like some of the pissants around here who can't hardly ride but can sure wear a hat."

Lonny felt his face flush.

"They were the nicest boys – more or less – when we were growing up. But as soon as they got old enough to smoke in public they bought new boots and a big hat and they think they're God's gift to women. To the whole world, for that matter. If my little brother Terry gets that way I'll kick his behind. I call him my *little* brother because I'm older than him but he's taller than me – taller than you, too," she added, looking back at Lonny, "but he weighs less than a fly. He can throw a rope pretty good. It's about all he's good for."

"I'm no cowboy," Lonny said to the horse. He still held him by the halter. "I worked at a riding stable before getting drafted."

She kept at her work with her back to him. Lonny liked her. She was nice looking, though he figured the guys in his unit in Korea wouldn't give her a top rating. She looked healthy, fresh and strong. He liked her way with her horse. He liked her brown hair in the long pony tail. He liked how she looked at him, her eyes bright and sort of teasing but friendly, not mean, and how she'd glance back at him now and then, as though she were interested, checking him out.

She finished with the mane, and when she turned around, her eyes scanned his face. Then she started on the horse's tail. She said, "So you were at the back end of a horse when you shouldn'a been? That how you got that scar?"

Lonny couldn't answer.

"Sorry," she said. "I get nosey sometimes. Ask questions I shouldn't. So, do you want to see the broncs? They got 'em in a corral. Just follow this road along here and you'll pass a barn and the corrals are next to that. Stupid place to keep the broncs because they'll have to lead them one by one all the way back to the stands and then underneath to the chutes."

Lonny stood silent, all the wrong words swirling in his head.

"Thanks for helping with Barney."

"You're welcome." Lonny let go of the halter. "And good luck to your brother. What's his name... Terry?"

"Terry Scholes. I'm Kristin. And that's not Christine, it's Kristin. With a K."

"I'm Lonny Stuart." He held out his hand. It felt naked and alone out there in front of him until Kristin took it, after what seemed a long delay to wipe her hand on her jeans. Her grip was soft at first, and then harder. He let go. He knew she saw his embarrassment – was it funny to her? I'm such a dope, he thought.

"Goodbye, Lonny."

"Bye."

He turned away, trying not to walk as fast as he wanted to. What he wanted was to run, but he held back, following the road toward the barn and the corrals and the broncs. *You'd think I'd never talked to a girl...* He saw Iseul's face then, her smile, the red lips. And then the smile went away and she looked sad. She looked really sad. He had seen that sometimes, her sadness. And then he'd feel sorry for her but she'd see that and right away cheer up and call him Soldier Boy and put her arms around his neck, happy, sexy, sure of herself – it was all an act to make a living... but maybe not always. He remembered the way she looked into his eyes sometimes. And then he'd think she really liked him. It hurt to remember that.

Her smile came back now, but immediately faded into a deeper sadness, deeper than he remembered actually seeing. After Cork's rough treatment he'd seen pain in her face sometimes, but there wasn't this sadness he saw now. Where had that come from?

He had stopped walking but now he moved on. Mavrokis and the other guys didn't seem to have any problem going to the whores. Lonny told himself he had at least tried to be nice to Iseul.

He passed the barn and looked for the corral up ahead because now he could smell it: horse, horse sweat, shit, piss. Good smell. He came around a shed and some trees and there it was.

He liked being around horses again. He figured he could probably feel at home anywhere there were horses. Kristin's Barney was a good horse. It probably had papered bloodlines from the looks of it. But it was Kristin's pet. Girls always made pets of their horses. Kristin had a nice face, kind of a sideways smile. He liked that, but there was always a question in it, and he didn't know what the question was. She'd looked angry when the horse nipped her. Her hand was like touching something alive... that's dumb, he thought. Of course she's alive. But it surprised him. Like getting a shock off a cat's fur.

In the corral the horses seemed peaceful enough. But they had spur scars on their shoulders, almost like stripes, and some had healed-over wounds around their heads. It was a rough life for a bronc. Probably short. And then dog meat. It made him sad to look at them. And suddenly his stomach dropped, he felt hollow, cold inside. It made no difference to Iseul that he loved her. She'd had to screw him so he'd pay her, so she could live.

He moved away from the horses and walked on, following the road. It made a circuit of the area and he soon found himself passing bleachers and then coming back to the grandstand, where there was another gate. It was closed but it opened from the inside and he went out and headed down Edith Street looking for Gabe.

He found him in The Downtown Café and joined him at his table. Gabe looked up. "I've been reading the local rag, Lonny-boy. Want to buy a ranch? Pick-up truck? Two-ton flat-bed? Saddle? Horse? Bull? Haybaler? They got it all here in the..." he turned the paper over to the front page "...*Edith Weekly Sentinel*. All you need to set up and get started."

"If I could buy all that, I wouldn't need to."

"What?"

"I remember my dad saying that. He's a salesman. Or was, last I knew. He used to read the want ads out loud sometimes. It was usually a business he wished he could buy, to be the owner and be his own boss. And then he'd say 'If I could buy it, I wouldn't need it.'"

"Meaning what?"

"I don't know. Never thought about it." A waitress came to the table and Lonny ordered coffee, though he didn't think he could drink it. "Hey, I know what he meant. If he had enough money to buy the business, he'd have enough to live on without working at all, and so there'd be no reason to buy it."

"My mother had sayings I never thought about. 'If it was a snake it would bite you.' And 'A stitch in time saves nine.' What the hell's a 'stitch in time' and what's it 'save nine' of?"

"Stitches, I guess. But if I could buy a ranch in this mountain valley I would, even if I didn't need it."

Lonny's coffee arrived.

Gabe shook his head. "What's here? Grass, trees, hills, cows, and cowboys. That's it."

Two teenage girls in jeans and cowboy boots got up from a booth at the back of the café and stopped at the register. Gabe appraised them with a long look. "And cowgirls," he said, lowering his voice, "sturdy and strong. Drop a kid a year, if family's what you want. Not me. I got two older brothers and a big sister. Brothers are married and making babies. But my sister and me, we're free spirits. She's an airline stewardess and fools around a lot. And in the Army, Lonny, I get plenty of free time to fool around. Lots of ladies, different countries. And at the same time I'm building a career and a retirement pension. With a couple of years in Vietnam I'll make rank and be set for life."

Lonny stared absently into the pool of black coffee in his mug, his hands folded around it. "You're talking about peacetime. You go to Vietnam you could get shot or blown up. You could step on a mine."

"Not me.

"Of course it's possible," Gabe said as they walked back to the fairgrounds, "that I'll get shot. But I'm lucky. I've always taken risks – like riding that Harley, never had a wreck, never will. And, no, *saying* this won't make it happen. I'm not superstitious. And *I* went to Catholic school! Those old nuns taught us we've all got a Guardian Angel, and my guy's doing one hell of a great job. He's making rank in heaven. I can be walking down the street with somebody, and say there's a ten dollar bill caught in the gutter. Every time it'll be me that sees it, not whoever I'm with. And one time I'm riding along in these hills and I see just ahead of me a bunch of rocks falling down on the road. So I pull over and stop to let the slide finish and right behind me some more rocks come down. But nothing touches me. I could almost *see* that big angel – I know he's got to be a big guy – up the hill like... like the prow of some fucking ship making the rocks fall away from me... Oh heavenly shit! Look up there, Lonny-boy. That ol' Harley's caught himself some quail."

"The girls from the café."

"Yeah. Too bad they're jail bait or we could have some fun.

"Hi ya, Ladies," Gabe sang out as they approached. "You don't want to get too close to my stud horse there. He's like as to bite little girls."

"He got no balls," said the taller girl, smiling, a brunette wearing a red bandanna loose around her neck. "It's a gelding."

The shorter girl, the blonde, seemed to hide behind her friend. *Just like me*, Lonny thought, hanging back a step behind Gabe. He checked his watch. "Gabe, I'm going in. I don't want to miss the bronc riding. It's up first."

"Okay, man, I'll find you."

Lonny was impressed by the skill of the riders. He wasn't bad himself, had always held on when a young horse tested him on a cold morning or any time it felt playful. A few crow-hops and kicks, but nothing like these twisting leaps, stiff-legged landings, head stands. He wondered if he could do it, stick on long enough to qualify. He knew they had to keep spurring the horse to make points, but he hated that part. He wouldn't be able to do that. Every rider but one got thrown. The one who didn't had drawn a horse who didn't have much heart for bucking that day. It was probably sick. Though from the stands he couldn't see well enough to tell.

When the calf-roping began Gabe still hadn't shown up. Lonny started thinking he might have to find another way back to Denver. But when the first rider burst out of the chute he forgot about Gabe. It went fast: the rider threw his rope out over the calf's head, and then all at the same time the loop settled and tightened, the horse planted his feet, and the rider leaped from the saddle. When the calf hit the end of the rope he flipped to the ground and the rider fell on him with his knees. He gathered together the calf's two hind feet and one front foot, held them with one hand and with the other hand took the piece of rope he held in his teeth, wound it around the feet, tied it, threw his hands in the air, and the crowd applauded. Then the rider loosened and reclaimed his ropes and the calf scrambled up and trotted off. Lonny was glad to see that. He'd thought its neck might be broken but it just looked happy to get away.

The next rider's horse didn't keep the rope taut, so the calf was back on its feet when the rider got to it. He had to wrestle the calf to the ground before he could tie its legs, wasting seconds on his time. Another rider came too slow out of the chute so he lost seconds catching up to the calf to throw his loop. But his horse did its job and the rider was at the calf before it could get up. Lonny liked this event. The rider had to be quick and strong, and he could see it took a smart horse, and one with big quarterhorse haunches to get that burst out of the chute.

Eventually he heard the announcer say "Terry Scholes on Barney" and it seemed only a second before Terry's loop was out and settling over the calf. Then Barney was sliding on planted feet and Terry was running down the taut rope. But the calf hadn't had a chance to get up to speed and so it had only spun around and was still on its feet. Terry reached under it, grabbed a hind and front leg, pulled and lifted, flipping the calf completely over and onto the ground and falling on it with his knees all in the same motion. Lonny glanced away, thinking he saw Kristin in the stands. When he looked back the calf's feet were tied and Terry's hands were in the air. Lonny applauded with the crowd while scanning the stands for Kristin's ponytail. Then he saw her... No, it was different girl.

Lonny couldn't see the point of the Brahma bull riding. There would never be a need to do that on a cattle ranch. It was the last event and still no Gabe. He bought a hot dog on his way out of the stands, ate it in four bites, and was licking his fingers when he came to the trees where Gabe had parked the bike. It was gone. He saw a piece of paper sticking out from under a rock set on top of another rock. He pulled it out. The note said, "Plucking quail. Café at 6. Lucky."

He looked around. A line of pickup trucks hauling horse trailers were slowly passing through the gate to the stables. He hurried past them, heading for Kristin's – Barney's – stall. He had no idea what he'd say.

He found her leading Barney to the back of an open trailer. Her brother Terry sat slouched behind the wheel of the GMC pickup, smoking a cigarette, the window rolled up most of the way and his hat pushed down over his forehead. It sounded like the picking of Flatt and Scruggs on the truck radio.

"Hi," Lonny said. "He did great! And so did Barney."

"Hi yourself. So you saw it. Yeah, I guess the twerp's almost good enough for Barney."

The horse tossed his head and backed away from the trailer. Kristin led him in a big circle ending back to the trailer and facing the ramp. Barney stepped onto it then stopped, put his head down, sniffed, snorted at the ramp, and backed up.

"Barney!"

"You need to tickle his butt," said Lonny.

"I know. I just thought he might be nice about it today. There's a rope in the stall. Would you get it?"

He got the rope and handed her an end then uncoiled it as he walked behind the horse to its other side. Then they pulled the roped taut between them so it rode up Barney's hind legs. He laid his ears back but ran up the ramp and shoved his face into the manger inside the trailer. They heard his big molars start grinding hay. Kristin got in beside the horse and clipped his lead rope to the bar at the manger. She came out and Lonny helped her raise the ramp and latch it.

"I haven't got a boyfriend," Kristin said. She kept her eyes on her work as she slowly coiled up the lead rope. "I was going with this guy I've known forever but I saw him with this other girl and at first I was shocked and mad but then I realized I really didn't care, not at all, except for the sneaking. Jas and I broke up just after New Year's but we're still friends." She laughed and looked at Lonny. "I remember him in first grade. He wet his pants when the teacher called on him."

Lonny remembered his own humiliations in school.

"You don't think that's funny?" said Kristin. "It happened to lots of kids when we were little."

"Yeah. But it wasn't funny for the kid who wet his pants."

Kristin leaned against the back of the trailer. "You're really different from the guys around here."

"I look different anywhere."

Kristin spoke sharply: "That's not what I meant. I meant the guys around here love to laugh at other people. Where're you from, anyway?"

"Minnesota... sort of."

"Sort of?"

"I haven't been back for two years. All I've got is a sister and she's living with foster parents. I just got out of the Army a couple days ago."

"That explains the short hair."

"Kristy!" Terry had stuck his head out of the truck window. "You ready to go yet?"

She stepped out from behind the trailer. "Keep your pants on, Terry! You could help, you know. Look around the stall and see if we forgot anything."

Terry slid out of the truck and slammed the door. He glanced at Lonny as he slouched by. Kristin rolled her eyes.

Terry made a noisy inspection of the stall while Lonny explained to Kristin how he'd come to the rodeo. Something clattered into the metal bed of the truck. "You forgot your damn curry comb," Terry said. He climbed back up behind the steering wheel. "C'mon, Kristy, let's go."

"Little brother needs his supper," Kristin said.

"I wish I could see you again," Lonny said, surprising himself.

"Yeah?" She thought a second, then pulled a folded up program from her back pocket. "You can look me up sometime." She opened the program to the list of contestants. "There's my address: Circle T Ranch, Edith, Colorado."

They heard the truck's engine start up and Kristin shoved the program into Lonny's hand. "Gotta go." She kissed him quickly on his scarred cheek then ran away around the trailer. He heard the passenger door slam. As they pulled away he heard Barney stomping nervously on the floor of the trailer.

They had reached the gate when the rig stopped and Kristin came running back to him. "Would you like to come to dinner?"

"Yes, but I can't. I've got to meet Gabe at six. I'm riding with him back to Denver."

"Well he can come, too." She looked at her watch. "It's almost six now. Where do you meet him?"

"Downtown Café."

"Lonny, they close at two. They don't serve supper."

"Well shit! I guess I'll have to wait outside there and hope he shows up."

"Tell you what. If he doesn't show by six-thirty say, call me. There's a phone booth at Myer's Conoco. It's a little further up Edith Street. I'll give you my phone number. You call me and I'll come get you."

They walked to the truck and Kristin got a business card out of the glove box. "My dad had these printed. I told him it was a waste of money. I keep the books for the ranch. Five hundred of these and we've got almost no one to give them to."

"If Gabe doesn't show, how do I get back to Denver?"

"There's a bus goes through Dalton City about noon. I can drive you over there in the morning."

"You're putting me up for the night?"

"Well we can't let you sleep out in the rain!"

"It's not raining."

"It might. What do you know about mountain weather?"

Chapter 15 Gabe

Lonny waited by the phone booth in front of the Conoco station. He watched the sun go down behind the western hills, putting all of Edith in shadow. For a brief while yellow sunlight seemed to catch on the highest peak to the east, before it freed itself and disappeared. The temperature dropped as the night came on. Lonny waited, watching up and down the broad, nearly empty street. Toward the east end of town three pickups were angle-parked in front of the Eight-Ball Bar. Two more pickups and a car clustered a little beyond that, at another bar, probably. To the west he saw nothing on the street but one car, parked or abandoned far down near the fairgrounds. A lone street light came on, marking the crossroad at the center of town. And then a white pickup came into its light from behind the hardware store on the corner. Kristin? It turned and came up Edith Street and stopped at the curb in front of him. Lonny opened the door and got in.

"It's seven o'clock," Kristin said. "He still didn't show?"

"Nope. I'm not real sorry about it."

Kristin did a u-turn. "I'll bet you're hungry. What's this Gabe like?"

"Sort of a hot-shot, gung-ho Army. Kept telling me I should have re-up'd. Said I could fool around and build a career and a retirement pension all at the same time. I only met him a couple days ago, like I said. Seemed like an okay guy. I'm a little worried something might have happened to him."

"Like getting in a fight? We could check the two bars in town. Is he a drinker?"

"He's all Army so it's likely, but I don't know."

Kristin pulled another u-turn. "The bars are up past the Conoco."

At the first set of pickups she stopped and Lonny went into the bar. He soon returned, said Gabe wasn't there, that the bartender didn't recognize the description. But at the next place, The Old Town Saloon, Lonny got an earful from the old man behind the bar.

He made Lonny wait while he lit a cigarette and took a deep drag. "That first drag's the best... Anyway, there *was* a guy in here looked like what you say – tall, crew cut, big shoulders. He parked a motorcycle out front." He took another deep drag, let the smoke drift out of his nostrils. "That was about four-thirty, I'd say. He had a beer and then he was playing pool with Colin Ork when Billy Stark came in and asked me who owned that motorcycle out front. I pointed out your friend there playing pool and Billy goes over and interrupts the game and starts talking to him. Gets right in his face." He took another drag and then coughed, and coughed again, and the coughing continued till he took a sip of beer from the glass he had standing on the counter behind him. Finally he got his voice back and went on. "I didn't hear much of what ol' Billy said but it looked like trouble to me and I was about to tell those boys to take it outside when they did that all on their own. They went out back." He tilted his head toward the back door. "A couple of other guys followed them. After a while they all come back in, except this Gabe friend of yours. Billy goes straight through and out the front. Then I hear that motorcycle start up and go off."

"So what happened to Gabe?"

"Haven't seen him again."

"So he's still out back? Did you look?"

The bartender shrugged. "Someone said they saw a drunk out there sleeping it off."

Lonny ran out the back door. His eyes took a while to adjust to the darkness. He made out a garbage can that had lost its lid and fallen part way over against another can. And then he saw Gabe on his side lying with his back up against the fallen can. Lonny knelt down, put his hand on Gabe's shoulder and looked in his face. It was bloody and swollen.

"Gabe. Gabe." Lonny touched his cheek. It was warm. "Gabe, wake up. Can you hear me?" He shook him very gently. Gabe let out a groan. "It's Lonny, Gabe. Wake up."

"Lonny." He opened one eye. The other was swollen shut. "Helluva fight. The other guy. Dead?"

"He stole your bike."

"Wha?"

"He stole your bike."

"Th' sombitch... STOLE MY BIKE?" He stirred, tried to sit up.

"Easy, fella." Lonny helped him sit back against the garbage can.

"Guess I los' uh fight. Guy's like a bull. Head like... f'ckin' shell casing."

"I'll get you some water."

The bartender dispensed the water without comment, a faint smile around his eyes.

Gabe was able to hold the glass and sip while Lonny went back to Kristin to ask her to drive the truck around to the back of the bar.

"Hurts to breathe," Gabe said when Lonny and Kristin knelt down beside him. "Broke rib, maybe."

"We've got to get him to a doctor," said Kristin. "There's an emergency clinic over in Dalton City. It's about a half hour drive."

They laid Gabe on the bench seat of the truck with his knees up leaving just enough room for Kristin to drive, squeezed against the door. Lonny rode in the back, sitting on a folded-up saddle blanket with his back against the cab.

While the emergency room doctor tended to Gabe, Kristin called home and then she and Lonny found an open restaurant where Lonny ordered the meatloaf special.

"I'll have coffee and a piece of that cherry pie I saw when we came in." When the waitress left Kristin grinned and said, "I had dinner at home, but not dessert."

"You've sure been nice to a couple of bums."

"You're not a bum. I don't know about Gabe."

"I hope he's not hurt too bad."

"I know why he got beat up. Billy Stark, that's Elly Ann's uncle. When I was driving over here whenever I went around a bend your friend would shift a little and groan something like 'Oh... Elly, you hurt so gooood...'"

"I was afraid of that. Does this Elly have brown hair, sort of dark eyes – brown, maybe – wears tight jeans?"

"Real tight. And did you leave out 'well-developed' on purpose, and 'cakes on the red lipstick?'"

"Yeah. So Elly Ann must be one of the girls we met before the rodeo. There were two of them. Elly was admiring Gabe's Harley. She looked about sixteen, in spite of the make-up."

"She's seventeen, going on thirty."

"Do you think they'll press charges?"

"It happened once before. Once that I *know* of. They made a deal. There were lawyers involved. The deal was that if there was no statutory rape by this kid Easton Glover then there was no assault by Billy Stark. Billy beat the kid from here to Sunday. He survived, though, and the Glovers moved away, to Oregon, I think."

Lonny's supper arrived with Kristin's pie and coffee. He dug right in.

"I see you're a good eater," she said. "Not like my little brother, though. He puts a pig to shame."

When he'd cleaned off half his plate he came up for air. He sat back, wiped his mouth and drank off his water.

"Why the uncle?" he said. "Why not the father? Or a brother?"

"Elly Ann doesn't have a brother. And her father wouldn't hurt a fly. But there's something weird about that uncle. They're real close, if you know what I mean, Elly Ann and Billy Stark. I don't know if they *do* anything, but it's weird."

"You don't have that sort of uncle, do you?" He went back to his meatloaf and mashed potatoes.

"I do have an uncle. But he's in Pueblo and I'm twenty-two." She patted his hand. "Not to worry, Lonny. I'm not trouble, not that kind anyway." She let her hand rest on his momentarily, then drew it away, trailing her fingers over the back of his hand. "How old are you, by the way?"

"Twenty-one this month."

"What day?"

"The twenty-eighth."

When she finished her pie, she rested her elbows on the table and cradled her coffee mug in her hands, taking small sips while Lonny ate.

Finally he put down his fork.

"We should get back to the clinic," Kristin said.

They stopped a nurse approaching them in the hall and asked about Gabe Williams. "Two cracked ribs," she began, "and a broken nose and four stitches over the left eye. He'll be fine in a month or so."

"Can I see him?" said Lonny.

"He's sleeping. We'll keep him overnight. Unless there's a problem, the surgeon will discharge him in the morning, about ten o'clock."

Kristin and Lonny went outside. It was dark, moonless, and very clear.

"Stars come right down on your head here," said Lonny. "It's amazing." He tilted his head back, his mouth open.

"You could eat one for dessert. It's okay. We've got lots."

"Would it be hot, do you think? Or cold?"

She looked up, thinking. "Both, like when your fingers get so cold it feels like burning."

"Like cold whisky going down your throat."

"Yeah, like that. Are you a drinker?"

"No. I don't like what it does to me. I'm dumb enough without it."

"You know it's not very attractive to a girl, running yourself down like that. It's better than bragging but not much."

He couldn't think of an answer to that. He looked up at the stars again. "The constellations, do you know them?"

"Just the ones everyone knows, the Big Dipper, the North Star off its lip, Orion's belt and sword. We should go. You can stay at the ranch and I'll bring you back in the morning."

"That's too much driving for you. And I don't want to make a lot of trouble for your folks. You've been awfully nice to me, but I should stay here. There's probably a motel, or they might let me sleep in the waiting room in the clinic."

"There's a motel a ways down this street. I'll take you there."

She waited in the truck while Lonny checked in. The clerk's eyes looked over Lonny's head when he asked for a single. He caught the woman's glance. He said, "She's not staying. She just gave me a ride over here."

"Right. Just sign here." The clerk put a thick finger by the X on the registration card. Lonny wrote his name and she gave him a key.

He walked down the row of rooms and Kristin followed in the truck. At 113 he stopped, opened the door with his key, went inside and turned on the light. Kristin came and stood in the open doorway.

"Not too bad," she said. "Though the cowboy stuff's pretty tiresome."

He stood looking at the bucking broncos on the bedspread.

"What happens when you get back to Denver?"

"I catch a hop to St. Louis or Chicago. Military transport. And then a bus to Duluth, or a train. I haven't told you, have I? That's where I'm from, Duluth, Minnesota."

She came into the room. "So then you're gone. Half way across the country. And you'll never see the great city of Edith again."

She was looking at the floor. He turned to her. "I'm not so sure about that. It's beautiful here. I love the mountains. And I like the people... I mean I like you, I like you a lot."

She lifted her face to him, her eyes appealing, moist. "You fool cowboy." She put her arms around him.

He held her and she squeezed him with her strong arms. He closed his eyes and kissed her on the neck. He gave the door a push and it clicked shut. He sat down on the bed and Kristin settled onto his lap. She tried to kiss his mouth but he turned his head. She kissed his eyes closed. "That old scar?" she said. Then she kissed his mouth. He lay back on the bed and Kristin lay on top of him, leaning on her elbows, her breasts above his face. He pulled her down, burying his face in her softness. He rolled her over and began unbuttoning her shirt. Then he was kissing her belly and she tried to roll away from him.

"Lonny, give me a minute."

He let her up and she went into the bathroom. He took out the condom that he carried in his wallet – thanks to the wisdom of Mavrokis. He undressed and got into bed. When Kristin emerged from the bathroom she wore only the shirt and panties. Her brown hair hung free, brushing her shoulders. He turned back the covers for her and she slid in beside him. They lay side by side, not moving, Kristin pressing her face against his chest. He began trying to unbutton her shirt again. She sat up and took it off then lay down again and he started to pull off her panties. She put her hand on his – "You do have a rubber?"

"Yes."

"Okay then." She raised her hips.

He rolled away from her and put on the condom quickly – he was far too aroused already. He came back to her and she slid under him, parting her legs. And then he was inside her and lay over her, not moving. She hooked her heels over his ankles and wrapped her arms around him. He began to move in her, very slowly at first, and then more urgently. She held him tighter and whispered, "Slow down, Cowboy, we've got all night."

He stopped and held there, on the edge. She relaxed her arms. He pushed up onto his elbows to see her face. But the movement spilled him over. He groaned, and a light and then blackness flooded through his brain.

He lay still then, holding her, his face pressed into the pillow beside her face, lost in her soft hair. Then he realized he was crying, silently. He took a deep breath then let it out slowly. Kristin shifted under him. He rolled off her and lay back. She nestled against him. Her eyes were closed and she seemed asleep.

He thought of the stars outside, how bright they were, and so near. But he couldn't see them now because of the roof. And the ceiling. His eyes traced a crack in it near the door. Iseul's room. "You a good man," she'd said. "Quick. No fuck round." Right. He wanted to go outside now. He wanted to put his clothes on, feel his boots on his feet. He wanted to go outside and take a long walk under the black sky and the white stars, hit the pavement hard with his heels, swing his arms. Where was he, anyway? Some town he'd never heard of. Colorado! Some mountain town. In some old motel. He looked down at the girl beside him. Kristin. A girl named Kristin. From his solitude he looked at her, this girl on his arm. A strand of her hair lay curled on her forehead, the end of it just touching an eyelash, barely touching it. He bent down and with his lips touched her cheek, just the lightest touch, like a breath. Her eyes opened, and she was there with him, arching her eyebrows. She opened her mouth as if to speak, then closed it. A question withdrawn.

"I really like you," he said.

"I like you, too, Lonny." She pressed her lips to his chest then rolled away from him. "I hope you come back some day." She gathered up her clothes and went into the bathroom.

Lonny stood by the GMC as Kristin climbed in. He closed the door for her and she started the engine then rolled down the window. She reached for his hand and held it to her cheek.

"Circle T Ra..." she said, choking off the word and turning her head away. She put the truck in gear, gunned the engine and drove off.

"Where's th' Harley?" Gabe had opened his eyes and seen Lonny standing beside his bed.

"I don't know. No idea. How are you feeling?"

"Beat up. I lose th' fight? Or's 'at bull dead?"

"I think you lost the fight."

He said something Lonny couldn't make out.

"What was that?"

Gabe slowly shook his head. "Hard to talk. All swollen. Harley out front th' bar?"

"No. I told you last night. The bartender said someone drove it away."

"Shit. Check m' pants. Keys." Gabe flexed his arm up from the elbow and pointed at the wardrobe door. Lonny opened it and went through all the pockets of Gabe's pants.

"Here's your wallet. About fifty bucks in it. No keys, man."

"Bastard stole m' bike!" Gabe tried to sit up. "Call the f'k'n sheriff!"

"Are you sure you want the sheriff in on this?"

Gabe looked at him, puzzled, then collapsed into his pillow. "Chick said she was nineteen."

"Seventeen. Elly Ann's seventeen." He relayed what Kristin had told him about the girl and her uncle.

"Thought as much. But hot! Man, gotta get m'ass outa here."

"There's a bus for Denver comes through in a couple hours. Twelve-thirty. I checked."

Gabe closed his eyes. Lonny sat down on the edge of the bed and looked around. There were two more beds in the room, empty. In the wall opposite the door a window framed a scene of forest and grassland sloping away, a range of mountains in the distance... east, he thought, checking the lay of shadows. Denver would be just over those hills.

Gabe grunted. "Can you raise this damn bed? I want to sit up."

Lonny found the crank handle and gave it a few turns.

Gabe winced as he leaned over to his side table and filled his water glass from the pitcher. "This y'r envelope?" he said.

"What envelope?"

"On th' table." He put down his glass and picked up the envelope. He tore it open. "M' keys! N a note." He scanned it, then dropped it on the bed. "Joke?"

Lonny picked up the note and read it aloud: "'Saw your Harley-Davidson down a ravine. Keys were in it. Mile east of Edith. Heard you were here. Happy trails.' Sounds like they wrecked your bike and want you to know it. Somebody must have brought that to the reception desk before I got here."

"Gotta find that bike. M' buddy in Denver, his truck's got a winch. Get me a phone." His face was regaining mobility in spite of the swelling.

Lonny found a nurse to bring in a telephone. Gabe called his friend and eventually got him to agree to come with the truck and pick him up that afternoon.

"If I can't repair it, I'll sell it for parts. The chick... seventeen? Christ. Miss Elly Ann's no virgin." A leering smile in spite of his swollen face. "So, you come help wi' th' bike?"

"I'm taking the bus to Denver."

"Wi' me broke up here?"

"You could take the bus with me. Heal up at home for awhile, then come back for the bike."

"No! Gettin' it now! 'fore they wreck it more."

"They're not going to bother messing with a bike down in a ravine. And probably no one else will even see it."

"You're not helping?"

"Your friend's got a winch. If you've got to get it now, you two can handle it."

"You son 'v a bitch! I gave you a ride t'a f'kin' rodeo. Could 'a been half-way to Texas!"

"Goodbye, Gabe. I hope you heal up okay."

"Get out, you prick!"

Chapter 16 Homecoming

Still in uniform, his duffle stowed at the Greyhound station downtown, Lonny stood on the hilltop beside the warm brick wall of Quincy Adams School. Below him on the playing field what looked like a fifth or sixth grade class was playing softball. As he watched, a left-handed batter, a lean boy with blond, almost white hair that he kept brushing back from his eyes, popped a short fly to right field. It dropped between the right fielder coming in and the second baseman going out. The batter was safe but the runner from first, having waited near the base until it was clear the ball would not be caught, tagged up and ran for second and seemed to arrive at the same time as the ball thrown from right field. Did the runner's toe touch the bag before the shortstop on second caught the ball from right field? There were no impartial witnesses, except the teacher of the class and himself and he knew his opinion didn't count. The argument grew heated. He saw a girl running in from left field. Looked like his sister... little Becky? Not so little anymore.

"Out! Out!" she yelled. "She's out!"

And now it seemed to Lonny that the ball in the shortstop's hand did touch the runner before her foot touched the bag. He looked at the teacher on the batting team's bench, shielding her eyes from the sun.

"Mrs.Zimmer, Annie was safe by a mile!"

"She was out, Mrs. Zimmer!"

"You're blind!"

They were all looking at the teacher, waiting for a decision. She reached into the black handbag beside her, and a moment or two later Lonny saw her arm jerk up and a coin glint in the sunlight. She let it fall on the ground and then leaned over it.

"Heads!" She announced. "The runner is safe."

The batting team cheered and the fielders glumly started back to their positions. Lonny saw Becky stop and stare up at him.

"Lonny!" she yelled. She waved violently. Lonny waved back, suddenly embarrassed, the focus of some twenty pairs of eyes.

The game resumed and players struggled through another inning until the gym class came to an end.

Brother and sister walked home together up Oxford Street, a steep half-mile, past mansions set back behind dark evergreens and deep lawns, and then near the top of the hill past more modest houses closer to the street. They walked through the pretty hilltop community of Morley Heights, and then, leaving city sidewalks behind, followed Summit Street down the other side of the hill to Morningside, the country road that met Summit Street beside a swamp. The croaking frogs fell silent when Lonny and Becky approached. After they passed and turned up Morningside the chorus resumed.

"It's like they're swearing at us," said Becky. She tossed a stone back into the swamp and the frogs went silent again.

"Cowards," Lonny said. "They won't say anything to our faces. Reminds me of a kid in Seattle."

"Who was that?"

"Never mind. I'd as soon forget it."

"Big mystery man."

"You've got secrets," Lonny said. "Who was that boy? You told him you weren't taking the bus. He looked pretty disappointed."

"Oh him. Calvin. He's just a boy in my class."

"Uh huh. 'Just a boy in my class.'"

She punched his shoulder.

Else Ekman fluttered her hands when Lonny came in the door. Then as though she'd been pushed from behind she rushed forward and wrapped him in a hug and gave him a peck on the cheek.

Hjälmar Ekman stepped out from behind Else. "Lonny! Gee Whiz." He stuck out his big hand and Lonny took it. "Now that's a man's hand. Are you out now? You're free again?"

"He's more free than he was before," said Becky. "He's almost twenty-one."

"Well whaddaya know? You can vote then. You can take out a mortgage on your house. You can go to jail if you get yourself in trouble."

"Hjälmar!" said Else. "Jail! For goodness sake! Lonny, did you know your sister's going to high school in the fall?"

"Not high school," said Becky. "Junior high."

"Yeah. She wrote to me. I got lots of letters from Becky."

"You bet you did, and I got maybe one for every three I sent you."

"Oh Lonny come out to the kitchen." Else took his arm. "You must be hungry. There's rhubarb pie. You used to love rhubarb pie. Ekman keeps some rhubarb growing in a sort of green house he fixed up. Hjälmar, you make the coffee."

"There's some left from lunch."

"Ahh! Make fresh! It's not every day Lonny comes home from the Army... from Korea!"

"Yah. Okay."

Holding the glass pie plate in her hands, Else turned suddenly from the refrigerator: "Oh Becky! Your father called this morning. You were already gone to school. He said he's coming. He's driving but he's not sure when he'll get here. It will be a day or two so he'll call again. He said he wants to celebrate that you're graduating from grammar school."

No one spoke. Becky stared at Else. And then the moment passed. "Well sit down," said Else. "Both of you. Brother and sister. All together again. Pie for you, too, Becky?"

"Yes... Wait, is Daddy bringing Clare?"

"His wife? He didn't say, honey, so I don't know. He called from I think he said Fargo. He's driving. Oh, I said that."

Else took hold of her husband's sleeve. "Hjälmar, don't you think you better get up that siding before he gets here, Becky's papa?"

"Yah, I guess I better do that."

"Get Lonny to help. You could do it now. Before supper even. And paint it tomorrow. And then it will be all done finally."

Ekman sighed. "Yah. You're right. I better get started." He stopped at the back door. "Lonny, come out when you've had your pie."

Outside behind the big shed Ekman pulled off the heavy black tarp and looked at his salvaged stock of shiplap. He shook his head. The old paint would have to be scraped, the nail holes filled, the split and damaged ends trimmed off. He fetched his saw horses from the shed and set then up by the lumber. Then back in the shed he gathered tools. The crosscut saw he'd had sharpened last winter – it hung on a nail over the workbench. He found his claw hammer on the bench under the bag of electric outlet boxes he hadn't installed yet. He was still hunting up the paint scraper and the box of finishing nails when Lonny showed up, having changed out of his uniform into one of Ekman's flannel shirts and his spare overalls. They found the box of nails, and then they found the scraper under it.

"We'll need the nail set. It's here somewhere." Ekman stirred his thick fingers around through the small junk on the workbench.

"Are these the right nails?" Lonny said. He opened the box. "Here it is." He held up the nail set he found lying on top of the nails.

"I guess I put that there when I ran out of siding. Gee, that was a while ago, before you went in the Army, anyway."

Becky had gone to her room. She lay on her bed listening to the sawing and scraping going on outside, and to the pounding on the wall that sounded like it was inside. You go along, she thought, every day is pretty much like another and then one day Lonny comes home after being gone for two years and almost the same day Daddy shows up! And then it's Lonny's birthday, and then my graduation day! All at once! And everything changes... maybe, somehow. I wonder if Lonny will stay home now? And is Daddy going to take me back to Seattle? ...to Clare? Oh God. I want to stay here with Else and Grandpa.

Her father, she saw him sitting in a car, his hands on a steering wheel. It was a grey plastic sort of wheel, with a chrome ring inside it. She'd seen one of those in a new car parked along Oxford Street. It was a pretty car. And he's wearing a hat and a suit. No, he wouldn't wear a hat inside the car. Was Clare beside him? She suddenly felt a little sick to her stomach and rolled onto her side. Why would he bring Clare? She wouldn't want to see me. And why didn't he take the train? It comes straight to Duluth. She sat up and leaned against the headboard. Maybe they're sightseeing. They're on vacation and just now thought of coming to see me. I wonder how far they're going. Chicago? New York? She thought of the atlas on the shelf under the coffee table in the living room. But she stayed on the bed. I'm older now, she thought. Clare might like me now. Lonny said I looked pretty in the picture I sent him.

"Oh the heck with Clare," she said aloud. She remembered the time she took a black crayon and scribbled over Clare's face in her drawing. Daddy didn't mention her in his last letter. That was Christmas. Maybe Clare ran away, like Mom did... She stiffened and stared, seeing nothing. *Ran away like Lonny did... and I did...* A feeling came over her she'd never known before. She felt it in her body. It was strange, as though it didn't fit, it didn't fit her body. It was a terrible feeling. She kicked her legs as if to kick it away. Her eyes grew blurry and her face tingled and seemed to swell as though she had a fever. She felt hot and then cold. She couldn't stand it. She jumped up and ran out of the room, past the living room couch and out the front door, letting the screen door bang shut behind her. Barefoot she ran down the center of the two-rut driveway. She ran till she reached the road and stopped. She started right, then left, then right again. She couldn't choose. She stood there, trembling in the long rays of the setting sun, starting to cry, her long thin shadow lying across the road.

*   *   *

Alan Stuart hung up the phone and listened for the coins to drop. Automatically he wiped the return box with his finger. He'd gotten a free nickel once and always checked. He came out of the phone booth and admired again the gleaming chrome grill of his new Buick. As he walked back to the gas pumps and Clare waiting in the car he planned a speech. I'll just tell her outright, he decided. I'm going to see Rebecca, and Clare will just have to put up with it. She's my daughter, for Pete's sake.

Clare was reading a local paper as he settled in behind the wheel. He leaned back to see: the real estate section, of course. He started the engine and pulled away from the pumps and out onto the road.

Clare put down the paper. "Well?"

"'Well' what?"

"Whom," she said evenly, "did you call while I was in the bathroom?"

He took a deep breath. "I tried to call Becky but she wasn't home. I talked to Else. It turns out Becky's graduating from sixth grade. That's a big thing, and I didn't realize it. I really should drive over to Duluth and see her. It's been years, and it's an important event in the kid's life."

"What?" Clare looked at him, stunned.

"It's a big thing, Clare. I really should go see her."

"I don't believe this. We had a plan. We worked it out, where we'd go, what we'd do."

"We can change our plans a little. It would mean a lot to Becky, I'm sure."

"You had this in mind all along! Your little secret! You'd drop me off in some cheap motel in a nowhere town like Fargo and then drive off to visit your precious daughter."

"Clare, for Pete's sake, what's so strange... no, what's so *underhanded* about a father wanting to see his daughter graduating from grammar school?"

"I don't give a damn if you want to see your daughter. You can see her any time you want. And seeing her now saves you a trip. Fine. We could have planned for it. What's underhanded is your goddamn secrecy!"

"I swear I hadn't made any secret plan to see her and I didn't even think of calling her until we passed the Northern Pacific station back there in Fargo." He turned slightly in his seat to face her. "Look, when the kids and I took the train to Seattle – what was it? five-six years ago? – we'd had about an hour's stopover in Fargo and we took a little walk outside the station. And when I saw the station again I thought of Becky and wondered how she was doing. And while I was waiting for you I thought I'd give her call. And then Else mentioned her graduating from sixth grade."

"I see. The idea just came to you then. Outside the station. God, your phoney innocence! Why did you take us through Fargo, anyway? Isn't this far north of Minneapolis? That's where we're headed, remember? And then a ferry down the Mississippi?"

Alan studied the road ahead, both hands on the wheel.

"Answer me. Why so far north? You were headed for Duluth, admit it."

He sighed. "Well, nuts. It's all ruined now. The thing is, I wanted to surprise you. I wanted to show you where the river starts, where it flows out of Lake Itasca. I thought you'd get a big kick out of it, like I did, when I first saw it. You can jump across the river there, at Itasca. It'd be fun to remember that little stream when we're on the ferry going down the Mississippi and it's so wide you can barely see either shore."

An ironic smile on her face she shook her head slowly. "You're pretty good, Alan. But not real good. I've met weasels more accomplished than you."

"Now Clare..."

"No, no, no," she sang, cutting him off and waving an upraised finger. "It's okay. I'm sure I'll be marvelously entertained, jumping back and forth across the Mississippi while you're mooning over

165

your grown up little girl. I assume there's a tourist trap at this Lake Itasca. Probably a steak house and a bar between souvenir shops. God damn it, Alan! Where's that map!"

She reached across him and grabbed the Minnesota map from the door pocket, unfolded it and spread it out over her lap and the dashboard in front of her.

"You're blocking the windshield! How can I see to drive?"

"Oh too bad. We'll have a wreck and you'll miss the graduation. Here's Fargo." She jabbed the map with a red-painted fingernail. "When is this graduation, anyway?"

"There's no ceremony, as far as I know. I just want to stop by Ekman's to see her. Wish her well. Maybe give her a present."

"'Maybe...' Ah, here's Minneapolis. Allen, I'm sure you've got a present hidden in the trunk... Looks like it's not so very far. Okay, Alan, tell you what." She collapsed the map and began folding it, ignoring the creases. "You drive me to Minneapolis and I'll check into a decent hotel downtown – I suppose there's a downtown in Minneapolis? – and then you can drive back up to Duluth. Stay as long as you like. And I'll do some exploring. Maybe I'll find something lively going on. Or I could do some shopping, go to a movie. I might even be glad to see you when you come back."

"You *could* come with me, you know. You and Becky might even hit it off now. She's older, might have, you know, woman interests."

"Uh huh. 'Woman interests.' I haven't seen the kid in years but I waltz in and set her down and tell her about her period and the birds and the bees."

"I'll bet she doesn't know another beautiful woman like you with her own real estate business."

"Give it up, Alan. I'm hungry. I want to stop for lunch as soon as we see something that looks like a restaurant and not a diner. We can bring the map with us and pick the route to Minneapolis. And then we'll drive like hell and get there before dark."

"Well, if that's the way you want it. But I do wish you'd come with me."

"Swedish Home Cooking," the sign said, in blue script against a white background. It looked like a tidy little place just off the highway. It had a pale blue entry door and there were lace curtains in the windows. A bell tinkled when Alan pushed the door open and followed Clare inside, proudly. She is one classy lady, he thought to himself, as he did whenever they made an entrance. As at last week's office party, when he was presented an award for Top Sales: First Quarter. Oh she made him look good, knows how to dress, how to make people like her right off. What an asset.

A young waitress in a lace-trimmed blue apron seated them at a table by a window and gave them each a menu.

"What's that secret smile, Con-man?"

"I shouldn't tell you. You'll think I'm trying to flatter you."

"I've seen that self-satisfied look before. You got away with something, right?"

"I was thinking what an asset you are to a man like me."

"Asset. I'm not sure that's flattering. But I'm too hungry to think about it. What's *pitti panna*?"

"It's a kind of pan-fried hash, with potatoes, barley, some other things I forget, with cardamom and pepper. And slices of hot dogs or baloney, and a poached egg laid over the top. Not very elegant but it *can* be very good."

"That's just the sort of peasant grub I wanted to avoid. The salmon might be good, with small potatoes and brussel sprouts."

They ate in silence, which continued until their dishes were cleared and coffee served in flower-patterned porcelain cups, which Clare admired.

She lifted her cup. "Well they do try, don't they?"

"I wish you'd reconsider and come with me."

"Tame the tigress with salmon and a pretty cup?"

"We're a team, Clare."

"It's you that keeps forgetting that. What other secrets lurk behind that handsome face?"

"Now you're flattering me." He smiled, pleased by the compliment and relieved the fight was over. In a serious voice he said, "Clare, we hardly ever mention the kids, not since I took Becky back to live with my mother in Duluth."

"There was quite a bit of discussion a couple years after that, as I recall, when your mother died."

"Right. That left Lonny on his own, and we let the Ekmans take in Rebecca."

"Not 'we,' *you* let the Ekmans have Becky."

"Clare, you couldn't stand either of my kids."

She glanced around the restaurant. The lunch crowd had mostly evaporated, leaving only an elderly couple lingering over dessert, and a slightly balding man in a business suit relaxing with a cigarette and coffee. "I don't want to talk about this in here. Let's find someplace outside, a park maybe. I need to walk around."

The waitress directed them to a state park some five miles further on. When they arrived Alan found a place to park in the shade and facing a grassy meadow populated by a few widely spaced birches and poplars with a slow-running creek meandering among them. A paved walkway followed the creek, crossing and re-crossing it on narrow wooden bridges.

After the first bridge Clare said, "Okay, let me get something straight. Do you blame me for your not having had Lonny and Rebecca with you? No, wait, let me put it another way. If it weren't for me, would you have been living with the kids all this time?"

"I had custody."

"You just can't manage a straight answer, can you?"

"Well how do I know what I'd have done? If I hadn't met you, well, maybe I'd have been with someone else, and maybe she would have really liked the kids and we'd have all been together. I don't know."

"Oh my God." It was barely a whisper.

"What? What is it? That I might have found another woman if I hadn't met you?"

She looked up at him, her mouth open, as if waiting for lost words. "You don't get it," she said finally. She put her hand gently on his arm. "They're *your* kids, Bozo." She thought a moment: "And I do believe you now, partly anyway, the part about not knowing that Becky was graduating. And something else, are you aware that Lonny will be getting out of the army in six months?"

"Ah, well sure, that's about right. Yes."

"No, it's not right. He was drafted for two years. He went in in March. So he must have gotten out a couple of months ago."

"That was a mean trick, Clare."

"I suppose it was. Like a mirror. A mirror can be pretty mean sometimes."

"You think I don't love my kids because I'm a lousy accountant?"

"I think... I think the mirror just went cloudy."

They walked on without speaking. Eventually the walkway began to loop back toward the parking lot.

"Clare, I can't decide now whether it would be better for Becky if I go to see her or stay away."

"That sounds like the right question, anyway. What's best for *her*. But I'd say it's too late to ask it now. You said you were coming. She's expecting you."

Lonny woke to the ringing of a telephone. It seemed far away. The ringing was suddenly louder, and then it was quieter again. He opened his eyes and saw a door closing. The kitchen door. Ekman's kitchen. The phone's in there. Someone just opened the door and went through to the kitchen to answer the phone. I'm in Ekman's living room.

He threw back the sheet and blanket covering him on the sofa and sat up. He heard Else's voice in the kitchen. Then water running. He stretched and stood up. There on the chair were the work clothes he'd borrowed yesterday. He pulled on the overalls, went to the bathroom, decided he'd shave later, then went into the kitchen.

"Lonny. Your uniform, I hung it up in the hall closet."

"Thanks Else."

"You'll want to get into Lena's house, I think. The tenants moved out a couple weeks ago. We thought you'd be coming home earlier." Else put the lid on the percolator and plugged it in.

He scratched his head. "I really appreciate your taking care of the place for me, you and Hjälmar."

"That was nothing. Look, you're barefoot. Aren't you freezing?"

Chapter 17 Home Economics

Lonny borrowed Ekman's Ford to fetch his duffle bag from the Greyhound station. Downtown at Montgomery Ward he bought two pair of jeans, a warm flannel shirt and a light blue dress shirt. He looked at jackets but they were expensive and he couldn't decide among them anyway. He needed underwear and socks and more shirts, but he'd done all the shopping he could stand to do at one time and was headed for the door when he passed the shoe department. Sneakers – he couldn't wear his GI oxfords or combat boots all the time. He bought sneakers and then he drove home to Lena's house.

The rose bush was still there, all leafed out by the front porch. The house looked much the same, except shabbier, and it seemed smaller. He got out of the car and walked slowly all around the house. It needed paint, that's for sure. He laughed when he saw the plywood still there covering the utility room window. He'd nailed it up himself after Becky broke the glass trying to hit him with an apple. She'd really thrown it hard! She had a temper, that girl. The apple tree looked great, and it still had a few blossoms left on it, high up. Where Becky used to climb. Where he'd found her the day Lena died.

He brought his things inside and saw that the tenants had left the place in pretty much of a mess. The whole house needed a thorough sprucing up, he decided, suddenly appreciating an Army tradition: you get a new Commanding Officer, everything gets scrubbed or painted or both. In his old room upstairs he dug into his duffle bag for his comfortable well-worn fatigues, took off his summer tan uniform that he'd worn to town, and put on the fatigues. He drove the Ford up the hill to Ekman's and found the man himself painting the siding they'd put up the day before. Else came out offering coffee which Lonny declined but asked to borrow cleaning materials. She loaded him up with a bucket, scrub brush, sponge, rags, a box of Spic and Span and a can of Old Dutch cleanser.

Thus supplied he walked back to Lena's house – it'll always be Lena's house, he thought – and set to cleaning.

About noon Becky came over and found him on hands and knees scrubbing the living room floor. "Dad hasn't called yet."

"He did say it would be a few days."

"Will you be glad to see him?"

"Sure. Why not?"

"I feel bad about how we ran away from him, just like Mom did."

"Ma did run away from him, but it was Clare I ran away from. And from that rotten school I had to go to, and you didn't run away at all. Dad *brought* you to live with Grandma and me."

"Still it feels like we all ran away from him. But I'm mad at him, too."

She folded her arms and leaned against the wall near the door, her legs crossed at the ankles. She wore a white blouse and bib overalls that she'd nearly outgrown.

"Yeah. But you want to see him anyway." Lonny put down the scrub brush, rolled off his knees and sat on the floor facing her. "Clare's the problem, not Dad."

"Clare is his doing!" said Becky.

"Well, I'm not mad at anybody. I miss Lena, though."

"Me, too." Becky looked around the empty room. "I can almost *feel* her in here. Are you really going to live here now, in Lena's house?"

"It's our house, Becky, yours and mine."

"I know that, but it's still Lena's house. Hey, big brother, if you live here, then you've got to pay me rent for my half."

Lonny shook his wet brush at her and she jumped away, laughing. "Tell you what," he said. "I'll only use half the property. I'll live in the house but I won't use the yard."

"Oh no. It's *all* half mine."

"Well then, I'll only be here half the time. During your half I'll be out working or something. And I'll give you a bill for half the cleaning I'm doing. And you can pay the whole bill for that window you broke."

"*You* broke. You shouldn't have ducked. And I didn't tell you to clean. And..." She paused to think. "And it's the property that's half mine, not the time."

"How'd you get so smart? I go away for two years and come back and you're like a lawyer in the movies."

"I'm not so smart."

"You've always been smart." Lonny rolled back onto his knees and started scrubbing the floor again.

"Lonny, have you ever heard from Mom?"

"Nope."

"Has Dad?"

"No idea. When he gets here, ask him."

She slid to the floor and sat with her back against the wall. She watched her brother scrubbing. The water in his bucket was getting very dirty. She ought to get up and change it for him.

"Lonny, what are you going to do?"

"About what?"

"Well, are you going to get a job or what?"

"I don't know. Haven't given it much thought. I saved a lot of my Army pay."

"You were gone a long time."

Lonny got up to change his scrub water. When he came back he noticed Becky hadn't moved from her position against the wall. He put down the pail and got back to work. He had developed a rhythm and it felt good.

"You seem really different from when you left," Becky said.

"You, too. We're both older. And seeing as how you're a half-owner I should ask your opinion: this whole house needs painting. Should I start with the outside or the inside?"

"There! That's what I mean."

"What? What are you talking about?"

"Your wanting to paint the house. Scrubbing the floors. Getting a high school diploma. That's not Lonny. Lonny's either in the woods doing who-knows-what or you're at the stables messing with horses. Next you're going to tell me you want to go to college, and you've got a girlfriend, and you're getting married and you're going to move to California or Korea or China or maybe the moon!"

He looked up, surprised by the outburst. The girl's face was flushed and she looked ready to cry. He sat back on his heels.

"What's got into you? I'm not moving to California. I haven't said any of that stuff. I want to fix up the house."

"And then sell it and leave again!"

"I don't want to sell it! I can't anyway. It's half yours, remember? You could help me. You want to help with the painting?"

"I think it looks fine! Paint it yourself!" She jumped up and ran out the door. He followed her outside and stood on the porch watching her run up the hill. He watched till he saw her turn in at the Ekman's driveway and go out of sight behind the trees. Then he saw her at the front door as she pulled it open then disappeared inside.

It was mid afternoon before he finished scrubbing all the floors. His old room upstairs needed much more than cleaning and paint. The beaverboard walls and ceiling showed blisters and sagged in places. He should rip it all out and replace it with something better. Maybe Ekman knew how to plaster. He was going to need more money than he'd saved from Army pay. That meant finding a job. Doing what? Maybe he should have stayed in the Army, as Gabe said, hung on for another eighteen years, retire, and *then* start my life? That's nuts.

He brought the scrub brush and pail to the enclosed back porch, washed his hands and face there at the laundry tub, gathered the borrowed materials together and headed up to Ekman's.

"Sit down, Lonny. I'll make you a sandwich. Cheese and pickles, you still like that, I think?"

"Thanks, Else. I want to get set up in Lena's house as soon as I can. I need a mattress and some new kitchen stuff. I've got most of the cleaning done, but I want to paint everything, too. Inside and out. But before I do any of that I've got to get my old Chevy running so I can haul things home."

"My, my. I should get Ekman to hear you talk."

"I've got to find a job, too. I'm going to need money to fix up the house."

Else set a plate in front of him bearing a ham sandwich on thick-sliced homemade bread. She took a bottle of milk from the refrigerator and a glass from the dish drainer and set them beside his plate. Then she sat down at the table, wiping her hands on her apron. She adjusted her glasses, folded her hands and rested them on the table edge. She waited until Lonny was chewing a second mouthful of sandwich; then she said, "You've got money in the bank, you know. You and Becky together."

He swallowed and drank some milk. "What money?"

"Rent money. From your house. But I took some out for taxes and things." She smiled. "Just a minute."

Else left the kitchen and came back with a little red ledger book and stood beside him. She opened it to the last page of entries, pushed Lonny's plate aside and set the book down in front of him. "See there." She pressed her index finger on the page at the bottom of a column. "Your balance with the last rent payment."

"Holy cow! I didn't think there'd be this much. Part of it's yours, isn't it, yours and Hjälmar's?"

"No, no. I already took some out like I said. For 'management,' they call it. Every month. See here." She pointed to an entry. "I talked to a company that takes care of rented houses to find out what they charge, and then I cut it in half because Hjälmar and me we ain't no big company. He said we should take it all but I said no and I think he was kidding anyway. We never had to do much. *He* did some fixings. He never did the front steps yet. They're loose and maybe rotten."

Lonny studied the neat column of figures, the itemized entries. "Else, you were doing all this for Becky and me while I was just fooling around in Korea."

"'Fooling around,' huh." She gave him a jostling hug with her strong right arm, as if to settle his addled brain. "You were defending our country and we was defending your house and little sister."

"Thanks, Else." He relaxed into the hug. Then he sat up. "Else! I don't have to get a job after all!"

"Huh! You and Ekman! This much money won't last long."

"I'm just kidding. Besides, it's half Becky's."

"That's right. You look out for your little sister."

"She's not so little anymore."

"Yes she is. She don't look so little but inside she's still little. She ran into her room a while ago and was crying but she wouldn't say what was wrong. Did you say something to her?"

"No. *She* said a lot of crazy things. She said I was going to get married, and I was going to go to college, and I was going to move to California. I didn't say any of that."

"She's scared, poor thing."

"Of what?"

"You're not so dumb as that."

"She's afraid I'm going to leave again?"

"Lonny, her mama left, and her papa lives far away, and her grandmama died, and her brother joins the Army. And now her papa is coming, but it's only a visit and then he goes away again. She's not so dumb to be scared, don't you think? I get scared for her just thinking about it. You want coffee now?"

He nodded, took another bite of his sandwich and chewed slowly. He remembered Becky hitting him when he left for the

Army. *You're always leaving*, she said. He'd thought it was just teasing.

"I guess I didn't think about how it was for her, everybody leaving."

"Well you did think about it, but maybe not so you knowed it. You thought enough to bring Becky to me and Ekman."

"Yeah. They wouldn't let me take care of her. But I didn't think I was *leaving* her. I was just down the street."

"Ya. She was happy here. But then you went to the Army and she was sad till she got your letter. After that she was happy waiting for letters you wrote to her. That was good you wrote to her so much. When you wrote you was coming home it was hard for her to wait. She got crabby sometimes, and it wouldn't take nothing to make her cry and she'd run into her room."

"Else, I left her once before that."

"Ya. Ekman told me. You ran away from Seattle."

"I didn't even say goodbye to her." He felt miserable all over again remembering when he was on the train and thinking about Becky waking up and finding him gone. He realized now it must have been just like when he and Becky had waked up one morning and found their mother gone. When she wasn't in the kitchen as she usually was. And his father was standing in the living room, smoking. He never smoked in the house. Lonny had felt scared and didn't know why, just that something awful had happened. He'd said "Where's Ma?" and his father had glared down at him and said, "It looks like your *mother* has run off with another man." Then his father went out and stood on the porch.

*   *   *

The Duluth Herald listed three ads for auto mechanics. One required far more experience than Lonny'd had in the Army. The other two seemed like possibilities, one a Chevy dealership, the other an independent shop. He decided to try the shop first, partly because it was located in Lakeside, a quick shot about four miles straight down Summit Street toward the lake. He and Stig, when they were kids, used to coast most of the way on their bikes, down past the golf course and Indian Head Bluff, then down a long curving steep part to where the road leveled out and its name changed to something he could never remember. It was about ten blocks of easy pedaling then to the lake, through a city neighborhood of small houses. Going back home was the hard part, pushing their bikes up that long hill, especially on a hot day.

"Do you have your own tools?" The big mechanic glanced back at Lonny over his shoulder as he unscrewed the drain plug from the differential of a '58 Edsel. He had it up on a hoist over his head. The plug came out and black viscous oil poured into the wide mouth of the oil catch on a stand under the car.

"Some," Lonny said. "But in the Army the motorpool supplied all the tools."

"So what did you work on in the Army? Willys Jeeps?" He faced him now, turning the plug in a rag to clean it. In his coveralls and grease-stained painter's cap, he stood a head taller than Lonny and he looked him over, head to foot.

"Jeeps, yeah, and Ford and Chevy staff cars, some deuce-and-a-halfs. I just got back from Korea."

"So, that scar on your face... Looks like a bottle cut. You get in bar fights?"

"Go to hell." Lonny started to leave.

"Just a minute, young fella. I need know who I'm hiring."

Lonny stopped and looked at him.

"Talk to me."

"It's not from brawling."

The mechanic smiled. He held out his hand, looked at it, almost black with dirty oil, and let it drop. "I'm Broder Young. I own this shop. Who're you?"

"Lonny Stuart."

"Stuart. Wait a minute. I knew a Stuart in high school. I knew *of* one. He played baseball, I think. Varsity."

"Could have been my dad."

"S'pose it could. Well, then, Lonny Stuart, I don't know what kind of mechanic training you boys get in the Army. I've hired three kids out of high school auto shops. The last one was pretty good. Stayed with me about a year, but he's run off to Minneapolis. The others didn't know much, and they didn't care to learn."

"I didn't have any real training, just OJT. That's on the job training."

"I know what it is."

"In Korea they assigned me to the motorpool when I got there. That's where they needed a body, I guess. I said I'd worked on my own car."

"Did you rebuild engines?"

"In Korea? No, but I swapped out a couple, pulled out a bad one and dropped in a rebuilt. And I did a few valve jobs."

"Look, Stuart. Till I see how much you know I'd have to pay you as an apprentice." He quoted a wage only slightly higher than the stables had paid.

It was much too low, but Lonny thought about it. He looked around at the shop. It was well-equipped and neater than most he'd seen. And from all the cars parked around there seemed to be lots of work.

"I can't live on that," he said, "much less buy tools. But if I can use your tools I'll give you a week at that wage. After the week I want twice that much. You decide if I'm worth it. If you do, I'll buy tools."

The big man put the drain plug in his pocket and held out his hand after wiping it carefully on the rag. "Fair enough," he said, "but I'll dock your pay if you lose my tools."

They shook hands.

"If you've come ready to work –" Lonny nodded – "you can finish this Edsel. Grease, oil change, transmission pan gasket, fluid, new filters all around. If you're not sure about anything ask me. Don't guess. Did you bring coveralls? No? There's an old pair hanging in the crapper. You can use that today. Tomorrow bring your own."

Driving home that evening Lonny saw clipped to his visor the letter he'd forgotten to mail to Kristin. He stopped by a mailbox, hesitated, then dropped it in. Immediately he regretted it. Fantastic schemes for retrieving the letter raced through his mind. But there was no reasonable way to get the letter back. He got in his car and thought over what he'd written. He hadn't said anything sappy or that he liked her a lot. And then he was sorry about that because he didn't want to hurt her in case it was true that *she* liked *him*, as it seemed at the time. And he really *had* liked her a lot. Besides her being about the only girl who'd ever shown any interest in him.

He put the Chevy in gear and pulled away from the curb.

But a girl who'd go to bed with a guy she just met! And the way she talked about that Elly Ann that Gabe went off with – as if she wasn't just like her. "If she lets *you* in, Bunky, you sure as hell ain't the first." Cork's "words to the wise," from the biggest asshole in the unit. What he did to Iseul.

It was Monday today. He could imagine Kristin reading the letter Wednesday, maybe Thursday morning. God! he was glad he hadn't said anything sappy. She'd probably just laugh at him. Show the letter to her friends, or that stupid brother of hers...

No. She wouldn't do that. He remembered her face, how she looked at him that night, the way she choked up just before she drove away. She really had liked him. And he liked her. They were like good friends five minutes after they met. He liked her a lot. He should have told her. He should have put it in the letter, and if he was wrong and she laughs at him then she laughs at him and there you are and so what?

Maybe she'll write back. Or maybe he should write another letter right away and tell her... something. No, he should wait. He hadn't said anything mean. It was friendly, really. Maybe she'll write back.

Chapter 18 Kristin

"Have you seen him again?"

"Who?" Kristin had a ledger lying open and flat before her on the big oak desk. She went on entering ranch expenses from the receipts skewered on a spike driven through a pine block.

"You know 'who.' Your funny-looking friend at the rodeo." Her brother Terry tossed the week's *Henton County Register* into the wide waste basket beside the desk.

"Lonny. And he's not 'funny-looking.' He's got a scar is all."

"Well, have you seen him?"

"I haven't seen him. Not that it's any of your business. Don't you have something to do, little brother? Push cows around? Get some virgin in trouble?"

"I don't think there's a virgin in the whole damn county."

Kristin closed the ledger and gathered the receipts into a neat pile. "He lives in Minnesota, if you must know. That's where he went. He'd just got out of the Army and he was going home. Our little rodeo was a side trip." She pulled open a drawer, took out a manila envelope and laid it on the desk.

"And you were another."

"Another what?" She wrote "Expense Receipts, June 1961" on the outside of the envelope.

"Another side trip." He rocked in the old swivel chair to make it squeak.

"Uh huh." She slipped the receipts into the envelope, closed it up and wound the string around the button on the back.

Terry put his feet up on the desk next to the envelope. He was wearing work boots.

Kristin held out her hand, "Lend me your bandana a second?"

He pulled it from his back pocket and handed it to her. "You're not going to cry, are you?"

"Fat chance." With a sweep of her arm she knocked his feet off the desk then wiped the top with the bandana.

"Hey!"

"Thanks," she said, "here's your red rag."

He inspected it, holding it up to the light from the window. He gave it a shake and a snap then held it up again. Satisfied, he put it back in his pocket.

"You sure it wasn't prison this Lonny just got out of?"

"Ooo, a bank robber, maybe, headed to where he stashed the loot."

"You haven't heard from him, have you?"

She left the envelope lying on the desk and sat back in her chair with her hands folded and her elbows on the armrests. She looked out the window over the desk at the hills rising a few miles to the east of their valley ranch.

"No. I haven't heard from him. He was nice, too. But he seemed sad. Not sad on the surface, you know, but inside. As if something... I don't know. As if he'd been hurt. Really bad. Maybe a long time ago."

"Lousy kisser, eh?"

Kristin sighed. "I guess there's still some hope. Not much. But you *are* young. You might manage it yet."

"What? Manage what?"

"To become human. I really haven't given up on you."

"I don't know, Krissy. You're human enough for both of us."

"Go away, little brother. I'm tired of you."

"Not possible." He stayed put.

Kristin thought about what she'd said – that Lonny seemed sad, deep inside. It was a strong impression now, though she hadn't thought about it before. She remembered how he looked when she was loading her horse. He was shy then. And when she ran back from the truck to invite him to dinner he looked happy as a little kid. But at the motel he'd been sort of strange. It was her doing, their making love. She probably shouldn't have done that. Scared him off... No, that wasn't it. She was getting into her truck to leave, there was something then. The way he looked. Really hurt.

The chair squeaked beside her.

"You still here?" she said.

"Kristin?"

"What?"

"Do you miss Mom?"

"Sure."

"It'll be two years next month."

"Yeah."

"I hate cancer. She never saw me ride a bronc."

"She never saw you smoke, either."

"Think Dad'll marry Mrs. Whatshername?"

"Hoenfeldt. Probably."

"It's gotta be time for lunch. I'm hungry." He stood up.

"Thank God."

"Why?"

"Terry's hungry. All's right with the world."

A letter arrived two days later, postmarked Duluth. Kristin put it in her shirt pocket, and when she finished her morning chores she saddled the paint gelding they called Mosey and rode up into the eastern hills. She stopped at a lookout where she could see the ranch buildings in the valley below. Above the hills on the west side of the ranch rose huge white clouds that seemed to look back at her across the valley. She waved to them. Mosey shook his bridle. She dismounted and let the reins drop to the ground.

She stroked the horse's warm neck. It was damp with sweat and smelled richly of horse. "Now you stay there like I taught you. Your reins are tethered to that spot on the ground. You can't drag them."

She moved a few steps away, lay down on the grass and took out the letter. Leaning on her elbows she studied the return address. Then she rolled over on her back, slipped her finger under the sealed flap and opened the envelope. The letter was written in ink on a single sheet. Very neatly.

21 June 1961

Dear Kristin,

Thanks for all the help with Gabe (though he didn't deserve it.)

I'm living in the house that my sister Rebecca and me inherited from my grandmother. We used to live here together, me and Becky and Grandma Lena. I am fixing up the place and there is lots to do, including painting it all, inside and out. Becky still lives with the Ekmans nearby. They are foster parents to her. Our real dad sends them money for her. The county says he has to do that.

Becky just graduated from 6th grade and she's going to junior high in the fall.

I'll be 21 in a few days. I think you said you were 22. Else (Mrs Ekman) says a man can't ask a woman her age. I don't see why not.

I don't know what I'll be doing yet. I might try to get a job as a mechanic. The stable where I used to work closed and the place is a dairy farm now. The Nowickes (the people I worked for) have moved away. I wonder what they did with all their horses?

I didn't want to go back to the stables anyway. Ekman says something will turn up. Else says I should go dig something up. I like the Ekmans a lot. They've taken real good care of Becky.

I hope you're o.k. I'm sorry for all the trouble I caused you. Me and Gabe. I wish I had got to see your ranch.

Your friend, Lonny

"He's not coming back," Kristin said aloud. "At least he wrote to me." She heard Mosey ripping off tufts of grass and his molars grinding, a deep, grumbling sound that she always found comforting. Then she heard the horse shake himself, plates of saddle leather slapping together and the bridle jingling. She turned over on her side and looked back at the horse.

"Itchy under that saddle, Mosey? Don't you lie down and roll now." She turned onto her elbows and looked at the letter again. The lines were all perfectly parallel to the top and bottom. Very neat handwriting. Not one correction, no crossings-out. He must have written a draft and then copied it. And if he made a mistake in copying he must have started over.

"Maybe he liked me a little after all, Mosey." She scanned the letter again. "But he sure didn't say so." She lay her head down again. Well, sure, he liked me. *Maybe* more than that. But a thousand miles – fifteen hundred? – and a shy cowboy on the other side of all those miles. And I'm no great beauty. Hell.

She rolled over on her back. "I've got to get out of here, Mosey. *This* fall! I'll go to Fort Collins. Dad said he'd pay if I get good grades. If I just fool around the money stops. That's a fair deal, don't you think, Mosey?" She sat up. "Mosey!" She scrambled to her feet. "Hey! Hey you bad old beast!"

The horse had moved away toward a more lush patch of grass – but he trapped himself by stepping on a rein, which pulled his head down. And there he stood, the rein taut and his hoof firmly planted. Kristin lifted the foot and caught up the reins.

"See, I told you," she said, patting the horse's neck. "When your rein's on the ground it's just like you're tied to a post."

She led him back to where she'd left the letter on the ground and picked it up. She folded the page back into the envelope and slipped it into her shirt pocket, swung up into the saddle and rode home.

She led Mosey into his stall in the barn and started to remove the halter when the soft brown eyes of the horse stopped her. "Well, heck, Mosey, that's what you think? Yeah, I think so, too. I'll write him a letter tonight.

Chapter 19 Cake in a White Box

Alan arrived in Duluth on a Saturday morning. He drove past
the train station which he'd last seen from the inside – when he and
Lonny and little Becky had said goodbye to his mother and
boarded a train for Seattle and a new life, a new life that hadn't
worked out so well, "so goddamn well," as Clare would say. He'd
lost his kids. Clare seemed to blame him, which wasn't fair. She's
the one who made it so hard. But he hadn't lost them, really. The
connection was still there, though it was stretched. Like a rubber
band. And now it did seem like a stretched rubber band that was
contracting and pulling him along toward his old home and family.
He drove slowly, reluctantly, through Duluth's downtown along
Superior Street, past the old Glass Block department store, past the
bank where Kate had begun her life separate from him, past Mode
O' Day, the women's clothing store with its irritating marquee, all
the letters in different pastel colors. Then past the warehouse that
had always stood empty, probably since the day it was built, its
dark windows looking even darker than he remembered them.

He drove by the gas station where he'd had a flat fixed one Christmas Eve, and had given a big tip to the scruffy kid who did the job, out of gratitude and because it was Christmas Eve and he'd been happy, bringing home presents for his wife and baby son. He passed the park with the Viking long boat that he'd always assumed was genuine until pretty Esther Holmes in a history class at East High had laughed at him and set him straight.

The feeling that he was being pulled along – dragged – grew stronger as he came up Fourth Street and turned the corner at his old high school. He wished at least that Clare were with him. Even more he wished he hadn't seen the train station in Fargo that made him think of Becky and aroused the impulse to call her. What he wished above all was that he was with Clare in Minneapolis, having lunch right about now in a nice place with a white table-cloth and smartly dressed people around, and Clare would be all bright and looking sharp.

On Woodland Avenue he pulled over to the curb and stopped the car. What could he possibly achieve by going on? He'd see Becky. She might not be glad to see him. He'd feel guilty, and he shouldn't, because she herself had wanted go live with her grandmother. And maybe he'd say that, and then there'd be bad feeling all around.

And Lonny. Weird coincidence that he's back from the service just now. He'll be all grown up. Bigger than me, maybe. Strong. The Army will have changed him. He might have grown out of his shyness.

Alan looked at his watch. One o'clock. He decided to continue on up to Woodland. If he got some lunch there maybe he'd feel more like getting this reunion over with. There used to be a café near the bus turn-around. He remembered now that he and his Morningside teammates had gone there for sodas after just barely losing a ball game to a Woodland team. They lost by only one run, which was better than they expected since they were just a bunch of neighborhood kids. Woodland was a real team. They all had red jerseys that said *Woodland Tigers*. They even had a coach.

The café was gone, the one he remembered, but a bakery had taken its place. He saw there were a couple of small tables inside by the front window. They would probably serve coffee. He parked the Buick and went in. As soon as he saw the cakes on display he got an idea and told the white-haired woman behind the counter he wanted a chocolate layer cake with some writing on it in white icing. He wrote out exactly what he wanted it to say on a slip of paper and handed it to her.

"That's a lot of writing," she said. "It don't fit on a layer cake." She had a heavy accent, Swedish or Norwegian. Alan never could hear the difference.

"Oh. Well then, how about on a flat cake? That one there." He tapped the glass in front of a chocolate-frosted one.

"I guess I could fit it on there. It's a yellow-cake, though, under the frosting."

"That's all right."

"The writing is extra. I have to charge by the letter."

"Of course."

He ordered a cup of coffee and a slice of rhubarb pie to have while he waited for the cake. He sat down at one of the little tables beside the big storefront window. Outside he saw a newsstand across the street and called to the counter-woman that he was going out to buy a paper. He was back in a couple of minutes with a *Duluth Herald*, the little bell over the door chiming his return. He sat down and turned to the sports section.

"What?" he said aloud. The Duluth Dukes were now the Duluth-Superior Dukes! His beloved Dukes had married the hated Superior Blues from across the bay. That had to have been a marriage of economic convenience. He asked the counter-woman about it when she set the white cake box down in front of him – with the lid open so he could see the writing.

She laughed. "I don't know nothing about baseball." He paid for the cake then ate his pie and sipped his coffee while skimming the rest of the paper.

During this time three women came into the bakery together, followed later on by a young girl with a little boy she held by the hand. And while the women tried to decide on a coffee cake for their afternoon meeting – they belonged, Alan surmised, to a sewing group, or aid society of some kind – the girl and boy quietly bought one cupcake apiece, paid for them, and went out. He watched them cross the street and sit down on the bench next to the newsstand. Then they started in on the cupcakes. Later, a man in a dark suit came into the bakery and held the door for the three women going out with their chosen coffee cake. After that a steady stream of customers came and went, the little bell over the door rarely silent. Alan enjoyed all the movement and talking in the room, the door opening and closing, the little bell dinging away. He felt immensely cheered up. It'll be good to see Becky and the Ekmans he decided – he remembered the Ekmans but not very well, neighbors up the hill, years ago – and it would be good to see Lonny all grown up. The cake will make a party of it.

But when he returned to the Buick and got in, placing the white cake box on the seat beside him, the quiet enclosed space brought back all his apprehension – and he wished again that he hadn't made that telephone call from Fargo.

Ekman sat in the wicker chair on his front porch whittling down the end of a stick of birch for use as a rake handle. Lonny sat on the floor beside him, leaning back against the wall of the house.

"How'd it go with Becky?" Ekman said.

Lonny looked out across the front yard, watching the road. It was mostly obscured by a hedge of rose bushes except for the gap made by the driveway. The sun had been out in the morning, but now it looked like rain clouds gathering in the west. A dusty black Hudson drove by going slowly up the hill. He recognized it.

"That was old Linkvist, wasn't it?"

"In the Hudson? Yes it was."

"He liked to blow his horn at us kids."

"He was doing that before you were born. My daughter Ellen's favorite story is about old Linkvist. He's always been *old Linkvist*, you know, one of those kind of folks. Seems Ellen and a couple of her friends were having a little snowball fight out in the street there in front of the house and old Linkvist comes along in his car, a really old Ford, which is what he had before that Hudson. Well, I guess he was afraid the Ford would quit on him if he slowed down, because if he drove any slower than he always does he'd be stopped or going backwards. Maybe that old Ford wouldn't idle. Anyway, he blows his horn and the kids take a while getting out of the way. They're busy, you know, throwing snowballs. So he blows his horn again, and he blows it *again,* and they finally get out of his way. And then as he goes by Ellen sees he's all red in the face and he shakes his finger at her and he yells – he's got his window open, you know – he yells, 'Don't you kids know enough to get out *o me vay ven ay toot me vistle*?'"

Lonny laughed. "I guess Ellen and her friends must have worn him down, because he never yelled at us. Just 'tooted his vistle' and went on by."

"We all get old. Even Linkvist gets older."

Ekman folded his clasp knife, stretched out his leg and put the knife in his pocket. "Speaking of Ellen reminds me," he said. "You did talk to Becky, didn't you?"

"Yeah...?"

"Else told me Becky's worried about you leaving again."

"I talked to her. I explained all over again why I couldn't tell her ahead of time that I was going to run off from Seattle. I couldn't because they'd have gotten it out of her and stopped me, or she'd have had to lie and I didn't want her to have to do that, and she was little so they'd have gotten it out of her anyway. It seemed better all around just to take off."

Ekman worked to smooth the whittled taper with a piece of rough sandpaper. "Was she happy with that?"

"Sort of, I guess. She'd heard it all before anyway. She said she knew all that but it didn't make her any less scared. I promised her no more surprises. Like I told her ahead of time when I was going to join the Army. Because I did, I told her ahead of time. But she's worried about Dad coming today, too, and wants me to be here. I told her I wasn't going anywhere. Poor kid. I feel real bad about what happened to her when she was so little. Ma leaving, and then Dad taking us far away from Grandma Lena, and then me leaving. ...Hey, looks like Dad's here."

Ekman looked up and saw the big Buick turning into his driveway. Lonny got up and brushed off the seat of his pants. "I'll go tell Becky."

"And tell Else to put the coffee on." Ekman blew the sawdust off his work and inserted the smooth tapered end into the ferrule of his leaf rake. He stood up, leaned the rake against the wall, then stepped off the porch to greet the visitor. "Good afternoon," he said. Alan was getting out of the car, buttoning the jacket of his blue business suit. He left his hat in the car.

"Hello. Hjälmar Ekman. How are you? Many years since we were neighbors. I'm Alan Stuart." He held out his hand.

"Ya. That's who you are." Ekman grinned and shook Alan's hand. "You're Becky's and Lonny's papa. Come on in, we're all expecting you."

"Just a minute." Alan turned back to the car and retrieved the cake. "A little something for the celebration."

He preceded Ekman into the house and was met in the living room by Becky, her hair freshly combed and the tears washed from her face. She had put on a dress with little pink flowers on white cotton. Lonny, in the clothes he wore when he went to work – jeans and a checkered shirt – stood up. Else held a tray bearing her china coffee service.

"Hello! Mr. Stuart," she said. "This was a wedding present from Ekman's mama and papa. We brought it with us from Sweden. That was nineteen twenty-eight. Oh my, thirty years ago? Come in! Sit down." She set the tray on the coffee table. "Hjälmar, take his hat."

"He doesn't have a hat."

She ignored him. "Coffee will be ready in just a few minutes. Here's Lonny and Rebecca. Haven't they grown? Becky made her dress herself... with only a little help."

Lonny watched his father. He seemed a little overwhelmed by the greeting.

Alan stood in the room, looking from one face to another. "Goodness," he said. "Thank you, Mrs. Ekman. Yes, it *is* a beautiful set of china. Oh, and here's a little something for the celebration. To go with the coffee." He handed her the white cake box. Then he turned to his daughter. "Rebecca, hi. And Lonny. Wonderful to see you both looking so healthy, growing up." Lonny held out his hand. Alan took it and looked him over. "You're a man, Lonny! Good Lord. The Army didn't do you any harm, did it?" He turned back to Becky. "And here's the graduate. Smart, pretty, getting big. How's my girl?" He reached out his arms.

Becky stepped into his hug, a little stiffly. "I'm glad you've come," she said. A small voice.

"I'm glad, too, honey." Then Alan held her away from him and looked her over. "What a fine dress you've made."

"I'll see to the coffee," said Else. "Ekman, you can help with this." She held the cake box by the strings. He took it and they went into the kitchen.

Alan said, "Well, here we are then. It's been a few years, hasn't it? Since you ran off, Lonny, and scared us half to death."

"Yeah." Lonny sat down on a side chair. Becky dropped onto the sofa and Alan looked around. "Take the big chair," Lonny said. "You're the guest. Clare's not with you?"

Alan sat down. "No, she's in Minneapolis. I dropped her off. She had things to do. We're going to take a boat down the Mississippi. Supposed to go all the way to New Orleans, but I doubt we'll go that far. Clare's keen on the idea but I think it'll get boring. At least the boat will make stops at different places along the way. This is a vacation for us. We both work pretty hard."

"Do you know where Mom is?" said Becky.

"Whew! You get right down to business, don't you, Becky? Just like Clare. No patience for small talk just to break the ice. She's all business, that one. Well, the answer is, I don't know. The divorce papers went back and forth through a lawyer in Chicago, so obviously she was there at one time. She's not in the Chicago phone book, and Information can't give me a number for her. Other than that, I haven't tried to find her. Did she ever contact you?"

"No. Did she hate us?"

"Oh no, honey. Of course not. Not you or Lonny. She didn't have much use for me, though, apparently. I don't know, Becky, she never explained. She just *left*. I tried to stop her that morning. I even grabbed her and held on to her arms but she fought me off. That lady had made up her mind to leave right then. And she never gave me a clue she was unhappy with us."

Lonny changed position on his hard chair. He hated to hear his father lie. Even Lonny had known something was wrong. He'd felt it. Probably Becky had felt it, too. It was like a swamp in the house sometimes. And sometimes it felt like winter and someone had left the back door open.

"But let's look to the future," Alan said. "Aren't you just a bit excited about going to high school in the fall?"

"Junior high," Becky said. "I guess so."

"Did you get good grades this last year?"

"Yes."

"What's your favorite subject?"

"Did you know that Lonny got his high school diploma in the Army?"

"No! Lonny, you kept that a secret from me. Congratulations to you, too. I thought you hated school."

"I did. I never hated learning things, though."

"What's the diff... Well, right, they aren't exactly the same thing, are they? So was it a home study program of some kind?"

"Yeah. And this older recruit, a buddy of mine, sort of acted like a teacher."

"Lonny, I've often wondered – since your mother told me once – that when you were a kid and I was away on business you spent all your free time in the woods, if you weren't at Grandma Lena's. What did you *do* in the woods?"

"Not much."

"Track animals? Shoot birds? Catch frogs in the swamp?"

"I never shot birds. I watched frogs sometimes."

"You watched them? That's all? When I was kid my friends and I used to catch frogs."

"What did you do with them?"

"You know, I don't remember now what we did. The fun was all in catching them. Probably we just threw them back."

"I knew a couple of kids here that caught frogs and blew them up with firecrackers. I hated them for doing that."

"Right. That's a terrible thing to do."

"I loved being in the woods. Once I followed bees to their hive and when I went back to check on them a week or so later they were gone and it looked like claw marks on the tree, so I figured a bear got to their honey."

Alan laughed. "The bear got the honey before you did."

"I never wanted the honey." Lonny looked at his father, sitting there in Ekman's well-worn chair in a fine blue suit, white shirt, nice, maybe expensive, tie. He tried to see him as a kid catching frogs.

"So fooling around in the woods was more fun, say, than baseball?"

"Baseball... The woods were a lot less trouble. Becky plays baseball."

"Softball," she said.

"Good for you, honey! Did you know that I played baseball in high school?"

"No."

"Well I did. I played shortstop on the varsity team. Did you know that, Lonny?"

"I think Mom mentioned it once."

"Did she? Well... Becky, you play softball. Are you a team player?"

"We didn't have real teams, Daddy. Mrs. Zimmer divided up the class different every day. We played softball in gym class when it wasn't raining."

"You need to be a team player in business," Alan said. "I have a sales team. We have to know each other, depend on each other, work together. That's how you win."

"Becky's a good player," Lonny said. "I watched her the day I got back."

"Here we are!" Else came into the room carrying Alan's cake on her breadboard, followed by Ekman with the coffee. He filled the serving pot, then looked around for a place to put the percolator. He set it on the floor next to the door to the kitchen. Meanwhile, Else had placed the cake on the coffee table, and Lonny and Becky silently read the writing on it:

Congratulations, Rebecca!
We are always together
in our hearts.

No one said a word. Even Else was still, just standing there looking at the cake with all the others. Finally Ekman said, "I hope somebody decides to serve that cake pretty soon. It sure looks good to me."

Alan said, "Becky, would you cut it?"

She looked at Lonny, saw his slight nod. "Okay."

In what was left of the afternoon, Lonny and Becky accompanied their father on a tour of his childhood home – Lena's house. They stood in the living room where Lonny's sleeping bag lay open in the middle of the floor.

"What happened to all of my mother's furniture?" Alan said.

"It's out in the shed. I put it there so it wouldn't get messed up from all the cleaning and painting."

"Couldn't you even use a mattress?"

"The renters ruined all of them. They're going to the dump."

"The dump! I used to go up there and shoot rats when I was a kid. I had a twenty-two. Don't know what ever happened to it. Maybe it's out in that old shed somewhere. What do you think? Let's go find it!"

"Dad, the shed's stuffed. You'll never find anything in there."

"No? Well, okay. But if you ever find my old twenty-two, let me know."

They moved on to the kitchen.

"You've cleaned the ceiling. That must have been a job. And the same old cupboards! New paint, though, right?"

Lonny nodded, and then his father noticed the closed door on his right.

"And this door. This opens to Mom's bedroom." He paused. "You know, I'm real sorry I couldn't come back for the funeral. Did Mrs. Björnquist handle everything all right?"

"I don't know," said Lonny. "I guess she did."

"Clare had been hemorrhaging so bad I didn't dare leave her alone in the hospital. In my letter I said it was a miscarriage, didn't I?"

"I don't remember that. You just said she was in the hospital."

"Oh. Well maybe I thought you were a little young for that information."

"What's a miscarriage?" said Becky.

"Becky!... Ah, well, it's a little complicated. Clare was going to have a baby, but something went wrong in the process, in the early part of it. You see there wasn't really a baby yet. And the pregnancy just stopped and Clare started bleeding instead. That's what "hemorrhaging" is, bleeding inside."

"That's awful. Does it happen a lot?"

"Well... Look, Becky. You're a little young for this. And I don't think I can explain so you'll understand it right."

"Is Clare okay now?" said Lonny, interrupting Becky who was starting to protest.

"Yes, she's fine. But I was sure worried about her for a while." He saw Becky's dark looks and hugged her to his side. "Honey, you'll learn all about that sort of thing soon enough. Just be glad that Clare's all healed up and she's fine now."

Becky forced a half-smile, looking at the floor.

Alan released her. "I'd sure like to see your grandmother's room." He opened the door and took one step inside. He stood there quietly, looking around.

Then he stepped back into the kitchen, blinking his eyes. "Clean as a whistle, Lonny. Except for the worn linoleum, there's no sign of the former occupant." His eyes moved toward the stairs beside the back door. "Same upstairs?"

"I haven't finished up there," Lonny said. "I'm pulling off the beaverboard. It's falling apart."

"Okay if I go up anyway?" He started toward the stairs.

"Sure, Dad. You and Becky go on up. I'll wait outside."

It felt strange and uncomfortable, his father's asking *him* for permission. And he realized he felt sorry for him.

Becky was holding her father's hand when they came out onto the narrow front porch. Alan said, "You've done a lot of work on the old place."

"There's a lot more to do."

"Always is. When you own your own home there's *always* a lot more to do. It never ends. There's a lot to be said for renting."

Back at Ekman's place Becky showed her father some of her artwork from school and it seemed to her that he genuinely admired it. Later, they all went out to see the Ekman's garden plot, and Alan told about the little garden he planted and tended in back of Lena's house when he was a boy. He stayed to dinner and told stories from his sales trips. After dinner, Becky and Else went into the kitchen to wash dishes and make coffee.

"Now that the ladies are out of the room," Alan said, "I can tell about the first time I tried to establish a client in Spokane."

"Is that so?" said Ekman. "Well, I'm not sure about me, but I guess Lonny's old enough, and he's been in the Army." He winked at Lonny.

"It's not that risqué, Mr. Ekman."

"Well, then. Let's hear it."

"It was a few years ago. My boss was happy with the sales I was bringing in and decided to expand my territory. He gave me the section of Washington state where this other salesman wasn't producing. And I found out why. In Spokane I walked into the biggest furniture store in town and found out they'd never even seen one of our reps. The other guy must have spent a lot of his time on the road in 'personal business,' as we say. So I walk into this store and look over the merchandise they have out on their floor and see they've got nothing to compare with the quality of the products we sell. A floor salesman comes up to me – it says 'Andrew Castle' on his name tag; I always check name tags and memorize the names. A young guy, he comes up to me and I ask to see their buyer. He tells me she's out to lunch. 'She' is out to lunch! So I ask him where she goes for lunch and he looks me over and sort of grins and says, 'Well, I don't know if I should give out that information.' I take a couple of bucks out of my wallet and he picks them out of my fingers. 'But I guess you're okay,' he says: 'City Café,' and he tells me where it is. I head for the door then realize I don't know who I'm looking for and I ask him her name and what she looks like. 'Candace Crouch,' he says. 'Just ask a waitress.'"

Alan glanced over at the kitchen door. "Well, to make a long story short, I find this City Café in a sort of seedy part of town and it's more of a bar than a café. I figure the kid is having his little joke on me and I'm curious to see how far it goes. So I go in and look around and see a couple of kids who were obviously too young to be in there; they're playing pool, and other punks are standing around watching. There are booths and scruffy looking folks eating what looked like bread drowned in gravy, you know the sort of thing, and there are a few people at the bar – old guys – and at one end of it a couple of youngish women wearing too much make up. I go up and order a beer and ask the bartender, a tough looking broad – woman, excuse me – if Candace Crouch is there. 'Where you from, Mac?' she says. 'Not from here,' I say. 'I'm a sales rep. Trying to establish a base here in Spokane.' 'Let's see your card,' she says, and now there's a little crinkle at the corners of her eyes. I show a card and she looks at it. "Who do you think this Candace is?' she says. "A buyer for Stromberg Furniture,' I say, 'but never mind. It's pretty clear somebody's playing a little joke on me. Who *is* this Candace Crouch?'

"'That's her,' she says nodding toward the end of the bar. 'The brunette with the red hair bow. But she calls herself Candy, not Candace. She got out of prison two days ago and came straight back here where she started.' That's all she says, and waits for me to ask. So I lay a fiver on the bar and ask, "Started what? And what was she in prison for?'

"'Five bucks will buy you a lot of beer. Do you want it all now?' she says. 'I don't want any more beer,' I say, 'but I'd sure appreciate just a little more information.' 'Keep your money,' she says. 'What Candy started was turning tricks, but she went to prison for blackmailing one of her johns. He came in here looking for her one night, got drunk and tried to assault her. I called the cops,' she says, 'and the whole story came out. He lost his job and left town.' 'And his job was?' I ask. 'City attorney,' she says."

"Gee whiz," said Ekman. "That's quite a story. Any of it true?"

Alan smiled. "Oh, most of it, I think." He winked at Lonny. "It was a few years ago. I don't go to bars much anymore."

Lonny didn't see the wink. He sat with his chair pushed back away from the table, his hands folded in his lap. He studied his hands and thought about Korea and Iseul. Like his Army buddies, his father jokes about whores. But stupid Lonny goes and falls in love with one. And then she disappears. Stupid Lonny gets himself ditched by a whore. Wouldn't Mr. Alan Stuart get a laugh out of that?

"Did you go back to the store?" said Ekman.

"You bet, and I'm glad you asked. I went right back, but on the way I stopped in at a Walgreen's and bought a pack of note cards and a little bottle of cheap scent. Then I wrote a note to the boy in the store and doused it with the cologne. I tried to make my handwriting look feminine. It said something like "Andrew, Sweetheart, Thanks for the referral. Next time you visit, I'll give you a discount." And I signed it 'Candy C.' with a few x's and o's."

Becky opened the kitchen door: "There's some cake left. Anyone want a piece?"

"Sure," said Ekman. "That was good cake."

Lonny and his father shook their heads. Becky closed the door.

"Okay, then. When I got to Stromberg's Furniture I gave the note to another clerk I'd seen in the store when I was there before: an older woman but attractive in her way. And I didn't seal the envelope."

"Did you ever go back after that?" said Lonny.

"Sure. A couple of months later. Business is business."

Becky came back in with a tray. She gave Ekman his cake, distributed coffee cups, then took her seat at the table.

"Was the kid there," Lonny said, "this Andrew?"

Else came in with the percolator and set it in front of Ekman. "Coffee, Mr. Stuart?"

"Yes, please." Ekman poured. Then he poured for Else, Becky, Lonny, and himself.

"No, he wasn't there," said Alan with a satisfied smirk. "But the older woman was and I asked about Andrew. She said, 'He is no longer employed here.' Then she introduced me to the actual buyer, who really *was* a woman, but no Candace. And I left there with a big order."

"Who's Candace?" said Becky.

Ekman caught a look from Else.

"It's a long story," Alan said. "I've been boring Mr. Ekman and your brother."

"Daddy, you're staying over, aren't you? You can have my room if you do. I'll sleep on the couch."

"Ya," said Else. "You stay here tonight, Mr. Stuart. Have a good breakfast in the morning."

"That's very kind of you, but I really should get back tonight. Clare will be expecting me."

"You could call her," said Lonny.

"She'll be out late. She was going to a concert tonight."

"But you're at a hotel. You could leave a message for her."

"Well, yes, I could do that."

"Don't you want to stay over?" said Becky.

"Oh, sure I do, honey. Goodness, you're all sure making me feel welcome. I'll stay then. But you keep your room, Becky. I'm sure I'll be fine on the couch."

Becky woke to the sound of a car door slamming shut. She propped herself up on one elbow and tried to see. It was dark in the room. She heard the car's engine start up and then the crunch of gravel under rolling tires. Was her father leaving? She threw back her covers and ran out into the living room. In the weak moonlight she saw the empty couch where her father had slept, the sheet and blanket neatly folded on a cushion. She dashed out the front door and stood on the porch just in time to see the red tail lights of the Buick flowing out onto the road and disappearing behind the trees.

Chapter 20 Lena's House

"Lonny, wake up!" Becky knelt beside him on the floor and shook him. "Wake up!"

He opened his eyes. Becky's red puffy face hovered above him, her eyes like sores. She scooted away and sat against the wall hugging her knees. She was barefoot but had pulled on her jeans and a green flannel shirt.

Lonny raised up on his elbows. "What's wrong?"

"Daddy's gone. He left in the middle of the night. I heard something and woke up and ran out and saw his car going away. Why did he leave like that?"

"He didn't leave a note?"

"Oh sure, he left a stupid note. Two of them, one for us and one for the Ekmans." She pulled them out of her shirt pocket and read aloud.

"Dear Mr. and Mrs. Ekman, Thanks for everything. I got to worrying about my wife Clare and couldn't sleep so I thought I might as well get an early start. Say goodbye to the kids for me.

Yours Very Sincerely, Alan Stuart. But he crossed out that 'say goodbye' part and wrote this other note. *Dear Becky and Lonny, Sorry to leave without seeing you again in the morning. I got to worrying about Clare all alone in Minneapolis so I decided to get an early start. I love you both very much. I hope we can have a longer visit next time. Dad."*

"Let me get dressed," Lonny said. He unzipped his sleeping bag, rolled out of it and pulled his pants on over his shorts. Then he headed for the bathroom. Becky got to her feet and began pacing around the room, her hands shoved into her back pockets. She stopped at each window to look outside; now and then with her bare toes she kicked at Lonny's rumpled sleeping bag on the floor. The toilet flushed. Becky ran out of the room and up the narrow stairs off the kitchen to what had been her bedroom after coming back from Seattle. Through the gable window she looked out at the road in front of the house. She remembered exactly how it was – getting out of the taxi and hugging Grandma Lena. Getting a hug from Daddy before he got back in the taxi. And then the taxi going away. There was always a car going away.

She heard Lonny call her name.

"I'm up here." She trotted back down the stairs. I don't care if he's gone," she said, meeting Lonny in the bare kitchen. "I did at first, but the heck with him."

He tried to put his arm around her but she shook him off. "Let's do something," she said. "Go out in the woods. You used to show me places and tell me about things."

"Can I eat first?"

"Eat! That's what men do, isn't it? They eat. Then they go away. And then they come back and eat and go away again."

"Ekman never goes anywhere."

"And he's the best man I ever met!"

"Let's go see him. And get some breakfast."

Lonny put on his shirt and they started up the road together.

"You haven't said what you think about it," Becky said.

"About what?"

"About his leaving!"

"What's there to say? He wanted to leave as soon as he got here."

"How do you know?"

"I could tell. And you could, too."

"No, I couldn't!"

"Becky, you weren't *really* surprised when he left, were you?"

She stopped walking. She stood with her toughened bare feet on the gravel road and started to cry. This time when he put his arm around her she pressed against his side. She stopped crying and wiped her eyes on the cuff of her sleeve. "I did check once. Before I went to sleep I checked to see if he was still there on the couch."

When they came to the Ekmans' driveway, Becky broke away. She ran to the porch and up the steps. At the door she turned back and said, "Wait two minutes before you come in." Then she disappeared inside.

Lonny looked at the door standing shut between him and the friendly cup of coffee he wanted. He sighed and sat down on the porch steps with his elbows on his knees. He looked at the road and imagined two little red lights going away in the darkness, the taillights of his father's Buick, and years before that, the taillights of the car that took his mother away. He hadn't seen that, only imagined it from his father's account of the night she left.

Darkness and red taillights... and a GMC pick-up going away, somewhere in the Colorado Rockies.

But now the sun was up and it felt warm on his left shoulder. He turned his face to it with his eyes shut. It felt good. And today he was twenty-one. Inside there's coffee and breakfast, and Hjälmar and Else and Becky. He opened his eyes. And out there, far down that road is Florida and good old Mavrokis. And Gabe's in Denver, or headed for Washington. And Iseul's in Korea. And Kristin...

"Lonny! You can come in now." Becky held the door open for him.

"It's about time. You wake me up and then you starve me." He followed her through the living room and when he entered the kitchen Ekman began singing "Happy Birthday," joined immediately by Becky and then by Else whose high soprano fairly trilled above the other voices. On the table next to his plate – laden with fried eggs, a slice of ham, and a toasted slice of Else's homemade bread – were two wrapped packages. One was flat and about the size of his breakfast plate, and the other he thought might be a book, a thick one. He grinned as they sang and looked from Else to Ekman to Becky to the gifts and all around again, lowering his eyes, looking up, shifting his weight from one foot to the other. The song ended and Becky clapped her hands and said, "The flat one's from me."

"You're a man now," said Ekman. "Sit down and eat like a man."

Else smiled and hummed quietly, her fingers moving up and down on her apron.

"I didn't..." Lonny shook his head.

"You're surprised, aren't you?" Becky said.

"Yeah, Squirt. I'm really surprised."

He sat down and reached for the flat package just as Becky snatched it away: "Eat first, presents after."

"Good idea," said Lonny.

Steam rose from the coffee as Else filled his cup from the percolator, and then she refilled Ekman's. He tilted his chair back and watched Lonny attack his eggs. Else sat down at the table and Becky stood with her hand resting on the back of Else's chair.

When he wiped up the last color of egg yolk from his plate, Lonny took another sip of coffee, then reached for Becky's present, but he hesitated: "You're not going to grab it away again?"

"Go ahead, open it!"

He carefully removed the wrapping and found a framed pencil drawing of a young woman in a long gown, her hair flowing down to the middle of her back, and she was holding the hand of small child. They were shown in side view, the woman and child walking together, apparently in a park, the child, in a knee-length dress, trailing a step behind the woman. Becky had added some light coloring to the picture. Lonny looked at it for a long time.

"How did you do the color?"

"I used pencils, colored pencils."

"I really like the picture, Becky."

"I can't do faces yet," she said.

They were turned away, slightly, from the viewer.

"I like wondering what the woman is looking at," said Lonny. "I guess the little girl is looking at her mother, if that's who the woman is."

"I looked at a picture in a book but I didn't really copy it."

"Thanks, Squirt. I like the picture a lot."

"Hjälmar made the frame for it."

"He made a nice one, too."

Lonny unwrapped the other gift – a wooden box with a hinged lid. Opening the box revealed a small set of knives for carving wood.

"You used to carve birds with a pocket knife," said Else. "That's what Becky told us."

"Yeah, I did."

"It was a chipmunk and a loon," said Becky.

"But I used a hunting knife. That sure was a long time ago." He held one of the knives in his hand. "These are really nice. But I don't know how to use them."

"You'll figure it out," said Ekman.

"I'll find you a book in the library," said Becky.

That night, down the hill in Lena's house, Lonny woke to the sound of distant thunder coming in through the open window. He lay in his sleeping bag with his arms folded behind his head staring up at the ceiling through the darkness. He thought about his father and how he handled everything yesterday, how easy he was, comfortable, though it was somehow obvious to Becky and himself that he didn't want to be there. He at least *seemed* comfortable. It must be a talent, and Lonny wished he had some of that talent himself. The man could tell stories and jokes and seem like he was having just a great time. Maybe, Lonny thought, I should have tried to play baseball like Dad and not spend so much time alone in the woods. I wasn't always alone, though. Stig was with me sometimes and it was really fun. But it sure was weird to see him again, that time with the horses. He was wearing sneakers to ride a horse! And he'd gotten fat, and talked about electronics and high school. He was so different, nothing like when we'd fooled around in the woods together. But why did I run away from him? You'd think I was scared or something, but I didn't *feel* scared, just creeped out somehow. That was so weird, it makes me kind of sick to think about it.

He closed his eyes and wondered what Mavrokis was up to. He liked remembering Mavrokis, and imagined the Professor finding some other dope to teach and straighten out. Gabe should meet up with him.

And then he thought of Kristin, how she looked at him when she was sitting up in her truck and it was dark. The engine was running but she hadn't turned on the headlights. Then she turned them on and drove away. The hour before that they'd been in bed together, making love. And they'd only just met that day... *So who's she with tonight?* It was an angry thought, but it hurt, too. And it probably wasn't fair. He really didn't know her very well but what he knew he liked. He sure liked being with her, and how she could do things, and how she looked, and talked. It was good making love with her but then it scared him afterwards. Because would he ever see her again? ...He'd never see Iseul again, the real Iseul. All he'd ever see would be the image in his mind, how she looked when she called him Soldier Boy, her small breasts, her eyes... always sad, almost always. But the image wouldn't stay, it kept dissolving and he kept trying to bring it back. Finally he let it go and it seemed to break apart and float away on a black river... *up* river, and that's weird, he thought.

Then he was thinking of Kristin again. She did like him. She really did. He *could* see her again. He turned onto his side and pulled the sleeping bag closed around his neck. He settled himself to sleep and he thought of Lena, Grandma Lena in her old robe grumbling and swearing in the morning and making coffee. The bare wood floor of the house was hard and solid under him. It was Lena's house. His.

Epilogue

July 10 Happy Birthday, Lonny!
I know this is very late but you didn't give me your address, maybe because you didn't want me to write to you – if so, you shouldn't have included the return address on your envelope. For that little oversight, you're getting this belated birthday greeting.

It was terrible that Gabe got beat up so bad and I'm sorry for him. Elly Ann is real trouble. It's kind of awful to say, given what happened to Gabe, but for me the evening was the best I've spent in years. So, no, you weren't any "trouble" for me. Though I guess you are now...

If you had stayed a few days, we could have had a nice time on our ranch. I would have put you to work, of course. I'm sure you're a better worker than my lazy brother.

*It must be nice for you to be back in your old home –
and now it even belongs to you and your sister. If you ever
write again, tell me about your sister.*

"Your friend," Kristin

23 July 1961

Dear Kristin,
*Thank you for the card and the letter. I hoped you
would write back.*

*I thought I should stick around with Gabe and help
him get home, but I should not have bothered about him.
That next morning he called a friend in Denver who had a
truck with a winch on it, and they were going to salvage
Gabe's Harley which was down in a ravine. During the
night someone left a note and his keys. He expected me to
help. I thought he was nuts and I left. I wish I had gone
with you to the ranch.*

*I got a job as a car mechanic here in Duluth. I passed
the probation and now I'm earning twice what they paid
me at the stables. But so far I've been spending most of my
earnings on tools. I have to have my own.*

*I don't know what to tell about Rebecca. Except that
she's smart and I guess she's cute (she's my sister, how
would I know?) She likes to play softball and she reads
and draws and Else is teaching her to sew. We get along
good. I haven't told her about you. She would ask a
thousand questions and I wouldn't have the answers.*

*The Ekmans are Swedish and they told me that in
Sweden I would be called AutoMechanic Stuart. People
are called by their work, like doctors are here.*

Your friend,
AutoMechanic Lonny

*August 1st   Lonny! – News Flash! My dad is driving to
Minneapolis in a few days to a stock show and sale. I'm
going with him to help with the driving. It's a big truck*

and tiresome to drive. Call me as soon as you get this and give me your phone number and I'll call you from Minneapolis – it's only about a hundred miles from Duluth, isn't it? My phone number's on the little card. Don't lose it!

    Stockbuyer Kristin Scholes